DISCERNMENT

Sons of the Living God: Book I

Tina C. Brown

Discernment
Sons of the Living God: Book I

ISBN-13: 978-0-692-09598-0

Alive in Christ Publishing
7380 Spout Springs Rd #210-325
Flowery Branch, GA 30542

aicpublishing.com
tinacbrown.wixsite.com/website

www.529books.com

Cover: Tina C. Brown & R.R. Brown

Prophetic Novels
Inspired by True Events

This book is dedicated to the lost, to the weary, to the brokenhearted, to the hopeless: Jesus is the way. He will give you rest, heal your broken heart, and reveal true purpose. You are not forgotten; you are precious and valuable in His kingdom. You are accepted by God.

Contents

DISCERNMENT

Introduction

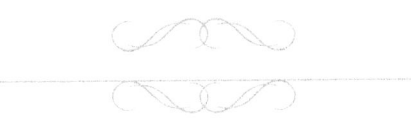

"Arise, shine; for thy light is come, and the glory of the Lord is risen upon thee. For, behold, the darkness shall cover the earth, and gross darkness the people: but the Lord shall arise upon thee, and his glory shall be seen upon thee. And the Gentiles shall come to thy light, and kings to the brightness of thy rising" (Isaiah 60:1-3 NKJV).

PART I

1

Depressed Much?

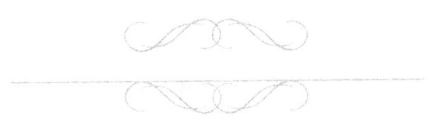

I let out a throaty cough. The air was saturated with men's cologne. I could practically taste it and it was burning my nostrils. His office was dark and ominous, except for a few rays of sun that fought their way through slivers of empty space in the closed wooden blinds. A built-in bookshelf towered over me as I sat in the leather loveseat. The decorative pillows distracted me. They didn't really fit; this was probably the doing of his wife. In addition to books, the shelf was crammed with pictures, awards, and knick-knacks from his worldly travels. There was a mahogany desk that was way too big, not at all in proportion with the room. The second hand of the large wall clock ticked loudly; yet, somehow time felt as if it were standing still.

"Do you know why?" he asked again.

His question finally registered. "I'm sorry, I didn't hear the question," I lied.

"Why do you think you'll end up pushing a shopping cart on the street? Why do you feel you'll be homeless?"

I couldn't help but watch his left leg rock calmly, crossed over the right. Green and yellow argyle dress socks peeked out of his slacks. The Italian loafers he wore sparkled as if he were shining them before my arrival. He wore a brightly colored button-down shirt covered with palm trees that appeared even brighter against his blotchy, sunburned skin. The first few buttons were open, revealing the gold link chain that was nestled in the coarse, light brown coils on his chest. The hair on his head was slicked back with too much hair gel by anyone's standards. His hand brushed his beard almost as if he were trying to show off his gold pinky ring.

He resembled a pimp more than a doctor. Maybe even a used car salesman more than a psychologist. The only thing he was missing was a tiny comb for his mustache. I wished that was sticking out of his shirt pocket. I have no idea why. I wondered to myself if he really thought his look was at all appealing to the opposite sex, or just in general. I suppose it didn't matter because he had been happily married for years now—at least it seemed that way from the family photos. But then again, things aren't always what they appear to be.

His daughter was in a couple of the pictures. The beautiful girl looked my age. Her complexion was like buttermilk, her long, thick, flaxen hair reached her waist, and her eyes looked just like the depths of the Aegean Sea off the coast of the Mediterranean—they were the deepest of blues. The picture captured her as the innocent, well-adjusted teenage daughter to a perfectly put together psychologist. I suddenly became sad for Doctor Lewis. I knew his daughter. It was Emily, a girl who attended the same high school as me. A picture only captures one moment. And in that moment, you could portray anything, even if it was a lie.

I had a few classes with Emily. We hung out in similar circles. She was nothing like that picture. Innocent is not a word I would use to describe her. She was overtly flirty. I'd overhear her and her friends talking about the parties they had been to over the weekends, how drunk they had gotten, and who they had hooked up with. Other days I saw her at lunch, and she would laugh with her friends, but she seemed sad despite her outward display of confidence. I wondered if Doctor Lewis knew his daughter like I knew her.

I silently scoffed to myself. This guy is of no help to his own daughter, but he thinks he can help me. Or maybe he doesn't think he can help me. He looks awfully perplexed in his big leather chair that matches that giant desk.

"Kristen, why do think you'll end up pushing a shopping cart on the street? Why do you feel you'll be homeless?"

"I don't know," I paused. "It's just how I see myself when I get older."

"I wouldn't worry about that. You seem like a bright young lady with a good future ahead of you." He scribbled something down on the legal pad in his lap. "After all, you're only seventeen. It's perfectly natural to worry about the future. It's okay to not know exactly what you want to be when you grow up. You'll figure it out. I'm sure you won't end up on the streets pushing a shopping cart." He paused with a content look, waiting for my response.

"Sixteen."

"Ah, what was that?" he asked, now a bit confused.

"You said I was seventeen. Um, when you were talking just now. I'm only sixteen. My birthday isn't until next week."

"Oh." He scribbled something else down quickly and then met my eyes again. "Well, either way, my point is still valid."

I glanced down at his shirt. "Hey, I forgot to ask you if you and your family had fun last week in…."

He grinned from ear to ear. "Aruba, yeah, we had a lot of fun, and maybe a little too much sun. Do you like my shirt? I got it at one of the little shops near where we stayed."

"Oh. Well, it definitely says Aruba." Screams Aruba is more like it.

3

"Don't think I don't know what you're doing. You know, one of these days you're going to have to talk to me. It's the only way we can get to the bottom of what's going on with you."

We stared at each other for what seemed like forever. It was like one of those old western movies—one person waiting on the other to make the first move. I had been coming to Doctor Lewis once a week for about two months now, and I still wasn't convinced that talking about my feelings would help me. So, I stubbornly sat tight-lipped with my arms folded, waiting on the tumbleweed's cue. We continued to sit in silence as the hands of the clock ticked deafeningly.

He finally cleared his throat and adjusted himself in his seat. "Well, it looks like we're just about out of time for this session, but I definitely want to pick back up on this the next time you come."

He stood and walked toward his office door and stopped abruptly, holding the door open for me.

I quickly walked past him, trying not to look at the chest hair that was staring back at me. I was thinking of ways to get out of my next appointment. These therapy sessions seemed pointless to me. He was just one of the many psychologists, psychiatrists, and counselors I had been to this year, and I wasn't feeling any better. Talking only made me relive the hurt and pain. We seemed to be getting no closer to finding out how to get rid of the depression that engulfed me. It was an hour a week I'd never get back.

He checked his gold Rolex as he walked closely behind me down the narrow corridor. We walked through another door that led into the waiting area of the doctor's office.

"Ah, right on time, Mr. Webber," Doctor Lewis said, looking the young man up and down.

The teenage boy sitting in the waiting area was a scrawny thing. He reminded me of a frightened Chihuahua—he almost jumped out of his skin when Doctor Lewis called his name. He was average height for a boy but looked extremely underweight. His appearance was disheveled. He wore khaki pants that looked like they spent most of their time on his bedroom floor or shoved in a dirty clothes hamper. His T-shirt was partially tucked in, wrinkled like his pants, and spotted with unidentifiable stains. He was well overdue for a haircut—it was greasy and unkempt, hanging down and hiding most of his facial features.

What's he in for? I wondered. I watched him as I walked out the door, but he never made eye contact with me.

Outside was a total contrast to the melancholy environment of Doctor Lewis's office. It was so bright that my eyes burned as the sunlight reflected off the parked cars. It was the end of August in sunny Southern California. Similar to a scorching skillet, I could feel the heat from the sun rising off the asphalt like it did every day around this time.

Right in front of the building was Doctor Lewis's car—a white-on-white BMW 760Li that was taking up two parking spaces. There wasn't a spec of dirt on it. Some days I'd get a sudden urge to kick his perfect car, though I hadn't followed through on it yet. I often imagined what my footprint would look like on the pristine paint job. Better yet, I wanted to see the look on his face when he saw that someone had left a mark on his beautiful car. Doctor Lewis worshiped that car as if it were his savior, but to me, it was only a car, nothing more. I wished it were as easy as that. As easy as something or someone being able to completely free me from the pain I carried. If only that person were Doctor Lewis. If only he truly had the power to cure me of this perpetual sadness that burrowed into the depths of my worthless soul. Even if he had that power, he'd probably only use it to keep his stupid car clean or ensure he had a lifetime supply of hair gel. I guess I can't really be mad at Doctor Lewis. He seems like he's trying to help, but it's clear that he can't supply what I need.

And that's when I spotted it. I froze as the panic set in. My heart raced. I could feel my palms becoming clammy. I wouldn't make any sudden moves because that's exactly what it wanted. As soon as I did, it would pounce. The slightest movement would coax it into a spastic frenzy. I thought quickly and decided to make my move cautiously, as to not disturb the small pigeon feather that lay on the ground in front of me. I HATED feathers. Well, I was deathly afraid of them, and that brought on the hatred. I tried to walk by the single feather as slowly as possible, but the demon feather had a mind of its own and began chasing me. I screamed and ran, putting myself far from the feather that was now gliding aimlessly in the light coastal breeze behind me. The crisis was averted, and my breathing began to slow as I calmed myself.

My mother sat in her car waiting for me like she always did after these appointments. I got into the front seat. My mom was doing a crossword puzzle on the back of some celebrity gossip magazine. Her straight, jet-black, shoulder-length hair blew lightly from the vents in front of her. Her cantaloupe-colored halter dress clung to her slim figure. It complimented her beautiful bronze skin that still glowed from whatever youth promoting moisturizer she had used earlier that morning. She diligently focused her big, brown, almond-shaped eyes on her magazine—her full lips in a pout and her brow wrinkled. She made a habit of keeping up with what was hot and new when it came to music, fashion, and celebrities. She was always young at heart. In some ways, she was more like a sister or best friend than a mother when it came to our relationship. It didn't help that she looked exceptionally young for her age, even though she did have me early in life. She'd giggle like a schoolgirl whenever people thought we were sisters. Her reaction was always a little more over the top when the compliment came from the opposite sex. I shook my head as I thought about how she acted when flattery took hold of her. She'd bat her eyes and toss her hair while lightly touching the poor, unsuspecting man's shoulder. And it worked every time. Flirting was something she had down to a science. I, on the other hand, always had a problem with science. Having the grace to hold a coherent conversation with a male was not one of my redeeming qualities.

"Lady Gaga refers to her fans as what?" she asked with a confused look on her face.

"Little monsters," I said as I put on my seat belt.

"That's right! I knew it was something like that."

I just looked at her, waiting for an explanation.

"It's a Lady Gaga crossword puzzle." She held up the magazine as if I couldn't already see what was in her hand. Every week she'd buy a new issue of her favorite gossip magazine and examine it from cover to cover. She quickly wrote her answer down, tossed her magazine in the back seat, and put the car in reverse. "Can you believe Aria is pregnant?"

"Who?" I asked.

"Aria."

"Again, who?"

"Aria Knight," she replied as if she had lunch with her last week. "Platinum recording artist and mega superstar. She's pregnant again."

I shrugged, uninterested.

We backed out of the parking spot and shot into oncoming traffic. A car horn violently blared from behind us. I glanced at the passenger side mirror to see a little red Mercedes convertible swerve from behind us into the next lane. He then passed us at an accelerated speed.

"So, are you excited to be starting school in a couple weeks?" She was oblivious to the angry man in the red convertible.

"Um, I don't know. I guess." I stared out my window. Having to go back to school was the last thing I wanted to think about. Although, this year wouldn't be so bad. It was my senior year. I would be captain of the dance team and captain of the cheer team. It was ironic that I'd be the leader for my high school's team spirit. I shook my head at the thought. On those chilly varsity game nights, I'd be the one to lead the squad in getting the crowd pumped up for our football team. It wouldn't matter, though, because all the pep in the world wouldn't help our football team win a game. Well, we did win one last season, but that was only because the opposing team's star players had mono.

But I was the ambassador for Belmont High's school spirit, and I'd have to play the part. I felt like my life was one big performance. At school, I would play the role of the bubbly-yet-poised popular girl, and at home, I would be the mindful and responsible daughter. If they only knew that I cried myself to sleep each night, hoping I wouldn't wake up the next day. Or that the only reason I tried out for cheer the year before was for the perks. I was excited when my cheer big sister, one of the seniors who left that year, gave me my laundry basket full of personalized goodies. Once I became part of the team, I realized how much I enjoyed it. But the happiness I felt was temporary. Sustaining happiness was what I longed for.

I was in deep thought as I played with the delicate ring on my left ring finger. It was one of my favorites. It was a birthday gift from my dad that my mother probably bought. She said it was from him, but it was more likely that he had forgotten my existence yet again. A freshwater pearl sat at the center and was encircled by two rows of diamonds. I watched the diamonds sparkle in the sunlight. It was my absolute favorite, but I'd trade it in a second for true happiness.

"Your birthday is around the corner, too. Do you know what you want?" my mother asked.

I leaned my head back on the leather headrest. "Yes, I want to die," I said in a monotone voice, closing my eyes.

"Oh, you're so dramatic."

I snapped up, watching her as she dug through the center console. She put her designer aviator sunglasses on and glanced over at me. "School will be fine like it always is, and I bet your father has something really nice picked out for you this year."

I glared at her in disbelief. "You do realize you just picked me up from a psychotherapist's office? One that I'm going to because I'm depressed and have been having suicidal thoughts? And your retort is that I'm dramatic?"

"Don't make this about that again. It's a chemical imbalance, and the pills will help soon. You just have to do your part and take them like you're supposed to."

"It's the way I feel, Mother! You think I can just switch this off and on? It doesn't matter what I do; I still feel this way. The pills aren't helping, that's why I don't want to take them anymore. Do you even know what the side effects of these new pills are?"

I pulled out a folded paper out of my pocket. "Common side effects include nausea, abdominal pain, anxiety, insomnia, trouble concentrating, unusual dreams, joint pains, muscle pains—"

"All right," my mother answered.

"Nervousness—"

"All right!"

"Unexplained rashes...." I continued.

I could sense her scowl.

"Dizziness, hallucinations, chest palpitations, difficulty breathing. This medication may cause suicidal thoughts or behavior—just to name a few. And this is supposed to help me?"

"Stop it now!"

I shut my mouth and looked out my window. This was the third type of anti-depression medication they had put me on. I was experiencing all but a few of the side effects from the ones I'd taken before. My body had always been overly sensitive, even to over-the-counter medicines. My mom promptly removed Nyquil from our household after I almost overdosed on it, even though I took the recommended dosage. She told me I was seizing after I had blacked out. When I began to come to, I vomited all over her cream Berber carpet.

After some time, she composed herself and was finally able to continue.

"Look, hon, I'm still trying to make sense of all this. Really, I am. I just don't get it. To be honest, I don't understand it. You're such a beautiful girl and so smart. I don't know why you would… how you could…." She grimaced slightly and shook her head. "…even think such things." She paused for a while before she spoke again. "You know, your grandfather committed suicide when I was just a little girl." Her face was solemn when I looked at her just then. Her body was in the car next to me, but she looked as though her mind was somewhere far off. "It was a week before Christmas when they found him. He hung himself in an old, abandoned warehouse not too far from our home. My mother, your grandmother, couldn't even get out of bed for weeks, even though we never saw her cry. Somehow, she found the strength to go on. I guess she did it because she had to."

My mother had told me about how strict my grandmother was during her childhood. My grandmother wasn't able to express her emotions. My mother always prided herself on being the total opposite of my grandmother. My mother's parenting style was a bit more liberal, unlike her conservative upbringing.

"Why didn't you ever tell me that before?" I asked, surprised.

"Because we didn't talk about it. My mother never talked about it. We didn't even go to the funeral. Well, Mom went, but your aunts, uncle, and I didn't go."

I had only seen pictures of my grandfather. One, in particular, was the photo that sat on our mantel in the living room. It was a black and white picture of my grandparents on their wedding day. They both look so serious; it was hard to make any assumptions about that moment that was captured forever. I would have to examine it again to see if there were any indicators that he was depressed. We finally entered the underground structure and pulled into one of the two assigned parking spots.

My mother put the car in park and took the key out of the ignition. She turned to face me. "Look, I want you to promise me that you'll seriously try to make an effort at getting better. I couldn't bear the thought of losing you, too. Okay, hon?"

"All right." I sighed, not sure it was that simple.

The place I called home was a 1,500-square-foot, two-bedroom, three-bathroom condo on Ocean Boulevard in Long Beach. We lived on the sixteenth floor, mainly because my mother refused the penthouse, which boasted expansive views of the ocean, Catalina Island, the Marina, and the city shoreline. We moved here years ago when my parents divorced. They had just finished construction on the building; it had been one of my father's projects. He bought the lot, though it wasn't cheap, and built these luxury condos. Projects like these are how he makes a living. His real estate development firm took up all his time, but he loved it. He always put it first, above all other aspects of his life. I guess that's why he's so successful at it—he was married to his career. That was the main reason he and my mother split. His job took him all over the U.S. Eventually, his company went international, and he began traveling out of the country, as well. He provided for us, of course, and we wanted nothing financially speaking, but his constant absence played a major part in my mother's decision to leave him. She'd beg and plead with him to be the father and husband we needed, but in the end, his first love won out over us. I still remember the first night we stayed here as if it were yesterday. My mom stayed up most of the night consoling me as I sobbed uncontrollably, asking her repeatedly why my father no longer wanted or loved us. I snapped out of that memory as the elevator doors opened to our floor.

"What do you feel like having for dinner tonight?" she asked, unlocking the front door.

"I don't care, whatever."

The open layout made the condo bright and airy, especially with the floor-to-ceiling windows that covered almost every wall. But the warm tones of taupe, beige, and chocolate with minimal pops of color made the space feel cozy. I made my way to my bedroom.

"I guess we probably should have picked something up on our way home," she said, standing in front of the open stainless steel refrigerator. "When did we buy P.F. Chang's?"

"Wednesday," I yelled from my room.

"We didn't have Chinese on Wednesday. We had pizza. Hon, didn't we have pizza Wednesday?"

"No."

"What?" she yelled back.

I walked into the kitchen to find her smelling the inside of a takeout container.

"We had P.F. Chang's last Wednesday," I replied.

She looked confused. "No, we didn't. We had pizza last Wednesday."

"What? No, we didn't, we had pizza this past Wednesday," I insisted.

"That's what I said, but when did we have P.F. Chang's?"

"Mom, we had it last Wednesday. Not this week, but the week before." Then I thought for a moment. "Wait, no, we had Mexican Wednesday before last, so that means P.F. Chang's is from the Wednesday before that," I said with a look of disgust on my face.

"Oh, well, do you want some of this? I think it's still good."

"Why don't we just order pizza?" I suggested.

2

Wildwood

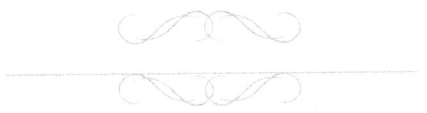

That night was a struggle. I tossed and turned, but after most of the night had passed, I finally fell asleep. In my dreams, I was somewhere unfamiliar. There was green as far as my eyes could see. I was in what looked like a forest. It might've been early morning, but it was hard to tell. The treetops formed a canopy that blocked out most of the daylight. The stillness in conjunction with the random sounds of insects and wild animals scurrying made my surroundings seem eerie. It was hot but different from the heat I was accustomed to in California. This was a sultry heat. The light mist that fell from the trees helped cool me some, but only by a fraction. I walked through thick brush, shrubs, and trees. Glancing down, I noticed I was barefoot, standing on a dirt road that meandered through the forest. That's when I heard branches snapping behind me. My heart leaped. I spun around but saw no one. I stood very still; careful of even breathing too loudly so I could catch where the sound had come from. Then I heard it again, coming from the other direction. I turned, searching the forest frantically. A young girl stuck her head out from behind one of the huge oak trees. Her face was pleasantly round with a warm, welcoming smile. She had long, chestnut-colored hair that hung in big, beautiful curls. She looked lost. She was wearing a long, white cotton nightgown with delicate lace detail along the edges. She was barefoot, her feet covered in mud and moss, but the nightgown was spotless. I sighed with relief.

"Hi, are you lost?" I asked.

She hid behind the tree and giggled.

I walked closer.

She poked her head out as if she were playing some sort of game with me. This time, I could see her better. Her cheeks were rosy. At that moment, a gust of cold air danced around me, producing a chill that ran up my spine. I almost didn't realize the little girl had taken off running. I ran after her, fearing she might be hurt by something evil lurking in the shadows of the forest. I was in pursuit of the young girl, no longer on the dirt path, as I pushed through the thick forest. I could see her stark white nightgown weaving through the plush green ferns and wild weeds that seemed to overtake the large oak trees. I came to an abrupt stop. I regained my balance just in time to find myself on the cusp of an enormous hole in the ground. I slowly peeked inside but couldn't see anything other than darkness. I wondered if that poor little girl had fallen to her demise.

Then there was a giggle behind me. I turned sharply to see the little girl standing a few yards away. Her hands were over her face, hiding her smile.

"You don't have to be frightened. I won't hurt you." I slowly took two steps toward her.

Her hands fell. She cocked her head to one side and her smile faded. "Why would I be fearful of you?" the girl said in a low, unnatural voice.

I paused, realizing her tiny body and face didn't match up with the terrifying voice that came out of her mouth.

"What?" I instinctively took a step back.

I began to feel fear rising inside. The girl walked toward me. I blinked, and in an instant, she was directly in front of me. Her face contorted. She grabbed my arms and her head whipped back and forth faster than humanly possible. For a minute, it looked like two heads were coming out of her small frame. I was terrified—frozen in place. I tried to scream, but it was futile. Then, with unbelievable strength, she shoved me. The force from her small hands sent me flying backward.

I was falling into the dark pit, screaming in silence when I suddenly woke up. My pajamas, pillow, sheets, and comforter were all soaked. My heart felt like it would burst right out of my chest.

I sat up to catch my breath and glanced over at the clock on my nightstand—3:15 a.m.

"Great, more side effects," I said, unable to shake the visage of the little girl from my mind. "Unusual dreams, check. Chest palpitations…" I put one hand on my chest, monitoring the erratic rhythmic pace, "…check," I said to myself, flopping down on my back. I've already checked the box with daddy issues, why not add these too. After a few moments of lying there trying to process what had just happened, I fell back asleep.

"Kristen!" my mom yelled from somewhere in the condo.

I could hear her coming toward my bedroom. I hated the sound of my mother calling my name so early in the morning, especially when I hadn't gotten a good night's sleep.

"Kristen!" she burst through my bedroom door. "You gotta get up, or we're going to miss our flight."

"Okay, I'm up, Mom," I groaned, shifting in my bed as proof that I was awake. There was a moment of silence, and I hoped she'd walked out.

"You don't look like you're up. You look like you're still lying there."

"Mom!" I shifted under my covers again, irritated.

"Get up, now!" She turned and walked out of my room.

I'd better be up by the time she comes back. I was so annoyed at this point, partly because of the lack of sleep, but mostly because I was not a morning person. I rolled over onto my back and sat up in bed for a moment, surveying my room. It was the same as it had been—everything neat and in its place. The large room was decorated to my mother's specifications. Out of nowhere, about a year ago, she decided to give the entire condo a little "spiffing up," as she called it. My walls were once eggshell, painted that shade when we first moved in. My life felt as mundane as the paint color. She only asked my opinion on one of the colors in her palette: blithe blue. It seemed ironic to me, considering the way I had been feeling.

I got up and grabbed my folded clothes. I had put them out last night, anticipating I wouldn't have time in the morning to search for something to wear. I laid them out on the blue and white striped wingback chair that sat in the corner of my room. On my way to the door, I grabbed my cell phone that sat on my small, white writing desk. I turned on the phone; I had twelve missed calls and eight voicemails. I sighed, turning my phone back off and placing it back in its original spot.

Stepping barefoot on the heated terrazzo tiles of my bathroom. Yes, heated tiles in Long Beach, apparently a selling point. I put my clothes on the marble countertop, examining myself in the mirror. Sometimes I would stare at myself, observing all of the different parts that came together to make me. I wasn't sure why I did this—it only reminded me how different I was to the rest of my family. I pulled my hair back, revealing the contours of my round face, my brow wrinkled in deep thought. My almond-shaped eyes and full lips resembled my mother's; however, on me, they weren't flattering like they were on her. I let out a labored sigh.

I have always felt like the odd one out. My mom's side of the family all had naturally beautiful bronze skin, which came from my grandmother's side of the family. She was a variable melting pot of ethnicities, the dominant being Indian and African American. I thought about that for a minute as I stared into my hazel eyes that popped against my manu-factured caramel skin. That was due to my many days out in the sun and frequent spray tans. Before my skin was always pasty, making my veins all too visible. My thick hair, a mess of chestnut waves that curled at the ends, reached the middle of my back. I immediately got out my blow dryer and flat iron and placed them on the counter.

My eye color was undeniably from my father's side of the family. His parents migrated from Turkey when my father was just a young boy. They were in pursuit of the American dream, just like any other immigrant, I suppose. My hair color was also a trait I received from him, as well as my thick eyebrows. I had a standing appointment every two weeks to get them threaded.

As I examined my face, I noticed it resembled the little girl in my dream. I jumped back and looked away. These darn pills were driving me crazy. A chill ran up my spine and goosebumps appeared on my arms. I ran my hand over my arm and saw a bruise, identical to the one on my other arm. They looked like tiny fingerprints. *How is that possible?* I paused, remembering my dream.

"The little girl," I whispered.

I tried to think of some other explanation. It was a dream. It wasn't real. Although, it seemed real...too real. Maybe I grabbed myself while I was sleeping. I put my hand over the fingerprints. Even though my hands are small, the fingerprints were smaller—small enough to be a child's.

"It's impossible. Or is it?" I shook my head. The only logical explana-tion was another side effect from the pills. Unexplained rashes, maybe.

I jumped in the shower before my mother came to check my progress. I was still in deep thought as I washed my hair. I got dressed in a Victoria's Secret pink sweat suit for maximum comfort during the plane ride. Even though I dressed casually, I would still straighten my hair and put on makeup to make myself presentable. This was a daily routine—all in prep-aration for me to get into character. The makeup helped transform me. It couldn't work miracles, but it was just enough to make me presentable. I often imaged what it might be like if I were exotic and beautiful. If I were beautiful, would it be enough to make my dad want to be a father to me? I was brought back down to reality every time I stared at myself in the mirror. I hoped my reflection would change, but to my dismay, it never did. It was a stupid thought, anyway. I finished getting ready in a mad dash, and we were off.

LAX was always the same, crowded. It was always full of people in a hurry to get to their destinations, and today was no different. We made it through airport security and boarded the aircraft. I made my way to our seats. I always got the window seat. My mother secured our carry-ons in the overhead bin and sat down next to me. The flight attendants had just begun their pre-flight safety instructions.

My mother squeezed her behemoth purse under the seat in front of her and was now fumbling with her seat belt. "I can never figure out these darn things."

"Before I forget, Mom, I need fifty dollars."

"Kristen, why on earth do you need fifty dollars?"

One of the flight attendants, a fiery redhead, flashed us a dirty look and shushed us as if to say we were disturbing the other passengers.

I rolled my eyes. "It's so not that serious," I said under my breath. "I'm almost out of my Juicy Tube, and I need more Studio Fix."

"I'd like to see you go one month without your M.A.C. and Lancôme," my mother whispered.

"It's your fault. You spoil me."

The flight attendant glared over in our direction again, but we both ignored her this time.

"Well, if I didn't, you'd probably just ask your father anyway."

I thought about her statement as she continued talking. I would have to ask Rita, my dad's secretary, for any advances on my allowance. She'd always administer them by transferring funds from my father's account to mine. It was an account that Rita set up in the first place. I had a closer relationship with her than I did with my father. But I never blamed her for all the missed birthday calls or cards. After all, there was only so much she could do. The rest would be up to him.

"We can go shopping when we get there. Maybe go into the city and make a day of it. What do you think about that?" She continued when I didn't answer. "We can eat at that little bistro you like so much for lunch. What's the name of that restaurant?" She closed her eyes tight as if to squeeze out the correct answer. "Oh right, Bistro 61. How does that sound? Doesn't it sound like fun?" My mom probably hoped that her enthusiasm would rub off on me.

"Yeah, I guess."

The flight attendants finished their presentation, and we were preparing for take-off. The redhead made her rounds, checking to make sure everyone had fastened their seatbelts and had all tray tables in an upright position. When she got to our row, she glanced over at us. Her face became stern, like a parent who was about to scold a child. She slightly shook her head but kept walking.

"I guess we can kiss our peanuts goodbye," my mother said, peeking down the walkway.

"What if the plane crashed and we all died?" I said, fiddling with the ring on my finger.

My mother turned to look at me with disapproval.

After a moment, I finally made eye contact with her. "What?"

"Why on earth would you say something like that?"

I shrugged. "I don't know. It was just a thought. I'm sure planes crash all the time. You never know when your time is up."

My mother stared at me, mortified. The man in the seat across from us was staring at me in horror as well. The top of his bald head shined, his eyes were fixed on us, peeking over the spectacles that hung low on the edge of his long narrow nose. His face was pale. I noticed he had the safety pamphlet in his hand. There was an awkward silence, so I turned to look out my window. The plane started backing up.

"Honestly, I cannot believe some of the things you say sometimes," my mother continued murmuring, but I blocked her out.

So what if I thought these things? Why is it such a big deal? As I stared out the window, I began to imagine different ways it might happen. Maybe the plane would go down in the mountains, and the impact would cause it to explode. I wondered what would kill us first, the impact, or the explosion. Or maybe it would go down in the ocean, and we'd be submerged underwater, which would totally suck. Who knows how far from land we'd be? I'd probably freeze and go into shock causing me to drown. Freezing to death wasn't exactly high up on my desired ways to go. Maybe I should've been listening to the redhead's instructions. But somewhere in between my enthralling fantasies of drowning and trying to remember anything the redhead said, I drifted into a deep sleep.

In my dream, I was walking up to a large, white house with huge pillars in front, surrounded by tall oak trees. On the outskirts of the property, there was nothing but green as far as the eye could see. It was humid. The sun was shining bright, directly overhead. Again, I was barefoot as I walked along the dirt walkway that led me to the front door. I opened it and walked in the mansion. It looked like it had been there for a hundred years. I walked into a foyer that had a grand staircase arched in a half-circle. Above was a large, crystal chandelier that sparkled from the sunlight. It shone in through the floor-to-ceiling windows. I looked more closely and noticed it was filled with cobwebs. In fact, I was surrounded by them. I ran into an adjoining room to get away and ended up in a room filled with animals. They all laid there on the floor and on furniture. I realized they were dead, and rigor mortis had already set in. I was standing next to a side table that had a squirrel on it lying face up. It looked as if it were sleeping. I leaned in to poke its stomach, and its eyes flew open.

I jumped up and screamed. My heart was pounding, but I was safely in my seat next to my mother, who was sleeping. At first, I wasn't sure if I had screamed out loud or not, but the plane was quiet. No one was looking in my direction, so I figured I was good.

"Mom," I said quietly, still scared.

My mother turned her head sluggishly to face me, but her eyes were still closed.

"I had a bad dream. It was so weird. I was in this house, but I don't know whose it was or where I was at." I paused for my mother's response, but she didn't say anything. "Mom, are you awake?" I touched her shoulder.

Her eyelids flew open, but her eyes were completely black.

"Mom…are you okay?"

She didn't answer. She began convulsing. Her facial features began to change, and she made these weird moaning sounds. Then she stopped and sat very still. She opened her mouth and a buzzing sound came from her throat. Suddenly, a swarm of bees flew out and attacked me. I screamed, but no sound came out. I shook my head and flailed my arms frantically to get them away, but they wouldn't leave. The silence was broken by the same crackling sound I heard in my dream the night before.

I jumped out of my sleep but was held in place by my seat belt. I was still screaming and flailing my arms around. My mother woke from her sleep, startled.

"What? What is it? What's wrong?" she asked, concerned—her body tense.

I calmed myself down some, but I was still unsure if I was really awake or still sleeping. I had grabbed both armrests, squeezing them tightly. My breathing was still accelerated as I tried to make sense of what was happening. The man sitting in the aisle across from us, along with others in first class, were staring, afraid to ask if everything was okay.

"Well, are you okay?"

"Yeah. I just had a weird dream, that's all."

My mother was still staring at me as I loosened my grip on the arm-rests.

"Really, I'm fine." I mustered up a half-smile.

She sighed. "You scared the crap out of me." She glanced around quickly. "And I think you frightened everyone on board."

"Sorry."

She slowly began to relax back into her seat, still peeking at me subtly out the corner of her eye.

"Really, Mom, I'm fine."

"Okay," she said, suspiciously. She paused for a moment like she was working herself up to say more. "Do you want to talk about it?"

There were two things my mother was deathly afraid of. The first being lizards and the other being all things scary. I appraised her face. "Um, I don't think that would be such a good idea."

"That scary?"

"Yeah."

"Oh," she said, apprehensive.

"It just felt so real," I said, thinking about my dream within a dream.

"Okay, well, hon, I'm sure whatever it is…everything will be all right. It was just a dream. It wasn't real. Like unicorns, leprechauns, or a leather Mahina under a $1,000."

I began to wonder if she was trying to convince herself or me. "You're comparing a Louis Vuitton purse to a leprechaun?"

"I'm just saying, there's no such thing as a real Mahina that you can buy for less than a few thousand dollars, just like there are no leprechauns or boogie monsters. You'll never find them. They aren't real. You have nothing to worry about."

"Yeah, I guess you're right."

* * *

It didn't take long to get our luggage from the baggage claim. Aunt Carol was at the curb waiting for us in her fancy SUV. We put our luggage in the back and climbed in. Aunt Carol hadn't changed much since the last time I had seen her a few years ago. Her jet-black hair was pulled back in a sleek bun. She reached over to hug my mother, then turned back to examine me from behind her black square-rimmed glasses. Her light brown eyes caught mine. Her fine face was full of glee, but she kept her conservative composure.

"You've gotten a little taller. What are you now, 5'3", 5'4"?"

I nodded.

"And even more beautiful than the last time I saw you. You might wanna cut that out—no one will take you seriously," she chuckled. "I guess you'll just have to talk to people to show them just how intelligent you are."

I mustered up an awkward smile and quickly averted my gaze. I fidgeted with my ring. Of course I didn't take her seriously. I scoffed at her use of the word beautiful. Being family, she probably feels obligated to encourage me of such things, just like my mother. Even though my family professed me as intelligent and beautiful, I knew it was all lies. I knew what I saw in the mirror.

When I was finally able to look back up at her, she winked at me. A police officer signaled for her to move along, so she turned around and merged with traffic. Aunt Carol and my mother had always been about the same body type—5'6" and slender, no matter what they put in their mouths. If I weren't the same way, I would hate them for it. Aunt Carol also looked young for her age, especially being the oldest. My mother was the baby of the family; there were four siblings all together. My Aunt Bridgette lived with Nana in Georgia, and my Uncle Andrew was living in Connecticut, where he owned a small investment firm.

My mom and Aunt Carol chatted as if they hadn't spoken in years even though they called each other at least twice a week. I kept thinking about my dreams and what they might mean. Why did that psycho little girl attack me? Why did it leave marks on my arms? My sweatshirt was hiding the bruises underneath. I tried to distract myself by looking out my window. We were on the freeway now, flying with the flow of traffic. The concrete in the city reminded me of California, but the green trees reminded me of the dreams.

"So what do you want to do for your birthday?" Aunt Carol asked.

"Well, Mom said we could go shopping in the city one day."

"Oh, okay, but what about on your actual birthday?"

"Maybe just dinner at home or something. We don't have to go out."

"Nonsense, we can go to P.F. Chang's. Is that still one of your favorites?"

"Yes."

"Then it's settled—that's where we're going." She glanced up at me in her rearview mirror with a smile.

I forced myself to smile back.

It was no use arguing with her, so I gave in quickly. I would much rather spend my birthday at home in bed, which was why it angered me so much when my mother said we were coming to Long Island this year. We used to come here every Fourth of July, but it's been more than a few years since our last visit. I began to feel uneasy. I'd have to put myself into character now. I'd have to smile and pretend to be happy about my birthday being here yet again. There was nothing happy about me existing another year. That only meant another year would approach—another year of being ignored, being rejected by the only person I wished would acknowledge my presence.

My father was the only one I wanted praise and attention from, even if it was a lie. He was nowhere and everywhere at the same time. His absence was a consistent reminder of how unwanted and hopeless I felt; a pain that burned deep inside me and seemed like it could never be quenched. I mean, yes, he's a good provider, but that wasn't what I wanted or what I needed. When he and my mother had divorced about eight years ago, he remarried right away. He had another family now. A family that he goes home to every night, a family that he takes vacations with, and daughters that have long since replaced me. He takes them to daddy-daughter dances, but I don't even get so much as a card on my birthday. It was just one day out of the whole year for him to at least acknowledge he helped make me, but even that was too much.

It took us an hour and a half to get out of the city and into Wildwood. The area was nice, peaceful. My aunt and her husband moved to Long Island when they first got married but moved to Wildwood about seven years ago. It was a beach community—family oriented. The house was located right on the coast.

We pulled into the three-car garage. It was a five-bedroom, five-bathroom quintessential beach house. Their décor was a mix between contemporary and traditional. There were two guest rooms, and my mother and I always shared the white one that overlooked the ocean. This was mainly because sharing a room with Aunt Bridgette or Nana meant listening to them snore.

We entered the two-story family room that opened into the gourmet kitchen. My cousins were lounging on each of the taupe couches. They jumped up once they saw us. The younger of the two, April, ran over to me first and hugged me. She was thin but athletic. She was only thirteen but was already a few inches taller than I was. When April turned her attention to my mom, Megan smiled and hugged me next. We were the same age.

Everyone said their hellos and took a seat in the family room. I remained standing.

"Um, I'm going to put my stuff away."

I grabbed my suitcase and headed for the white room.

3

Visitor

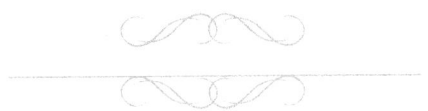

I shut the door behind me and stood there for a moment, taking everything in. I took a deep breath, effectively fighting back tears. Straight ahead through the French doors was an unobstructed view of the ocean. The waves were crashing into one another. I could see the clouds gliding across the sky at a snail's pace. The light of the sun cast vibrant layers of honey and topaz against the backdrop of the blue sky. I closed my eyes and took a deep breath. Thursday will be here before I know it. I tried to convince myself. I fought back my tears and decided I'd unpack to take my mind off the thoughts swirling around in my head. I laid the suitcase on the beige carpet, taking a seat on the floor to begin unpacking.

"Nana's here," my mother said as she walked through the door.

I just looked up at her. "Okay," I said, uninterested, as I put my underwear in the bottom drawer.

"So come say hello."

"Okay," I retorted sarcastically.

She stopped. "Are you still mad at me for making you come here?" Her arms were folded.

"I'm not mad, Mom." I continued unpacking, not making eye contact with her.

"I just didn't want you moping around the condo this year. You seem to like it here, so I figured visiting would help you get out of the funk you tend to get in sometimes."

I fought back the tears, taking longer than normal to answer. I thought I was doing a good job of keeping character with her, but I had obviously slipped up somewhere along the way. I wondered how much she noticed. Of course she knew I had been a little depressed for a while now, and that was the main reason I had started going to therapy. But I thought I was giving her the impression that I was getting better, not worse. It was no use, anyway. It was becoming more and more impossible to pretend for such long periods of time. School was one thing, but if I had to pretend at home for much longer, I might snap.

"Don't worry about it, Mom. I'm fine."

"Can you at least look at me?"

I sighed and looked up at her. "See? I'm fine." I mustered up a painful smile.

"Fine. Oh, by the way, guess who's coming out here for your birthday?"

"Who?"

"Well, he had to rearrange some things, but your father is coming out for a couple of days," she said with a sense of accomplishment.

"What?! Why?"

"Kristen, he's your father. He wants to come see you. He misses you."

"All of a sudden he misses me?" I got up from the floor and flopped onto the sea of decorative white pillows on the queen-sized bed.

My mother walked over to the other side and sat down. "He really is trying, hon."

"Seriously?" I rolled over onto my back. "You know, I'd love to see what him not trying looks like."

My mother lay down beside me. We both were silent, staring up at the coffered ceiling.

"I like this ceiling. It's almost like art. I could stare at it all day."

I sighed. "Yeah, I know. You say that every time we come here." I smiled for real this time. "Mom?"

"Yeah, hon."

We turned to look at each other.

"Is he really coming this time?" I asked the question even though I already knew the answer. It was quiet for a moment. "Did you speak to him or Rita?"

"I spoke to him. He said he wouldn't miss it."

She smiled at me, but I knew her well enough to hear the worry behind her statement. Even more so, I saw it behind her eyes.

She leaned over and kissed my forehead. "We better get out there before your grandmother—"

"Before your grandmother what?" The round old woman came through the door. Her black hair was pulled up neat in a French twist and her cocoa skin radiated against her royal blue pantsuit.

"Nana!" I jumped off the bed and ran to her waiting arms.

"Look at my little Krissy. Well, I guess you're not so little anymore." She kissed the top of my head. "You still listening to that devil music?"

"Nana, you think all music is devil music."

"Nope, not all of it. There are some good gospel artists out there."

"Then yes."

"All right. Let me get a good look at you."

I stepped away from her and turned in a circle.

"Humh, just as I thought. You're skin and bones. Don't you two eat?"

My mom shook her head in irritation. "Mom, of course we do."

"So you're cooking for this child?"

"I cook once in a while. We have busy schedules, so it's easier to grab something."

"Didn't I teach all of you how to make a good home-cooked meal?"

"Yes, but—"

"I don't want to hear it. You need to start feeding her properly. She's a growing girl. Of course, it's too late for you. There's nothing you can do about that now, but she still has time. Plus, you're a grown woman—you should know better."

"Yes, Mom," she said reluctantly.

"Anyway, I didn't come in here to start fussin'." She turned to look at me. "Everyone else is waiting to see you."

"Who?" I asked, surprised.

"Your cousin, Dennis, and Aunt Bridgette. He picked us up from the airport."

We made our way to the family room where everyone was gathered. I hugged Aunt Bridgette. She was wearing a tea-length black and white sundress. She was a little larger than her sisters, and her personality was even bigger. She wasn't as big as she thought, but I guess that happens when you're surrounded by sisters who wear a size four. Despite her insecurities, Aunt Bridgette was always well put-together. Her hair was also jet-black and full of beautiful wild curls that passed her shoulders by a few inches. Her makeup was always flawless.

"Ahh! I cannot believe how beautiful you are. Girl, you could be a model! You look like you even got a little color in your skin."

Everyone laughed.

"At least living out in California helped with something," Bridgette said, still giggling.

I made my way over to Dennis, Aunt Carol's son, and gave him a quick hug. Dennis was about 5'9" and muscular. His black hair was cut short.

"Good to see you, cuz. I hear you're doing well in school, honor roll and all that. That's wus up."

"Yup."

"Keep it up and stay focused."

"I will."

"All right y'all, I gotta go," he said, slowly walking toward the entrance.

"And where are you going?" Nana asked.

"Gotta meet up with some friends, but I'll be back for dinner tonight."

"All right, then. Be safe."

"Always." He ducked out in a hurry.

"Where's Michael?" Bridgette asked Carol.

"He's out playing golf with some friends from work. He should be here shortly. Are you guys hungry? It'll be time for dinner soon. I was thinking we could grill some steaks."

I loved when Aunt Carol made dinner. I could already taste the moist, charcoal-flavored steak in my mouth. My stomach growled in anticipation. The adults scurried into the kitchen to prepare our meal. Nana liked eating dinner around 5:00 p.m., so, of course, we all complied with her wishes. I sat down in one of the oversized armchairs.

"You on cheer again this year?" Megan asked.

"Yeah, looks like I'll be captain this year," I said halfheartedly.

She paused before answering. "I could've been captain of my squad if I wanted, but I opted not to," she said snidely.

"Oh, okay," I replied.

It was always a competition with Megan, especially since we were around the same age. I couldn't care less. It was pure coincidence that I had made captain. All the other girls were graduated, so I was the only one returning for the second year to varsity cheer. Since I was the only one who had experience, the girls decided I should be captain. It wasn't something I campaigned for or even wanted, for that matter. Regardless, my character would get the job done with a smile and a can-do attitude. I never really thought of myself as a leader. I'd rather blend in with the crowd. But for whatever reason, that rarely happened.

"My dad bought me a BMW for my birthday," Megan said.

"Oh, really? Wow, that's great for you," I said, trying show enthusiasm. For some reason, my replies always came out a little sarcastic.

She just looked at me, trying to assess my facial expression. "So, what are you getting?"

"Um, I don't know. I didn't ask for anything." Was she serious? I guess I hadn't thought about it what with all the suicidal thoughts lately. I sighed. That would be the extent of her problems…worrying about what color car would go best with her wardrobe. "I guess it slipped my mind."

"If I were you, I'd milk your dad for all he's got. Ask for a car, clothes, a new phone, maybe even a trip out of the country. I mean, he at least owes you that for never being around, right?"

And that did it. Why did she have to go there? Was she even thinking about how sharp her words would be? I could feel the tears welling up in my eyes. I wouldn't be able to contain them this time.

"I, um, have to go to the bathroom."

I quickly got up and walked into the guest bathroom and sat on the stone tiles with my back against the door.

I wondered how long it would take for someone to come looking for me. Not wanting to be bothered, I ended up moving to the walk-in closet nestled in a dark corner. I tried my best to muffle the sound of sobs that broke through my chest, wishing I were anywhere but here.

* * *

We all had dinner together that night. I pulled myself together enough to even smile and laugh at some of Aunt Bridgette's jokes. Dennis came back with his wife, Vanessa, and their two kids, DJ and Arianna. Uncle Michael, Carol's husband, had arrived while I was in hiding. It marveled me that Aunt Carol and her husband had gotten married straight out of high school and were still together all these years later. Aunt Carol got pregnant with Dennis her second year of college. Nana moved in with them to help while they both worked and went to school.

It made me think about my ten-year plan and the goals I set for myself. My teachers began to advocate the plan in my sophomore year of high school. We were to lay out goals and aspirations for the not-so-distant future. For many of my classmates, the future seemed like a lifetime away. But I knew better. I knew as soon as we graduated, we'd be in the real world. And that world was nothing like they perceived it to be.

My peers only saw freedom from their parents' control, but I knew it meant much more than that. It meant responsibility, although I didn't quite know to what extent. Nevertheless, I had mapped out my life for the next ten years. After graduation, I'd attend Cal State in Long Beach. After four years of college, I'd graduate with honors in my chosen field of psychology. I would then land a good job, get married, and begin having children a year later. Well, that seemed like the path I should take, anyway. The truth was, I wasn't sure what I wanted out of life or what the future held for me. Even though I made these goals, my destiny seemed bleak. I had planned everything out, but there was no depth to it. They were just words on paper. I truly wanted to do something I was passionate about—something that would wake me up each morning feeling elated to have another day to do it. But I wasn't sure where I'd find this desire, or even what this desire was. Because of that, the picture of me coming home to my fictitious husband and kids was always interrupted by a stupid image of me on the streets alone. It wasn't something I wanted for my life, but I couldn't escape it.

We ate steaks with baked potatoes, grilled green beans, and squash. The night ended with everyone gathered in the family room sharing funny stories.

"So a few months ago, Carol came to visit Mama and me," Bridgette said, already beginning to chuckle.

Carol, already knowing the story, shook her head in embarrassment.

"We were getting ready for bed, and Carol went to brush her teeth." Aunt Bridgette couldn't stop laughing.

Carol had to continue the story. "I was brushing my teeth, but the toothpaste tasted different. So I looked at the tube and saw I was actually brushing my teeth with Preparation H."

Everyone burst out laughing, except for the teens.

"What's Preparation H?" April asked.

"It's hemorrhoid cream," Bridgette said, laughing hysterically.

"Ew," April said.

"Gross," Megan said in a monotone voice, not looking up from her phone.

I didn't even realize she was listening. She got up and disappeared around the corner, probably going upstairs to her room. Dennis and his family left around 9:00 p.m. They live in the city, so they had a long drive ahead of them. The rest of my family would be up for hours, talking and laughing.

I made my way to the white room. I got my notebook out of my suitcase and lay down on the bed.

August 28

Dear Diary,

Today wasn't so bad. We got to Aunt Carol's house around 4:00 p.m. I really don't want to be here. Some strange things have been happening to me. I've been having weird dreams that seem too real. Maybe it's the new meds I'm taking. I hate taking medication. After all, unusual dreams are one of the side effects of these pills. In one of my dreams this little girl

grabbed me, and when I woke up, I had bruises on my forearms. Is that normal? I don't know

what to think. I want to tell someone, but will they think I'm crazy? I don't want to find out.

Mom says Dad wants to see me. It sounds so good, but I've heard this before too many

times. So many times I've waited for him to come see me. I waited at the window, waiting to

see my father's car pull up, but it never did. And the darkness inside me only got deeper and

darker. I thought the pain could never get worse. But it does with each day that goes by, each

day I'm still alive.

I lay there a moment, thinking about the dreams again. I felt a shiver run up my spine and goosebumps rising on my arms. I must be cold...but I didn't feel cold. This was a different feeling. I rolled up the left sleeve of my sweatshirt to see the hairs on my arm standing straight up. Maybe it was static from my sweatshirt. Upon examination, I noticed the bruises were gone. Did I imagine it? Was that a dream within a dream? I was so confused. Had it all been a dream? I rubbed my arm to get rid of the goosebumps. It wasn't working, so I yanked my sleeve back down. I rolled over on my back to distract myself with the detail of the ceiling. It was no use, so I decided to get ready for bed. When I got back from the bathroom, my mother was already in her pajamas. I took the right side of the bed, closest to the door. I got under the covers and tried to get comfortable.

"Do you want to turn the nightlight on?" Mom asked.

"What?"

"It gets really dark in here. The nightlight will let you see where you're walking if you have to get up in the middle of the night."

I wondered why she was acting so ridiculous. We've stayed here before and I never remembered us using a nightlight. Maybe my recent episode on the plane scared her more than I thought.

"No, I like sleeping in the dark. I'll be fine."

"Okay," she said hesitantly, not taking her eyes off me. She turned off the lights and got into bed.

As I opened my eyes to situate myself, I saw something at the door about fifteen paces away. I blinked a few times—it was something that looked like a ghost standing right next to me.

"AHHH!" I screamed, throwing the sheets over my head.

My mom jumped up and turned the lamp on. "What? What is it?!"

I slowly lifted the sheet and sat up, searching the room for the thing I had just seen.

"Kristen, what happened? Why did you scream?" She looked terrified.

I wasn't sure if I should tell her the truth. It was no use getting us both scared.

"Um, it was nothing…I just thought I saw a spider crawling on me."

"Oh my goodness, you scared me to death."

I laid back down, still looking around the room.

She leaned over to turn out the light.

"Um, Mom?"

"Yeah?"

"Maybe we should turn that nightlight on."

4

Rejection

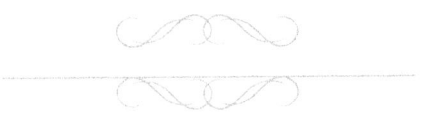

The next morning, Aunt Carol, Aunt Bridgette, and Nana got up early to get ready for church. My mother was still sleeping, but I lay there listening to them in the kitchen. I thought about the dreams and what I saw last night. I thought about the medications I'd taken in the past and the side effects I had experienced. There were a lot of crazy side effects, but I had never experienced anything like this before. Was I going crazy? Were these signs of a mental breakdown? I needed to talk to someone about what was going on. But who? No one would believe me if I told them what was going on. They would either lock me up in a mental institution or…well, no, I guess that would be it. What other explanation was there other than I was going crazy? I had always believed there was a God. I know Nana believes there's a God. She went to church faithfully, and I know she prays a lot. That was the one thing I hadn't tried yet. There was something inside me that kept telling me I needed to go to church, but I was still unsure if it would help. And then I made a snap decision; I jumped out of bed and ran to the kitchen.

"Can I come?" I said in a raspy voice that almost didn't sound like me.

Aunt Bridgette turned away from whatever she was preparing on the counter. Aunt Carol and Nana were seated at the kitchen table.

"Good morning," Nana said.

I cleared my throat. "Oh, sorry, good morning."

"You want to come to church with us?" Aunt Carol asked.

"Um, yeah, if that's okay with you?"

"Of course, it's fine. I think it's great you want to come. But you have to hurry. Can you be ready in thirty minutes?" Nana asked.

"Yes."

"All right then, go get ready and then come eat some breakfast."

"Okay." I ran to the room and gathered my things for a shower.

"What are you doing? Why are you up so early?" my mom groaned as she rolled over.

"I'm going to church with Nana," I said as I ran out the door.

My mom sat up in the bed, still half-asleep and bewildered.

My mom ended up joining us. The service was…interesting. There was a lot of standing up, sitting down, and repeating after the preacher and from a little pamphlet we received upon arrival. They sang a few songs. Of course, I didn't know them. The preacher was a woman who spoke for about thirty minutes about how we should accept God's will for us, no matter how devastating it may be. She gave an example of a person who was dying from cancer, and how that person must be at peace with the Lord's will for them. Now, I'm not an aficionado on the subject of God, but somehow that didn't seem right to me. How could that be? I mean, I understand everyone's time on earth must end at some point. But what if it wasn't God's plan for this woman to die? I wasn't even sure if what I was thinking made any sense. I just knew if it was God's will for her to die, then that would mean it was God's will for me to be crazy, and I would just have to accept that. Not only would I be depressed for the rest of my life, but I'd also be insane.

Everyone stood again to recite some phrase from the pamphlet, but I couldn't get up. It was as if my body were weighted down from the despair I felt. I sat in the center of the pew, surrounded by what seemed like mechanical robots, reciting what they had been programmed to. Did they really know why they were saying these things? Did this religious experience work for them? Or were they just going through the motions, not wanting to rock the boat? I could see some people looking at me out of the corner of their eyes, my family included. I was the only one who was still seated—the only one who couldn't, or wouldn't, conform.

"So, how did you like it?" Aunt Carol asked.

"Um, it was interesting," was all I could say.

I sat between my mother and Aunt Bridgette in the back seat, staring straight ahead. She changed the subject quickly after evaluating my reaction. They all began to chat among themselves. As I sat there, I felt so lonely. Before Aunt Carol asked my opinion of her church, she and everyone else in the car spoke about how nice the service was. I could only wonder if they were present for the same service. Maybe there was something wrong with me. Everyone else seemed to enjoy church. Why was I the only one who got nothing positive out of it? Clearly, there was no hope for me. I had exhausted all my options.

We drove around for a while and stopped at a few plant nurseries before going back to the house.

It was a beautiful day, so I sat out on the back deck. I watched the waves crash over and over. It was hot and sticky, but the cool breeze whipped around me, tossing my hair, making the heat bearable.

"What are you doing out here by yourself?" Nana sat down in the white Adirondack chair next to mine.

"Just thinking."

"Oh yeah? Anything you want to share?"

I smiled.

Her face wrinkled with worry, but her bronze skin was still smooth. It was clear that our youthful appearances came from her side of the family.

"It's nothing heavy, Nana. Just wondering what I want for my birthday, that's all."

I wasn't sure if she was buying it, so I turned my focus back to the ocean sprawled out before us.

"You're a liar," she accused, then turned to look at the ocean, too.

I was somewhat shocked by her words, but I didn't dare look at her.

"And a terrible one, at that."

I was quiet, hoping she would give up and leave me.

We sat in silence for a long while.

"Your mom says something scared you pretty good last night," she said, trying to prod. "It had to have been more than a spider that scared you so good it provoked you to go to church."

I finally looked at her in disbelief. How could she put two and two together so easily?

"You gonna tell me now?"

Could I tell her my secret? I thought quickly about whether or not I should tell her the truth. "You're going to think I'm crazy."

"How do you know what I'm gonna do or what I'm not? There's nothing I haven't heard or seen."

I scrutinized her facial expression after her last word was spoken. "Seen?" I asked, reluctantly.

She chuckled to herself.

"So he scared you good, didn't he?"

My eyes were wide with excitement. "You've seen him before?"

"Yes, plenty of times."

"Has anyone else?"

"No," she shook her head.

I couldn't believe it. I really had seen a ghost. I'd always been scared of horror movies, but I'd rationalize my way through watching them. I would tell myself I didn't have to worry about things like serial killers, ghosts, and monsters because the movies were never based in the same state as where I lived. Therefore, it wasn't real and could never happen to me.

But this had changed everything.

"Well, why does he come around here?"

"I don't know. He just does."

"I never really believed there were ghosts before, you know, white and glowing."

"Oh, yes, even the Bible mentions them."

"Oh, wow. Do they all look like people? Is there more of them? What does he want?" The questions flowed out one after another.

"I don't know the details. I just know it's a spirit and you shouldn't go talkin' to it, you hear me?"

"Yes, ma'am." I paused. "But why—"

"Here you are," my mom yelled as she came out of the house. "Hey, Mom, can I talk to Kristen alone?"

"Sure. I'm tired, anyway. I'm going to take a nap." Nana gave me a meaningful look, hidden from my mother's view, then got up and left.

My mother took her seat.

"What's up, Mom?"

She paused for a while. "Well, it's your father."

I could feel a knot rising in my throat. The pain in my soul heightened as if I needed a reminder that it had never left—only subsided. I began fidgeting with the ring on my finger. I exhaled and closed my eyes.

"He's not coming, is he?" I asked, saving my mom from the agony of being the perpetual bearer of bad news.

I knew how hard it was for her to say those words every time. I hated him for having her do his dirty work. Another rain check. I opened my eyes to stare out at the ocean, its crashing waves mimicking the chaos I felt inside.

"Honey, I'm so sorry."

"I know," I whispered back. The downpour of tears suddenly escaped.

For twenty minutes, I heard nothing but the crashing of the frothy waves against the pebble-filled beach. The wind continued to whip violently, and I wished it would somehow take me away with it. My mom put her hand on top of mine, but we never looked at each other. We just sat in silence. There was nothing left to say.

August 29

Dear Diary,

So Dad's not coming for my birthday. I don't know why I let him get my hopes up only to have them demolished again. I'm tired of crying over this...over him. He clearly doesn't care how much he's hurting me, so why should I? It's easier said than done. Last night was strange. I saw a spirit. He was a Native American dressed in traditional garb. He got really close and scared the crap out of me. He looked at me as if he had seen me before; like he was marveling at how much I'd changed since the last time he'd seen me. It was so freaky. Maybe he was someone who used to live on this land a long time ago. He would look like a regular man if he weren't all white and glowing. I thought I was going crazy until Nana said she has seen him, too. I cannot tell you how much it scared me. It made me want to go to church. I thought maybe God could help me, but that was a waste of time. I'll never get that hour of my life back. But Nana did say something about the Bible mentioning spirits or something like that. Maybe

I should get a Bible and see if I can find what she's talking about. Then again, I don't know how well that would go. The last time I tried to read a Bible, I couldn't understand a word of it. It might as well have been in another language. So what now? Well, I guess I'll have to figure that out myself, but I'll keep you updated.

* * *

Monday was my birthday, so we went into the city for a day of shopping and fine cuisine. I got all the things I needed and some extras on our excursion. I knew my mom was trying to cheer me up by showering me with gifts. It was always her futile attempt at giving me the happiness I yearned for. Nevertheless, I put on my happy face and showed no signs of the gut-wrenching anguish I was feeling inside. I got a few pairs of designer jeans, some shirts, blouses, and some dresses from Badgley Mischka.

We ate at Bistro 61 for lunch like my mom had promised, and afterward, we stopped by the TRL building in Times Square. Then we went to the MET. It was one of my favorite museums. The day was all about what I wanted to do and continued into the night when we went to P.F. Chang's for dinner. Uncle Andrew and his family came down to join us. Everyone was there. Everyone except the one person I wished would, just once, drop everything for me. The one person I wished would put forth the effort to make me feel like I was important, even if he didn't mean it. At this point, something would be better than nothing.

Every second I sat at that table, I was still anticipating his arrival. I was hoping he would surprise me and come anyway; that he would tell me he loved me—and mean it. I wished he would ask me question after question about everything he had missed out on and I would answer him with unguarded enthusiasm because the pain would be gone.

I was brought back to reality when I opened all my presents. My mother gave me the gift from my father. There were oohs and ahhs at the Harry Winston gift box. I opened the rectangular box to see a beautiful diamond tennis bracelet. It was breathtaking, but I had no breath left, so it didn't have the same effect on me as it did on everyone else. My mother helped me put it on. The sparkle of the diamonds was almost too much against my petite wrist. All I could do was stare at it. It was so ostentatious. Where would I wear this to? I couldn't wear it to school, lounging around the house, or even laying out on the beach. I wanted to be able to wear whatever he got me every day, but with this, it would be impossible. It was stupid of me to think my father had any connection to the bracelet. Rita probably bought it and arranged for the delivery. I wanted so badly for it to be from him, so he could be as close to me as my new bracelet was now. I glanced around the table at my family. Some were engrossed in conversation, and some were indulging in dessert. It seemed like life was passing me by as I sat in the same lonely state. He didn't show up, and the dark mass inside me grew larger.

*   *   *

The rest of my time in Long Island went by quickly. The following day we all went to the Bronx Zoo, and the kids loved it. Wednesday, we went down to the beach and ate lunch there. After that, we took the ferry over to Connecticut to visit Uncle Andrew and his family. I had no more incidents during my stay in Wildwood.

5

Spreading School Spirit

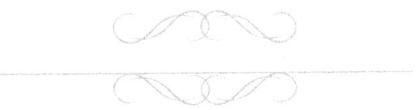

"How was Long Island?" Doctor Lewis asked.

"It was fine."

"Anything eventful happen?"

"Why? Um, I mean, what do you mean?" I was flustered but tried to play it off.

"Well, did you go out and do things? Like, did you go to the beach?" He seemed a little confused by my reaction.

"Oh, yeah, we went to the beach. My aunt's house is right on the beach."

"And how was your birthday?"

"That was fine, too."

"Did you get that bracelet for your birthday?"

Shoot, I forgot to take it off. Of course he'd notice it. I mean, who wouldn't? Even in this poorly lit room, the bracelet still sparkled and shined.

"Yeah," I said, folding my arms to hide the evidence.

"Did your dad buy it for you?"

Good guess.

"Yes."

"Was he there?"

I knew exactly where this was going, and I wanted to get off this train. "No, he had better things to do."

"Why do you say that?"

The anger had boiled up in me long enough. I could no longer hold it back. Like a steam kettle with no release, I felt I might soon combust. I had done so well for so long, but it was much harder to keep my composure now.

"If he wanted to come see me, he would've. He couldn't care less." I sighed, now angry with myself. I had gotten sucked into Doctor Lewis's vortex, and I wasn't sure how I'd get myself out now.

"And how does that make you feel?"

And there it was. I knew this was his plan all along. His progression of questions were all asked to get to this point, to get me to talk about my feelings. And, like an idiot, I took his bait. "What do you think? I'm not really feeling like skipping through a field of daisies these days."

I rolled my eyes folding my arms tighter. I could feel the bracelet forming an impression on the inside of my right arm, cutting into my skin. Unfortunately, it wasn't deep enough to overshadow the pain resurfacing from my father's absence this weekend. And definitely not deep enough to cause an accident that would excuse me from this therapy session. But I was almost sure it would at least leave a mark.

I messed up. I had been doing so well with not showing my emotions because I knew that's exactly what Doctor Lewis had been waiting for. He wanted to psychoanalyze if he hadn't been already.

"Kristen, you know, it's okay to be mad that your father hasn't been there for you. It's perfectly natural. I'm here to show you how not to let it bother you as much. I can help show you how to cope with all the emotions you're feeling, in a nondestructive way, of course. Will you let me do that for you?"

A numbing sensation began to spread throughout my body. I knew what I had to do now. I had to be the "agreeable" Kristen. This character will say all the right things. I would only pretend to take his advice. It was the only way to speed up the process so I could be deemed stable and stop coming to this place.

I nodded my head, not meeting his gaze.

"Good."

He seemed pleased, as if he had made some headway with me, and scribbled on his legal pad.

* * *

It was dark, just how I liked it. I rolled over in my bed. My alarm clock read 12:45 a.m. I got up to go to the bathroom. Through the dark, I opened my bedroom door and walked into the hall. I was about to turn the bathroom light on when I saw someone standing at the end of the hall, staring. I froze. I knew I had seen this person before. The picture on our mantle came back to my mind—it was my grandfather. I couldn't look away. He was wearing a tweed suit, similar to the one he'd been wearing in the picture. Not knowing what to do, I quickly walked into my bathroom. I stood there a moment, trying to work up the nerve to check if he was still standing there. Finally, I peeked into the hallway, but there was nothing there. I paused, waiting for the spirit of my grandfather to reappear, but he didn't. I went back into the bathroom and shut the door behind me. Why was this happening? Was it the medication? But Nana could see them, too. She didn't take these pills. Well, that's great; I'm just plain old crazy, no help from my medication needed. I used the bathroom and quickly got back into bed.

* * *

"Kristen! Kristen, are you up yet?" my mom called from somewhere distant. I was groggy from the deep sleep I was in. I was upset it was already morning. I got out of bed and walked through the hall to the living room.

"Mom?"

I glanced around the room. The picture of my grandparents caught my eye. I walked over to examine the picture. The fair-skinned man was average height, his fine hair slicked back. He stood next to my grandmother, who, in her younger years, resembled Aunt Carol. He was definitely the man I saw last night. But it didn't make sense to me. Why would my grandfather's spirit appear, especially since I've never met him before? Maybe he appeared because he knew I'd be able to see him.

I continued looking for my mother. She wasn't in the living room or the kitchen. I walked into her bedroom. "Mom? Where are you?"

"Kristen?" Mom called from the opposite direction.

Maybe she was in my bathroom. I walked out of her room to my hallway. My bedroom door was shut, but I knew I had left it open. I opened it and walked in.

"What the...?" I said, shocked. I had never seen this room before.

It was a good size room, much like mine, but the furniture was all dark-colored wood instead of the white wood finishes that filled my bedroom. I walked over to the huge bay window that looked out over the backyard. Directly outside the window was a huge oak tree. I turned away to get a better look around. It was clean and bright but a little out of date, not at all contemporary. That's when I heard a weird sound in the distance. I listened carefully to the buzzing noise that was getting louder. It sounded like a plane that was flying way too low. Then there was a loud crash that shook the floor so much, it made me stumble toward the bed. A volatile explosion of inferno-type heat consumed the room. Shards of wood, debris that was once the house, and broken glass came flying toward me. It happened almost instantaneously. But when the explosion occurred, time appeared to move in slow motion. The plane hit right by the tree. The blast broke the tree in half, causing it to catch fire and fall right through the window. I threw myself to the floor to get out of the way of the oak tree that was about to crush me. It fell to my right, destroying an antique armoire in its path. The heat from the fire permeated the floor like the currents of the ocean. Fire and smoke encompassed me as I lay on the floor, unable to move or breathe. That's when I felt someone grab my arm. I turned to see something unnatural and grotesque. It had absolutely no hair on its body, and its skin seemed to be melting off. It had no lips or cartilage where its nose should have been. I tried to free myself from its grip, but I felt more hands grabbing me—one by one gripping my shoulders, my hair, my other arm, my waist, and both of my legs. I realized the body of fire was filled with these creatures. They were desperately trying to free themselves from their torment.

My surroundings changed, yet again. It was no longer the bright, airy room it once was. Instead, the only light in the dark, cavernous dwelling was from the flames. The deafening sound of teeth grinding echoed in my ears and sent chills up my spine. I screamed, but it was no use. The sounds of the roaring flames and grinding teeth drowned out my cries for help.

I woke up coughing uncontrollably, now safely in my bed in the same position I was in on that bedroom floor. My body was hot and damp. My breathing was heavy and uneven. My throat even burned a little bit. I lay there wondering if I was truly awake this time.

"Kristen? Kristen, are you up yet?" my mom called.

My body froze. My eyes shot over to the door. There was no way I was getting out of bed this time.

My mom came into my room half-dressed. "Kristen, you got to get up, hon, or you'll be late for your first day of school."

"Mom, are you…really you?"

"What on earth are you talking about?"

"You already said that," I whispered to myself. I thought about her calling me in my dream. It felt like déjà vu. When I realized I was awake, I groaned and sat up slowly.

"Get up and get ready." She ran out of the room in a hurry.

Images of the sea of fire filled with those mutilated creatures were still fresh in my mind. The way they grabbed at me was terrifying. It was as if they were pulling me into my destiny—like they had been waiting for me all along. I shivered at the thought. The heat I felt from the explosion was so real…too real. I decided not to think about it anymore and instead focused on getting ready for school. At least I didn't have to think too hard about what I was going to wear. Since it was the first day, I'd have to wear my cheer uniform.

My best friend, Avery Morgan, got a brand new Audi at the end of last year. She picked me up for school. Avery was on cheer and dance with me, so we spent a lot of time together. She whipped in and out of traffic with no hesitation. I carefully examined the car.

"Wasn't your car silver before?" I asked, confused.

"Yeah," she said, messing with the climate controls.

Her long, honey-blonde hair was pulled up into a smooth, high pony-tail. Blue and black ribbons were tied neatly into an intertwined bow.

"Why is it white now?"

"Because I had to get a new one. I opted for the white this time instead." She looked pleased with her choice.

"And why did you need to get a new one?"

"Because the old one was totaled."

"What? You were in an accident?" I looked her up and down for any signs of damage.

"No, Rodney was driving and he crashed it, idiot. If he weren't so cute and the MVP of the basketball team, I so would've dumped him. I told my parents I did it because they would've freaked. I'm not supposed to let anyone else drive it. Actually, I wasn't even with him. He took it for a joyride with some of his friends. Anyway, it ended up being totaled. It didn't look all that bad to me, but whatever. So my dad got me another one, and Rodney promised to make it up to me." She glanced over at me for a moment. Her hazel eyes were beaming.

"Well, at least your standards are high." I shook my head.

"Shut up! Not everyone can have every eligible hottie drooling over them like you, you know."

"I do not," I said, looking at her with skepticism.

"Oh, come on, Kristen. You could have any guy you want. You know, Tyler Reed has a major crush on you. I bet if you show even the tiniest interest, he would totally dump Emily for you."

"Emily who?"

"Lewis. What other Emily could even be considered girlfriend material for Tyler? It's Tyler Reed." Her thoughts quickly took her elsewhere. "You couldn't have thought I was talking about Emily Finch?" she laughed. "What a loser."

"You know, I had a dream about Emily Finch over the summer."

"Yeah? That's weird. Why would you be dreaming about her?"

"I don't know. I mean, it's not like I was thinking about her or anything. I dreamed she was pregnant."

"Pregnant? I can't think of one guy that would touch her with a ten-foot pole, much less impregnate her. You must've eaten something crazy that night or something."

"Yeah, I guess so. I thought you and Emily Lewis were friends?"

"We are." She squinted her eyes at me.

"Well, if you guys are friends, then clearly Tyler's off limits."

"We're not besties or anything, so it's fair game. I mean, if he liked me and I wasn't so in love with Rodney, I'd go for it myself."

I stared out the window as she went on about Tyler, then Rodney, and then finally about her summer. Occasionally, I'd throw in a "wow" or an "oh, really" to give the illusion I was listening. The good thing about Avery was she rarely asked any questions and really just liked talking about herself. This was always fine with me because it gave me time to think. I wanted to talk to someone about what had been going on with me, but Avery wouldn't be that person.

We finally got to school. Belmont High was average size for a public school in Los Angeles with 4,300 students enrolled. We got to our regular table to find some sophomores sitting there, talking and waiting for the first bell to ring.

"Unbelievable! You sophomores want to get the—"

"Avery." I knew she was about to use a few choice words.

"Beat it, sophomores, you should already know this table is taken."

They quickly got up and left.

We both sat down.

"Did you see the look that one guy gave me? What a jerk. I don't know why they act like they don't know who we are."

"Avery, it's really not that serious."

"Are you kidding me? We have to let everyone know their place, or they'll try and walk all over us."

"Hey, guys," Carmen said as she took a seat next to me.

"Hi." I gave her a side hug.

"What's she going off about already?" Carmen's eyes went from me to Avery.

"I'm just saying. We have to let all these lower classmen know where their place is before there's a mutiny."

"I agree. Off with their heads!" Carmen smiled at me.

"If you're not going to be serious, there's no use in continuing this conversation. I'm outie."

"Really? I'm outie? That's so, like, 1990s," Carmen said.

"It's retro, I'm bringing it back." Avery grabbed her Louis Vuitton messenger bag and headed toward the quad.

"You don't have to go away mad," Carmen shouted.

"I'm not, just going to find Rodney. See you at nutrition."

"So how was your summer?" Carmen asked me.

"It was great. I went to Long Island and visited family. What about you?" I hoped she wouldn't notice how much effort it was taking me to be this animated.

Carmen rolled her light brown eyes and ran her fingers through her raven locks. Carmen was a beautiful Puerto Rican girl with a curvy figure she flaunted for all to see. "I was here. I had summer school."

"That sucks."

"Yeah, but at least it's over. Biology kicked my butt last semester."

"Didn't you get a C in that class?"

"Yeah."

"You do realize that's passing?" I smiled. I was falling back into character with ease after the long summer break.

"I know, but now I have an A," she smiled back.

That's when I saw Charlotte running over to our table holding a small paper bag in one hand and a Starbucks coffee cup in the other. She looked terrified. Charlotte was a petite sophomore with long, light brown hair, dark brown eyes, and an overly kind heart. Unfortunately for Charlotte, Avery knew that, too, and took full advantage of it.

"Am I early? Or am I late? Was Avery here?" Charlotte asked, her panicked voice pitching in odd places.

"She went looking for Rodney," I said.

"Crap! She's going to kill me. Her latte's getting cold. She's not going to be happy about that."

She wouldn't have to look too far because Avery was walking to our table with Rodney and a few of her fans. Avery called them her fans because they were fanatic about being around her. Being her friend would give them their own form of celebrity status that she already possessed. It was idol worship at its worst.

"Charlotte Westbrook! Where have you been? I almost starved to death because of you," Avery said.

"I'm so sorry, Avery. There was an accident with an ambulance, stretchers and everything. The guy didn't look so good," Charlotte said, still flustered.

"And what does that have to do with me? Where's my latte?"

Charlotte handed Avery the latte.

Avery took a sip. "Ugh! It's cold."

She handed the cup off to Ashley, a tall, slender blonde whose looks resembled Avery's. She idolized Avery the most. Ashley took the cup and threw it away.

"What about my muffin?"

Charlotte handed Avery the bag.

"Well, at least you did one thing right," she nibbled on the blueberry muffin. "You're all dismissed."

The girls slowly walked away. I felt so bad for them, but I didn't see anything I could do about it, so I kept quiet.

The bell rang. First period was creative writing with Mr. Swisher. He was laidback and young for a teacher. Most of the students liked him because of his unorthodox teaching style. I was excited about this class. I had never tried writing creatively before, but I did love books.

Second period was calculus with Ms. Marquardt. She seemed unsure of herself as she spoke, fumbling through her unkempt desk piled with stacks of papers. Her appearance was disheveled, and her mannerisms were comparable to a frightened alley cat. Her thin, brown hair was shoulder-length and wavy. It flew all about from static cling.

I had this period with Avery and Neil Schneider. I had become pretty good friends with Neil last year when we had history together. When he entered the classroom, he seemed pleased and disappointed at the same time. He sat at the empty desk on my right. Avery was sitting on my left. When she saw Neil, she rolled her eyes and turned her back to talk to Lisa; the powerhouse and voice of reason in our fearsome four. I quickly appraised Neil who, to my surprise, was no longer skinny and lanky. He had filled out some over the summer. He was tall with thick, black, curly hair and striking blue eyes.

"Hey," Neil said, smiling.

"Hi."

"How was your summer?"

"Good. How was yours?"

"Uneventful." He glanced at Avery quickly, then back at me.

"Are you going be okay?" I asked.

"Yeah. Of course, don't worry about me," he mustered up a half smile.

But I was worried. I wasn't sure if he was telling the truth. He had been hurt by Avery. They were a couple all freshman year and the beginning of sophomore year, but they broke up when Avery got her celebrity status after riding on the coattails of the most popular senior, Aubrey Carter. Aubrey ruled the school then. She was in almost every club, not to mention captain of the cheer and the dance teams. Everyone adored Aubrey. She took Avery in as a little sister when Avery made JV cheer, making Avery just as popular as she was. Not too soon after, Avery broke up with Neil. He was devastated. If that wasn't bad enough, Avery had been secretly hooking up with Neil on and off junior year. She didn't even tell me about it at first. It was Neil who had confided in me one day after school while we were working on a history project. Since he called things off with Avery last year, she was determined to make the rest of his time at school a living hell. If there was one thing Avery didn't like, it was being rejected, especially by someone she had rejected in the first place.

"You're lying," I said as I examined his face.

"I'll be fine." He ran his fingers through his hair. "I tried calling you a couple of times over the summer. Did you get my messages?"

"Oh, ah, I'm sorry. I didn't…have my phone for most of the summer. My mom took it as a form of punishment." It sounded more like a question than a statement.

He looked at me skeptically.

I didn't blame him. I didn't even believe my own lie.

"It's cool, don't worry about it," he said, turning to face the front of the class.

We were both silent for a moment. I felt so bad. Hadn't he been through enough? Did I have to pour acid in his wounds?

"I really am sorry," I whispered.

"Are you lying?" He turned his head to peek at me.

"No."

"Were you lying about the whole punishment thing?"

I sighed. "Yes." I leaned toward him. "It's just sometimes…I don't feel like talking. My phone was turned off for most of the summer. But it had nothing to do with you. Do you believe me?"

"Not particularly, no," he said, facing forward again.

"Okay." I tore a piece of my notebook paper out and wrote frantically. "Here, this is my home phone number. It's basically the bat phone, and what's good enough for Commissioner Gordon is good enough for you."

"Nice Batman reference," he said, taking the paper.

"Thanks. I figured you'd appreciate it. So are we good?"

"Of course," he smiled.

After nutrition, I had history and chemistry with Neil, which made things more bearable. At least I'd have someone I didn't mind talking to in a few of my classes this year. But as the day went on, I noticed it was getting harder and harder to commit to my character. It was like I didn't care anymore.

"What's your problem?" Avery said as we waited in the dance room for the other girls to settle down. We sat next to one another, Avery facing the mirrored wall and me with my back against it.

"What do you mean?" I asked.

"Well, you've been acting totally lame all day. You weren't even laughing when I made that hilarious joke about what Gwendolyn McKee was wearing today."

"That's because it wasn't funny," I said.

"It was too. Everyone was laughing. Even Rodney's friends thought it was funny."

"She heard you, you know."

"I know, I meant for her to." She fixed her makeup in the floor-to-ceiling mirrors. "Clearly no one else has told her how horrid she looks. I did her a favor."

"It seemed pretty crappy to me."

Avery finally looked at me, irritated. "I can't believe you're sticking up for her. She's such a freak."

"Did you ever think maybe she can't afford to wear the things we can?"

"No, why would I?"

"Right. Why would you?" I said softly.

I just shook my head. She looked confused. She was probably wondering what was going on in my mind. The truth was, I wasn't sure myself. I had never really voiced my opinions out loud before. I had always just gone with the majority. I was never one to rock the boat, so I wasn't sure why I had said anything at all. But I was tired of all the unusual and wanted things to go back to the way they used to be. I didn't want to cause problems with my friend, but that's what I would be doing if I let this continue.

"I'm sorry," I paused. "I think I've just been out of it because of my period."

"Oh. I know, I turn into a total witch when I'm on mine," she laughed.

A few of the girls behind us quickly glanced at each other, knowing Avery's comment was an understatement. And just like that, all was right again.

After school, Avery dropped me home. I found my mother in the kitchen.

"Hey, what are you doing home so early?" I asked, dropping my backpack on the floor next to the bar. I sat down on one of the stools and rested my arms against the cool granite counter.

"Oh, I took a half day," she said.

That's when I saw the bandage across her abdomen, the ends poking out from under a shirt that was too small.

"Oh my gosh, Mom! What happened to your stomach?"

"I burned it on the cookie sheet," she said as she smoothed the bandage gingerly.

I shook my head. Of course she did. My mother was notorious for hurting herself regularly. That was partly why she didn't cook much. Life for her was a constant obstacle course of danger. When she wasn't tripping over absolutely nothing, she was choking to death because she swallowed her saliva wrong. It was an involuntary function for the rest of the world, but for my mother, it took more effort.

"If I ever teach you anything, it would be to never operate a stove while wearing a bikini," she said seriously.

We stared vacantly at each other as I took in her statement before responding. "And, Mom, why exactly are you wearing a bikini to make cookies?"

"I wasn't." She responded as if what I had said was ridiculous.

"Okay," I said, trying to understand her logic.

"You know how sometimes I get an overwhelming urge to be a home-maker? Well, I was cleaning my shower."

I still stared at her blankly.

"So naturally, I had on my bathing suit."

This compulsion came over her often, but every time I caught her in the act of cleaning her bathroom, I was still dumbfounded.

"Of course," I said.

"Well, I got hungry, so I thought cookies would be a good snack before dinner. But I hadn't finished cleaning my bathroom yet, so...."

"So you were making cookies in a bikini." I shook my head at the absurd conversation. "All right, making cookies in a bikini is just plain strange, and evidently, very dangerous—lesson learned. Okay, well, I'm going to go do my homework."

"If you're hungry, they're chocolate chip," she said with a childish grin.

6

The Young Man and the Harlot

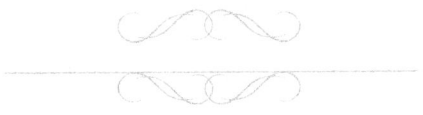

The next few months seemed to fly by. Football season was over, and we actually won a few games. I was the bubbly cheerleader again. I was the supportive friend I had always been before things had gotten weird. I laughed at all of Avery's demeaning jokes and pretended that they didn't bother me. Once again, I appeared to be happy at school by day but would cry myself to sleep at night. At least it wasn't every night like it had been before. I hadn't had a crazy dream or seen any spirits since before school started. I made a promise to my mother that I would try harder, so I began taking my medication as prescribed by Doctor Hampton, my psychiatrist. Finally, it seemed as if things were getting better.

"So everyone is going tonight. You have to go," Avery said, picking at her salad.

We all sat at our regular table for lunch outside, adjacent to the quad. Avery had been talking about the party that Tyler Reed was throwing tonight. She's still trying to push him and me together, even though he and Emily have been an official couple for the past four months. Momentous for any high school relationship of such a high profile.

"Why?" I asked.

"Because I think tonight is the night," she smirked.

"The night for what?" Carmen asked.

"I don't want to say who, but a little birdie told me that Tyler is so over Emily. He says she's way too clingy."

"Is she really?" Carmen asked.

"She's so desperate, it's pathetic," Avery answered, rolling her eyes.

"Well, what does that have to do with me?" I asked.

"Oh, come on, Kristen. I know you like him. Don't you?"

"Well, of course, but everyone at this table thinks he's gorgeous."

"Yes, but he thinks you're a goddess."

"Really? He said that?"

Avery nodded.

"You're making that up," I protested.

"Am not."

"Wait a minute. This little birdie wouldn't happen to be a big black guy, would it?" Lisa interjected.

"Okay, so Rodney told me. Apparently, he was talking about you one day in the locker room. And you, Veronica—"

"It's Ashley," she said timidly.

"Whatever. This doesn't leave this table. Understand?"

"Yes," she answered quickly.

"So it's settled. You're coming tonight, right?"

There was no use. She would not let it go.

"All right, I'll go."

The bell rang. Carmen and I walked to fifth period Spanish, while Avery went looking for Rodney. We were just about to enter the language arts building when….

"Kristen."

"Yeah?"

"Yeah what?" Carmen asked.

"Didn't you just call my name?"

"No."

Carmen walked in the building and I stood there a moment, looking around to see if someone else had said my name. I didn't know anyone walking by and none of them paid me any attention. I fidgeted with the ring on my finger. The second bell rang, and the crowd began dispersing. Maybe Carmen had been playing some kind of trick on me. She did like doing that sort of thing. I finally turned to walk in the building.

"Hey, what are you still doing out here?"

I jumped, startled. "Oh, hi," I said, trying to compose myself.

"Sorry, I didn't mean to scare you. You planning on ditching or what?" Neil asked.

"No. I'm just running late. What are you doing out here?"

"I'm stalking you," he replied in an eerie tone.

"Really? Well, you should know that stalking isn't romantic, it's just plain creepy."

"Good to know. Actually, there was a mix up with my schedule and I had to go to the office to have them fix it."

"Oh. So, are you going to Tyler's party tonight?" I asked, hopeful.

"Tyler's having a party?"

"Yeah, his parents are out of town, I guess."

"Well, if Tyler's having a party, I'm pretty sure I'm not invited."

"I'm inviting you."

"Thanks, but I don't think so. According to Belmont's popularity system, I'm ranked at the bottom, especially because of Avery's lies."

"Well, at least think about it."

After school Avery dropped me at home. Mom wasn't home from work, so I made some fish sticks and fries to hold me over until dinner. I went into my room and shut the door. I grabbed my notebook and sprawled across the bed.

February 10

Dear Diary,

Today I was standing outside of the language arts building when I thought I heard some-one call my name. Did I imagine it? It was only a whisper, but it was audible. I asked Carmen about it later in cheer class, but she swore it wasn't her. Who or what was it? Anyway, I refuse to give it too much thought.

Avery talked me into going to Tyler's party tonight. She said he thinks I'm a goddess. Of course, I've had a crush on him since tenth grade. But boyfriends only complicate things—as demonstrated with my friends. And my life is already complicated enough. Besides, if he knew me—the real me and not my representative—he'd probably think I was a freak. To-night, I will avoid Tyler at all costs.

I'm not sure when I fell asleep, but the sound of rustling papers woke me. It was coming from the opposite side of my bed. I turned back to see what my mom was doing, but it wasn't my mother. It was an unknown woman. She was bent over, rummaging through my nightstand drawer. Her silhouette was glowing against the shadows of the room. Although she was transparent, I couldn't see her face because she never looked up. Was this really happening again? I felt so groggy and confused; I couldn't keep my eyes open long enough to even be afraid.

I was roused by Avery's phone call. I tried to get out of going tonight, insisting that I was too tired, but Avery wouldn't hear any of it. Tyler's parents were in Paris on their second honeymoon, even though they'd only been married six months. His new wife was in her late twenties—thirty years his junior. It seemed gross, but whatever. Avery was just excited about putting her plan in motion. I was still caught up in what had happened earlier in my room. It had been a while since the last incident, and now I was worried.

I had told my mother that I was spending the night at Avery's, which I was, so it was only a partial lie. My mother would never allow me to go to a party with no parental supervision and guaranteed drinking. But Avery's parents never seemed to ask those hard questions. I wondered if they truly didn't know what was going on with her, or if they were just turning a blind eye. In either case, I was almost positive that their ambivalence had a lot to do with Avery acting out the way she did.

We pulled up to the house around 9:30 p.m. The driveway was filled with cars. Flower beds were pristinely manicured on the front lawn. I wore jeans and a T-shirt initially, but Avery vetoed my outfit. I ended up borrowing one of her Hervé Léger bandage dresses that hugged every curve of my body and some strappy Jimmy Choo's. Since Avery and I were around the same size, everything fit perfectly. Lisa and Carmen had given their parents the same story I gave my mom, so we all had gotten ready at Avery's. We all were dressed to murder the competition; Avery wouldn't have it any other way. However, I wasn't sure how this would help my plans to remain inconspicuous.

We entered the house. Music was blaring, and I immediately recognized most of the student body.

"Aye, yo, ma. You lookin' real spicy up in here."

Some guy was talking to Avery.

"Excuse me?" Avery asked, irritated.

"What's good? You gonna let me—"

"Mute it!" she shouted over the music. She turned around and looked at me.

The guy finally walked away, disgruntled.

"That was random," Avery said, searching the room.

"Who are you looking for? Is Rodney coming tonight?" I asked.

"I'm not looking for Rodney. I'm going to go scope things out, see if Emily's here yet. Be right back," she said with a sinister smile.

"'Kay."

Carmen and Lisa went to the bathroom together. I stood there in the corner of the living room, apparently holding the wall up.

"Hey you," Neil said as he gave me a nudge.

"Hey. What are you doing here?" I asked, pleasantly surprised.

"My friends and I decided to make an appearance. See what all the hubbub's about."

"You came here with friends?"

"Yeah, they're here somewhere. You been here long?"

"Just got here."

"Where's Satan's mistress?" he asked, searching the room. He spotted Avery directly across from us talking to a group of older guys. "Oh, there she is." He looked back at me as if he were seeing me for the first time tonight. "Wow, you look, ah, wow. You look good. Well, I mean, you always look good. I mean…. I'm just going to stop talking now and try to pry my foot out of my mouth," he said, shoving his hands in his pockets.

"Thanks," I said, embarrassed. "You look nice too."

His curls fell in just the right places. He was wearing worn, light blue jeans. He paired them with a long sleeve, button-down shirt. I never really noticed how attractive he was. Maybe it was the jawline, which was more defined this year. Or could it possibly be his sky blue eyes that were piercing into mine? Maybe he could see the fissures inside my soul? I looked away, breaking his gaze.

"So, you having fun yet?"

"Oh, yeah," I said sarcastically.

"What are you doing here?" Avery screeched, wedging between us.

"I heard there was a party."

"You weren't invited. No losers allowed."

"What's going on over here?" Justin asked as he walked up.

Neil was about 6'1" and maybe 170 pounds. However, Justin was taller and all muscle. Before I knew it, half the football team was crowded around us with their fight faces on.

"This loser thinks he can just crash," Avery told Justin.

"Look, I don't want any trouble. I'll just leave."

"And take your cornball friends with you," another voice in the crowd chimed.

Neil backed up toward the door, hands raised slightly to show he had surrendered and was leaving enemy territory.

"Bye, Neil!" I yelled over the crowd and music.

He saluted and left. The guys all dispersed with a look of triumph on their faces.

"You shouldn't let him weasel his way in by talking to you. People might start thinking you guys are friends."

I looked away and rolled my eyes. "Who are those guys you were talking to over there?"

"The one wearing the Abercrombie hoodie is Tyler's older brother, and those are his friends. They got all the liquor."

Adjacent to them, I recognized the group of girls that Emily hung around, but Emily was nowhere in sight. I hoped she would come soon.

"Hey, guys, what was all the commotion?" Charlotte asked.

"Charlotte, did either one of us ask you to come over here and start talking?" Avery asked.

"No," Charlotte replied, confused.

"Then why are you speaking out of turn? You totally interrupted my train of thought," Avery snapped.

"Um, I don't—"

"Mute it. That was a rhetorical question. Now go away," Avery said, disgusted.

Charlotte turned and walked off.

"Sometimes I wonder why I even put up with her. Oh. Hey, Tyler," Avery greeted sweetly.

I was glad I was facing the opposite direction because I was sure I looked mortified.

"Hey, Avery," Tyler responded. "Hi, Kristen."

I spun around after composing myself.

"Oh, um, hey," I said awkwardly. So much for being composed. Now I remembered why I didn't interact with boys more often. At least I was around the ones who looked like Abercrombie & Fitch models.

"Doesn't Kristen look hot tonight?" Avery asked Tyler.

His eyes met mine. "Yeah."

"Thanks. Emily is beautiful," I blurted.

Avery shot me a disapproving glance.

"So, where is the old ball and chain?" Avery asked Tyler.

"She's grounded, so I'm not sure if she's going to make it tonight. She was going to try and sneak out after her parents went to bed."

"Oh, really," Avery looked at me with a smirk on her face. "That's too bad."

Noticing his brother gesturing from afar, Tyler excused himself.

Avery grabbed my shoulders. "Why would you say that?"

"What?"

"Emily is so beautiful," she mocked. "Never bring up your competition unless you're belittling them or destroying their character. Have you learned nothing from me?"

"I don't think I can do this, Avery. It's not right. I think she really likes him."

"But he's not that into her. Didn't you see the way he was looking at you?"

68

"No. It's just…I'm nervous around guys. It doesn't come as easily for me as it does for you."

I hoped that my argument would finish this whole thing and she'd go run off to find Rodney.

"I know." She grabbed my hand and dragged me into the kitchen, where two of the college guys were mixing drinks.

"What do you have?" she asked the taller one. Something set him apart from the rest of the group. He seemed sketchy, like there was a dark secret he was hiding.

"There are some wine coolers in the refrigerator."

"We need something stronger. You got anything harder than that?" she asked provocatively.

The guy smiled and shook his head.

"Well, there's also vodka and rum."

"Perfect. Give me two rum and Cokes."

"You sure you can handle that, little girl?"

"I can handle anything you give me."

I rolled my eyes.

He handed us our cups, and we walked back into the living room.

"I'm totally going to hook up with him tonight," Avery said.

"I can't put my finger on it, but there's something off about him."

"Yeah, he's hot. Did you see how ripped he was in that shirt?"

"No, it's something else. I don't trust him."

"I think you're being a bit paranoid. But I know what will help calm you down." Avery glanced at my beverage.

I took a sip, feeling the heat slide down my throat and settle into my stomach. I followed it up with a couple Jell-O shots. By then, everyone had arrived. Or as Avery would say, everyone who mattered—everyone except Emily. Avery made her way over to where all the college boys were, but I stayed with Carmen and Lisa, making a conscious effort to avoid Tyler.

Suddenly, it was like a heat wave had washed over me. I felt weird and off-kilter. I decided to go splash some cold water on my face. When I made it to the guest bathroom, I locked the door behind me and stood in front of the sink, staring at myself in the mirror. I turned on the faucet and grabbed a paper towel, holding it under the stream. Water went everywhere, completely soaking the roll. I turned the faucet off and rang the paper towel out, then patted my forehead, my neck, and my exposed cleavage. I closed my eyes for a moment and reopened them. There was something different about me. I felt it permeating my core as I gripped the sink, my knuckles white. I relaxed, letting go of the porcelain. I examined my hand and stroked my thumb over each of my fingertips, feeling the sensation. I ran my finger over my lips and watched as I moved to my bare arms, the tips of my fingers tracing my skin. It was like I was touching myself for the first time. The look in my eyes was vacant and cold. A devilish smile appeared. Suddenly there was banging on the door. I stood there a moment, wondering how long that person had been knocking, unfazed by the anger in their voice. I opened the door.

The girl on the other side jumped back. "Ah, sorry."

I didn't break my gaze. She finally looked down at the floor. I walked past her and made my way toward the living room.

"That was creepy," I heard her mutter.

I was searching for Tyler like a lioness stalking her prey. Everything was all new to me, like it was the first time I was experiencing being in a human body. I spotted the college boy with the black muscle shirt. Avery was sitting on his lap as he talked to his friends. I still didn't see Tyler anywhere.

"There you are. I was looking for you."

I spun around. "Well, you found me. Now, what are you going to do with me?" I asked in a smooth voice that sounded nothing like my own.

"I, uh," Tyler said, flustered.

I moved closer and grabbed his shirt, resting my hand on his chest. I watched his reaction and smiled at how easy it was to mesmerize him. This would be much better than I anticipated.

"Where's Emily?" I asked, staring into his eyes.

"Uh, she can't come. She tried but she—"

"Well, maybe next time she'll think twice about lying to her parents. Or maybe not," I smiled.

Tyler looked confused.

"She just got grounded tonight. How did you know—"

"It's too bad that she would leave you here all by yourself like this."

"Yeah," he said, still gazing into my eyes.

I inched closer. "Do you want to kiss me?"

"I...."

Before he could answer, I kissed him. I ran my fingers up the back of his neck and pulled him closer. He kissed me back with the same passion. I broke free and backed away. I had him right where I wanted him. A look of bewilderment danced across his face.

"Did I do something wrong?" he asked.

I leaned in to whisper in his ear, my lips lightly brushing against his lobe.

"Don't you want to show me your room?"

"Sure. If you want," he stammered.

I grabbed him by his shirt and pulled him behind me as we made our way upstairs, away from everyone else. I knew exactly which door was his, and because of his excitement, he didn't even notice what was about to take place. We entered his room and I locked the door behind me.

"I don't think Emily would like me being in here alone with you."

I slowly began unzipping my dress. He watched, not missing a thing.

"Well, I actually don't know how much longer we're going to be together. We both want different things. You know?" he said, his voice uneven.

I slid my dress down and it fell to the floor.

"Oh wow, this is really happening," he said to himself.

I walked toward him; he slowly backed up until he fell backward onto his bed. I stopped at the edge and leaned over, whispering into his ear like before.

"You made this all too easy for me. If only you knew…." I smiled and caressed the side of his face.

"Knew what?" he asked, still intoxicated by my presence.

"'With her much fair speech she caused him to yield, and with the flattering of her lips, she forced him,'" I whispered.

"What?"

In a matter of seconds, I grabbed the side of his face, my razor-sharp nails slicing his skin. He let out an agonizing cry. My jaw dislocated like a viper about to devour its prey. I pounced and went for the jugular, sinking my teeth into flesh, muscle, finally hitting bone. He screamed hysterically, trying to push me away, but it was no use. I was way too strong for him. His warm body went silent and limp. I had completely snapped his neck. I loosened my grip and stood over his carcass. I could feel blood intermingled with torn flesh on my face. At that moment, I caught a glimpse of my reflection in his mirror.

7

Good Christians

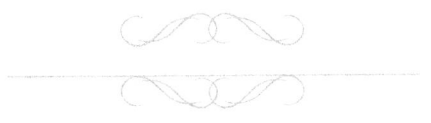

Ijumped out of my sleep with a gasp, my breathing erratic. I examined my surroundings. I was no longer in Tyler's room but Avery's.

"OMG," Avery said in a hoarse voice. She sat up slowly with her hand on her head. "I have a gnarly headache."

I gathered my thoughts quickly and calmed down.

"I know, my head is killing me, too," I said softly.

"Last night was awesome. You totally devoured Tyler," she said with a chuckle.

"What?" I gasped.

"I totally can't believe you hooked up with Tyler last night."

"I hooked up with Tyler?" I asked, still wondering what was a dream and what was reality.

"Yeah," everyone answered.

I hadn't noticed before, but Carmen and Lisa were also in Avery's king-sized bed.

"I can't remember anything past the Jell-O shots."

"Are you serious? You hooked up with Tyler and you don't even remember it? What a waste. Well, I think Spencer Hawkins is having a party next week, maybe you can try for a repeat."

"Absolutely not. I shouldn't have done…whatever, in the first place. What happened? What did I do?"

"Well, you didn't actually hook up with him, but you were sucking face most of the night. You were like this seductress. It was so cool. You had him and every other guy there spellbound. You've been holding out on me."

The way she described me was so familiar to who I was in my dream, but apparently, the latter part of the dream never happened, or else I might be in jail or locked up in a psych ward. I was so confused.

"Well, you certainly put on a show," Charlotte said from the couch.

I sat up slowly. "Oh. I didn't see you over there."

"I was the designated driver last night. You really don't remember anything?" Charlotte asked.

I shook my head.

"At one point, you were dancing on the dining room table for cash." Carmen laughed.

"Oh, no," I groaned.

"You didn't do too bad. Made a whopping one hundred and fifty bucks. We tried to stop you, but you were pretty determined," Lisa added.

"And see, my plan worked. All you needed was a little help from Jack."

"Who the heck is Jack? Did I hook up with him, too?"

"No, Kristen, pipe down. Jack Daniel's. We ran out of rum so we moved on to Tyler's dad's stash."

"Did you purposely get me drunk?"

"Yeah, and it worked. You loosened up."

"I can't believe you did that!"

"Really?" Avery said, surprised. "It sounds exactly like something I'd do. Anyway, you know, I think that guy I hooked up with last night might have stolen fifty bucks from me. But it was worth it. What time is it?"

"It's 10:47 and fifty-two seconds, fifty-three seconds," Charlotte answered.

"OMG, Charlotte," Avery snapped. "Really? Is it necessary to give the seconds? Don't answer that."

"I think I'm going to be sick." I sprang out of bed and ran to the bathroom.

"She's going to thank me later," Avery said, lying back down.

I swore to myself that I would never drink again if some higher power could help me feel better. I came out of Avery's bathroom to see the rest of the girls sitting around in her room, talking. Avery sat up in her bed while Carmen and Lisa sat on the couch.

"I hate Jack," I said as I sat down next to Avery.

"You still feeling sick?" Carmen asked.

I nodded. "I don't know how people do this all the time. I feel like I may have flushed part of my spleen down the toilet from all that heaving. There can't possibly be anything else left inside me to come up."

"It shouldn't be so bad next time."

"Next time? That's never happening again. I can't believe you made me drink so much."

"You didn't have to. It's not like I had a gun to your head."

I looked at Avery in disbelief.

"Okay, so I probably gave you too much to drink. Sorry," she said, unapologetically.

"Avery?" a husky voice echoed.

We all looked up at the ceiling.

"Yes, God?" Carmen replied.

Avery rolled her eyes and walked over to the intercom system.

"Yes, Dad?" she said into the speaker.

"Your mother wanted me to check in and see if you girls were awake yet."

"Yeah, we're up."

"Breakfast is ready."

"Okay, we'll be down in a sec."

"She'll be expecting you out on the back patio."

We all walked downstairs to the terrace out back. A beautifully dressed table of china and crystal had been set up with a Smörgåsbord of food.

"Hey girls! I thought you were going to sleep the whole day. You girls must have gotten in pretty late last night. I figured you might be hungry. I was going to take you all out for breakfast, but since you were still fast asleep, I decided we'd do brunch here instead," Avery's mother said. She moved the floral arrangement out of the way so that she could replace it with a platter of French toast.

Mrs. Morgan was tall with classic features—not surprising for an ex-model. Her blonde hair was perfectly styled. Her designer blouse and jeans were stark white and spotless. Her diamond-studded earrings glistened along with the huge rock on her finger. She was the stereotypical California housewife. I had always thought of her and Mr. Morgan as a modern-day Barbie and Ken—if Ken was a high-powered attorney and Barbie decided to settle down.

Mrs. Morgan smiled, flashing her pearly whites. It seemed more habitual than genuine.

"Nancy!" Mrs. Morgan beckoned.

The petite Filipino woman appeared out of nowhere.

"Yes, Mrs. Morgan?" Nancy said, her accent thick.

"Take these and put them inside. There is simply no room." Mrs. Morgan handed Nancy the floral arrangement. She took her seat and adjusted her ring, admiring it. We all followed suit.

"So, what did you girls do last night?" Mrs. Morgan asked, searching the table.

"I told you we were going to a party, Mom."

"Nancy, please bring the butter and jelly. How on earth does she expect us to eat toast without butter or jelly?" Mrs. Morgan laughed. "Now, what was that, Avery?"

"We went to a party last night."

We all began filling our plates. I was hoping some food would help settle my stomach. Nancy scurried out with the butter and jelly, then disappeared.

"A party?" Mrs. Morgan said, cutting into some pineapple.

"Yes. A guy from our school had a party last night and—"

"Wait, where is Riley? Sweetie, have you seen your brother?"

"No, but he's probably up in his room."

"Nancy, have you seen Riley?" She waited for a response that never came. "Well, I'm sure he's around here somewhere. Now, you guys went to a movie last night? Is that what you said?"

"No, Mom. Never mind," Avery said, irritated.

"All right. Did you girls did let your parents know you were going to be staying here last night?"

We all nodded.

"It's just an awful feeling not knowing where your child is." She took a dainty bite of toast and swallowed, her face showing disapproval. "Nancy! Come here, please." She waited for a moment and rolled her eyes. "What do you girls have planned for today? Anything fun?"

"No," Avery replied.

Mrs. Morgan appraised Avery's plate with dissatisfaction. "Avery, sweetie, what do think about joining me for my yoga classes? It will help get rid of your problem areas. Of course, changing unfavorable eating habits would also help," she hinted. "What have I told you about keeping up appearances? Girls, always remember that you should take pride in how you look because people are always watching, and if you ever want to marry well like I did, then that should be your main priority."

Avery put down her fork and pushed her plate away. She began eating from the fruit tray next to her.

Mrs. Morgan smiled. "Much better. Oh, before I forget, next weekend we're going downtown to help feed some of the less fortunate. I hate calling them homeless. Our women's church group will be organizing it. If you girls are free, you should come. It will be a blessing to a lot of people. Plus, giving back to the community makes you feel good. It's good to help others who can't help themselves. We're also raising money by doing a silent raffle and auctions to benefit the poor children in Djibouti, Africa."

Avery giggled.

Mrs. Morgan shot her a look of disapproval. It took everything in me not to laugh myself.

"That's also what being a Christian is all about. Of course, attending church every week is a big part of being a good Christian. But it's also our job to give back to the community. Although some people do bring things upon themselves, it's not my place to judge," she said arrogantly. "There are so many people out there who aren't as privileged as we are. Take Nancy, for instance. She would have a much different life if we hadn't taken her in. She makes much more now than she ever would cleaning offices at night or selling oranges on the side of the road like other people do."

We all glanced at each other, appalled by Mrs. Morgan's words. Avery never looked up from the table. The rest of us, along with Mrs. Morgan, caught Carmen's expression of disapproval.

"Not that there's anything wrong with that. I mean, someone needs to do those jobs, right? We all have our place in this world. But I like to think that I saved Nancy. She should be very grateful; this type of thing doesn't happen often for people like her. She even attends our church regularly. And that's what it's all about." Mrs. Morgan looked a bit uncomfortable at where the conversation had gone. "So, Kristen, do you attend church?"

All eyes turned to me.

I swallowed. "No." Was it that apparent that I needed help?

"You and your mother should come visit our church one Sunday. I'm good friends with the pastor. I'd be happy to introduce you two." She paused for a moment, collecting her thoughts. "I don't want to see anyone go to hell. A lot of people don't realize it, but if they don't go to church, that's where they'll go. It's a shame, really. You're such a beautiful girl. I'd hate to not see you in heaven."

She made it sound like getting into heaven was like getting into a nightclub. It was all about who you knew at the door, and as long as you had the money and looks to get in, you'd be chilling in the VIP section. Was that all that was needed to pass through those white gates? I never really gave it much thought. In her eyes, I was on my way to hell. Maybe she was right, but that was something I didn't want to think about right now.

"Oh, well, thanks, I guess. Where do you go?" I asked, appeasing her.

"You probably wouldn't know it by name if I told you, but it's the big cathedral on the corner of Ocean and Clark."

"Oh yeah, I know which one you're talking about. Looks fancy."

Avery rolled her eyes.

"We have a wonderful youth ministry for the teens, and quite a few of them come from a broken home like you."

And there it was. I was considered unprivileged because my father wasn't around. Maybe not unprivileged, but lower in whatever ranking class she held in her mind. Apparently, I was next on her list to be saved.

"Oh," was all I could muster.

"It's a beautiful church and you'll love Pastor Todd. Tell your mother that the two of you are more than welcome to come." She smiled as she was about to take another bite of her toast, but then stopped. "Nancy? Good heavens, where on earth is that woman? Nancy!"

"Yes, Mrs. Morgan?" Nancy said, standing behind her.

Mrs. Morgan jumped a little in her seat. "Oh, you startled me. Is this bread gluten-free?"

Nancy shrugged. "I don't know."

"Good heavens. I told you I don't eat anything with gluten now."

"Sorry, Mrs. Morgan."

"Take it away. Please."

I had a feeling that if we weren't all sitting here, Mrs. Morgan wouldn't have constrained herself. I felt sorry for Nancy. I wondered if she had a family of her own and a life outside of her job. She had to have housework of her own to do, maybe children to look after, possibly a husband to tend to. Did she have any hopes and dreams? Surely working for Mrs. Morgan couldn't be her idea of a dream job, but maybe she had no choice.

Nancy's eyes met mine. I smiled sympathetically. She returned the gesture, but there was hurt beneath the surface, maybe regret. Mrs. Morgan may have thought Nancy was different, but at that moment, I saw no difference between us; we were both hurting. The hurt may have come from different places, but the outcome was still the same.

Nancy grabbed the plate of toast.

"Oh, and Nancy? Let Riley know that breakfast is ready. He should hurry, it's getting cold."

"But—"

"Go get him and bring the blueberries."

Nancy left with a confused look on her face. We all stared at each other, missing the point.

"Morning," Mr. Morgan announced, his attention fixated on his phone.

"John, have you been upstairs?"

"No, I've been in my office, working—or trying to, anyway. Not that I could get anything done with all the yelling out here."

"I've been trying to get ahold of Riley so he can eat his breakfast."

"When he's hungry, he'll come down and eat. He's not a child anymore," Mr. Morgan said.

"Well, he is only ten."

"He's eleven."

"No, he's only ten."

"Katherine, I think I know how old my son is."

"Didn't he just have a birthday? He turned ten, not eleven," Mrs. Morgan replied.

Avery sighed. "Riley's eight and his birthday is in two months."

"Are you sure?" Mrs. Morgan asked.

"I'm positive," Avery said, annoyed.

"Look, young lady, there's no need to take that tone with me. It's a harmless mistake."

Nancy set a bowl of blueberries on the table next to Mrs. Morgan.

"Nancy, did you tell Riley it's time to eat?"

"No, Mrs. Morgan."

"Well, why not?"

"Because Riley isn't here."

Avery's parents looked at each other, then back at Nancy.

"Well, then where is he?" Mrs. Morgan asked.

"He went over to his friend's house last night and stayed there."

"Did you tell him he could spend the night?" Mrs. Morgan asked her husband.

"He broached the subject last week, but I told him to ask you."

"Oh." Mrs. Morgan turned back to Nancy. "And he left last night? When?"

"Um, seven. You were at your yoga class, and Mr. Morgan was still at work." Nancy gave them both a look of contempt and went back into the house.

Mr. Morgan cleared his throat. "Well, now that that's settled, I have to go into the office today if I ever hope to get any work done. I'll be home late," he said, walking away.

"Well, I guess that answers that," Mrs. Morgan said, delicately patting the sides of her mouth with her napkin.

"It's such an awful feeling not knowing where your child is," Avery said in a mocking tone. "Whatever."

Mrs. Morgan scowled.

On second thought, I may be on my way to hell, but if that's the case, Mrs. Morgan might not be too far behind.

8

The Truth Shall Set You Free

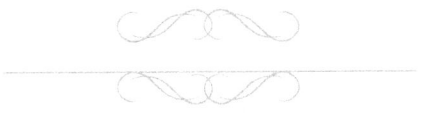

"**M**om?" I called from the living room.

"I'm in here."

I found her in her bathroom trying to straighten her hair, wearing only a bath towel.

"Are you going somewhere?"

"I'm going out with the girls tonight. We're heading to dinner and then out on the town."

"Are you coming home tonight?"

"I don't know, hon. It depends on how much I drink. I have to be responsible, you know."

I hoisted myself up on the bathroom counter. "Gotcha. Hey, you remember Mrs. Morgan?"

"That's Avery's mother, right?"

"Yeah. She invited us to her church. Apparently, she's very concerned about me coming from a broken home."

"Oh, I'm sure she is," my mother said sarcastically. "That woman—she's unbelievable. Such a hypocrite. The way she talks to people is disgusting. Her friends might think she's devout, but I don't buy her holier than thou act. Did she say that to you? If so, I'm going to have a talk with her and tell her where she can put her snide invitation."

"No, Mom, please, it's fine. I mean, it's not fine, but I'd just rather you didn't."

She studied my face carefully. "Fine. Apart from that, how was Avery's? What did you girls do last night?"

A terrible feeling rose in the pit of my stomach. "I went to a house party with boys. There was no supervision and tons of alcohol. I drank—a lot."

I waited for the wrath to begin. Her face was serious at first, but then she relaxed. She continued straightening her hair.

"Aren't you going to say something?" I asked.

"Nope."

"Why not?" I snapped.

"What do you want me to say?" she asked, parting another section of her hair.

"Yell at me, curse me out. Do something."

"Did you have fun?"

"Um, I'm not sure. I guess."

"Good."

"Good? Where is my mother and what have you done with her?"

She put the flat iron down and turned to face me. "I'm just glad you're going out and doing normal teenage stuff instead of moping around your room all the time."

"I was drinking Jack Daniel's, I did Jell-O shots, and I was dancing on top of a table."

"Oh, I did much worse when I was your age. Plus, I got pregnant. I'm not saying I like you drinking and going to unsupervised parties—we'll revisit that later—but it's better than the alternative."

Totally did not see this coming. My mom's very liberal, but this was unheard of.

"Mom, I want to talk to you about something."

"What is it, hon?"

"Well, I've been having these bad dreams. They feel so real. Sometimes I don't know if I'm dreaming or if I'm awake."

"You mean like on the plane when we went to Long Island?"

"Yeah. I won't go into the details, but they're scaring me. It stopped for a while, but I had another one last night. And…I've kind of been seeing things."

"Like what?" my mother asked, wide-eyed.

"Spirits," I whispered.

"What exactly have you seen?"

"They look like people, but they're translucent. It's weird; I can see every detail of their faces and clothes, just like I'm looking at you. It all seems so real."

My mother stared blankly for a moment, then turned back to face the mirror. I could see the worry lines etched on her forehead.

"You think I'm crazy, don't you?"

"No. I don't think you're crazy. I've seen things, too. Not like you, but I've seen things out of the corner of my eye, just shadows. It's been a while, though." She turned around and grabbed my face. "You are not crazy." Then she kissed my forehead and hugged me.

Her damp towel seeped into my clothes before she took a step back.

"Have you ever thought about asking them what they want?"

"No. Never. I normally try to ignore them."

We were quiet again.

"You know, I don't have to go. I can stay here with you if you want me to. We can have our own girls' night in. I can pick up some Chang's Chow Mein to-go, maybe even get a great wall of chocolate for dessert."

"Don't be silly. Go and have fun. I'll be fine."

"Only if you're sure."

"I'm positive. Please don't worry about me; I'm good."

My mom finished getting ready while I lounged on the couch, watching shows I had recorded.

"We're going to eat at this restaurant in West Hollywood. If you need me, you can reach me on my cell. Okay?" She gathered her things to head out the door.

"Okay."

"I'm not sure where we're going afterward, but I'll text you when I find out. See you later."

"Be careful, and text me to let me know if you're coming home or not."

"Okay."

"Be safe."

"Okay, hon, bye."

I ordered a pizza with the money she left me on the kitchen counter. Then I took a shower and threw my pajamas on.

I'd had enough Basketball Wives for one night, so I turned off the TV and went to my room. I sat at my desk and turned on my laptop. I decided to search the web to see if I could find any answers for what I had been experiencing. I typed in spirit sightings. A list of website links popped up about spirits, ghosts, and apparitions. The cursor didn't move. What was wrong with me? Why was I so scared? It's just a website, and it might give me some insight as to what is going on. I was just about to click the link when my phone buzzed.

"Ahhh!" I jumped in my seat.

It's just your phone, you idiot.

"Hello?"

"So, I've talked to quite a few people who have confirmed that Tyler and Emily are no longer a couple," Avery said with glee.

"You do realize that you are rejoicing over the heartache of someone who is supposed to be your friend?"

"You know, Kristen, I do all this work for you, and you don't appreciate it. That's kind of selfish."

"Avery," I said sternly.

"Make sure you wear something cute Monday."

My phone chimed in my ear.

"Hold on, Avery."

I glanced at my screen.

Mom: Hey hon. We're leaving the restaurant now.

"Sorry, it's my mom. I have to go."

"Just remember to dress cute, 'kay?"

"All right, bye."

I ended the call and tossed my phone on my desk. That's when I heard talking coming from the living room. It sounded like the TV was on. Didn't I turn that off? I got up and walked into the living room. The television was off. I paused for a moment, glancing around. Maybe I heard one of our neighbors? It was possible since we lived in a condo.

I went back to my room and sat at my desk, staring at my laptop screen. Just push the button. What's the worst that could happen? Then I heard it again. When I walked back into the living room, the TV was on. An episode of Ghost Hunters was playing. I grabbed the remote and hit the off button, then ran into my room and shut the door. Now I was wishing I had asked my mom to stay home.

Suddenly, my phone rang.

"Ahh!"

Pull it together, Kristen.

I grabbed my phone from the desk. "Hello?"

"Hey, it's Neil Schneider. You busy?"

"Neil, it's the twenty-first century. Phones have Caller ID. You don't have to formally introduce yourself."

"Is this a bad time?"

"No, I'm sorry. I'm not busy. What's up? Wait, tell me you're not calling because you heard about what happened last night after you left?"

"Um, no. What happened?"

"I got wasted and turned into the life of the party."

"Oh, really? I'm sorry I missed that." I could sense his smile.

"Yeah, well, I'm glad you missed it. Why are you calling?"

"Oh…. I, uh, wanted to get that assignment from you for chemistry class."

"Really?"

"Yeah."

My phone chimed again.

"Hold on a sec, Neil."

Mom: Hey, hon. Turns out I won't be coming home tonight.

Fear overpowered logic.

"Hey, what are you doing right now?" I asked, hoping I didn't sound desperate.

"Um…nothing, really."

"Do you want to come over and hang out?"

"Sure. I'll be right over."

"Okay, see you in a little bit."

Twenty minutes later, he showed up.

"Hey," he eyed me with suspicion as he came in.

We walked into the living room and sat on the couch.

"So…. Your mom doesn't mind me coming over at ten o'clock at night?" he asked, shrugging out of his jacket.

"She's not here.

"Oh. Where is she?"

"She's out with her friends." An awkward silence ensued. "Do you want something to drink or eat? There's some pizza in the kitchen if you're hungry."

"No, I'm good. I'm more curious to find out why you were down to hang at ten at night?"

"Well, it's kind of hard to say."

"Let me guess. Booty call?"

"No. But don't laugh when I tell you the truth, okay?"

"Okay."

"You promise?"

"Yes, I promise."

"I'm kind of scared to be here by myself, and my mom won't be back until tomorrow."

"Oh…okay."

"You're not going to laugh at me for being scared here by myself?"

"No. But nice pajamas," he teased.

I forgot I was wearing my flannel ones. Secretly mortified.

"Carol Burnett?" he asked, looking me up and down.

"Lucille Ball. You know, in I Love Lucy. See," I pointed to a section, "here she's the Vitameatavegamin girl when she did that commercial." My fingers moved to another section. "Here she's stomping grapes in Italy, and here she's the Chiquita banana woman when she thought Ricky was home sick."

"Oh, right. That's what I meant."

"How can you get Lucille Ball and Carol Burnett mixed up?"

"Sorry, I'm not up on my 1950s trivia."

"Everybody knows Carol came after Lucy."

"Is that common knowledge?" he asked sarcastically.

"It is."

"You know, I don't think I've ever seen you without makeup on."

"I don't wear it when I'm at home."

"You look the same."

I gave him a sharp look.

"No, I meant it as a compliment. You don't need it."

"Oh," I replied, shifting around uncomfortably.

"I've never seen your hair curly, either."

"It's naturally curly. I just straighten it."

"I like it."

"Thanks," I said, embarrassed.

"So, do those things moo?" he asked, looking at my bed slippers.

"Are you going to scrutinize me the whole time you're here?"

He laughed. "No, I was just curious."

"They're moose slippers, and they were a Christmas gift from my nana."

"So, what do you want to do?"

"I guess we can watch TV."

I turned on a new episode of Ghost Hunters.

"Have you ever watched this show before?" he asked eagerly.

"No."

"They go to different places to see if they are haunted."

"You watch this show?"

"Yeah, sometimes," he said, already engrossed.

"Do you believe ghosts exist?"

"I mean, there's a God, so why not? You can't have good without evil. Otherwise there would be no purpose for books, movies, TV shows. If you think about the premise for most movies, it's usually good versus evil."

"I never really thought about it before."

We watched the show in silence.

"Neil?"

"Yeah?"

"Have you ever thought to yourself that there has to be more?"

"More to what?"

"Life. I don't know, I just feel like there's more to it, like I'm missing something substantial. Have you ever felt that way?"

"You mean like why are we here on this planet?"

"Yeah."

"I guess it's crossed my mind a few times."

"I think about it a lot, especially more recently. Sometimes I'll to go to El Dorado Park and just sit and watch the ducks."

"By that pond?"

"Yeah. I go there to think. It's a really peaceful getaway."

"Getaway from what?"

"From school, this house…." I stopped myself. "I don't know why I'm telling you this. I just feel like there's more."

"Maybe one day you'll find it," he said sympathetically.

"Yeah. Maybe." My eyes focused on the TV show. "So have you seen spirits?"

"No, I haven't, but I do have a friend whose cousin's godfather saw one. Or so he said. But I don't know anyone personally. Do you mind if I put my feet up on this…?"

"It's an ottoman. Make yourself at home."

Should I tell him my secret?

"There's a website I found that has pictures of spirit sightings from people who spotted something supernatural."

"Do you remember the name of the website?"

He nodded.

"Would you show it to me?"

"Sure."

I went and retrieved my laptop from my desk. When I returned, I gave it to him and sat closer so I could see the screen.

He began typing away. I noticed he was smiling.

"What are you smiling at?"

"Just thinking, that's all."

"About what?"

"I was just wondering why you didn't call Avery to come over…or Tyler, for that matter."

"So you did hear. You're such a liar." I hit him with a pillow.

He blocked the shot and laughed, all the while making sure the laptop didn't fall.

"What did you hear?"

"I heard you put on quite a show for everyone when you weren't cleaning Tyler's teeth with your tongue."

I hit him again. "That's gross. I wish I could take it back. I'm sure Emily's hurt. Hey, how did you find out? No offense."

"None taken. One of my buddies took his chances and stuck around after I left. He saw the whole thing."

"That's just great. I'm sure I'll be laughed at for weeks."

"More like become every guy's fantasy at school. I hear you were dancing on top of furniture. It was a table, right?"

I groaned in horror and covered my face with my hands. I was clearly out of control and needed to be punished for my actions, but there seemed to be no relief in sight.

"Hey, you're not going to get in trouble for being out so late, are you?" I asked.

"No, I was actually at a friend's house. I told my mom I was staying over there tonight."

"What about your friend?"

"He thinks I decided to just go home."

"You didn't tell him you were coming here?"

"No. I didn't know if you wanted anyone to know."

"To know what?"

"That I was coming over here. It's late. Some people might automatically assume things."

"Assume things? Like what?"

Who cares if people knew we were hanging out outside of school? I didn't care about that. Although, I knew Avery would have a problem with it. Social status meant everything. Plus, she wouldn't want me fraternizing with her enemy, but at this point, I didn't care. I enjoyed spending time with Neil.

"People might think that we...." His cheeks flushed with embarrassment.

"That we what?"

"That we were hooking up."

"Who cares? We know the truth."

"Can I ask you a question? You don't have to answer if you don't want to."

"What is it?"

"Have you ever...you know?" he asked awkwardly.

"No! Tyler was my first kiss. It doesn't matter now, though, because I don't remember any of it."

"How much did you have to drink?"

"I don't know. Have you ever had that happen? When you couldn't remember things afterward? I have no point of reference because I've never drunk before."

"You're kidding?"

"Nope."

"I haven't. But I have heard of people blacking out when they drink too much. I've read something about that. They said if you drink too much too fast you'll be completely conscious, but the part of your brain that makes memories will be affected."

"I don't know. I had this weird dream last night and it was so real. I was at the party and, I don't know, it seems like something else comes over you when the blackouts occur. It's like there's something inside of you waiting to be awakened, and when you give it permission, it takes over," I said, staring off into space.

"What are you talking about?"

"I don't know. I'm rambling on about nothing again. Never mind. Did you find the website?"

"Yeah, this is it."

We looked at the obscure pictures and read vague testimonies of people who claimed to see supernatural phenomena. The whole time I was trying to work up the nerve to tell him everything, but I couldn't. Insecurity wouldn't let me. How was I supposed to know how he would react or what he'd say? After we looked at a few other websites, I put the laptop away. I wasn't any closer to figuring out what was going on with me. We began watching a movie, but soon we fell asleep.

When I awoke, it was 1:55 a.m.

"Neil, wake up. It's almost two o' clock in the morning," I said, shaking his arm violently.

He finally came to.

"What?"

"We fell asleep. It's almost two o'clock. Are you sure you won't get in trouble for staying out so late?"

"No, I'm good. But if you want me to go, I can go. I don't want you to get in trouble."

Was it worth the risk? I had fallen asleep and didn't have a nightmare. The fear had vanished, but I knew it would come back once I was alone again.

"Do you want to watch another movie?"

"Sure," he replied, still groggy.

It wasn't long before he fell back asleep. I figured I'd let him rest a couple more hours. I grabbed some blankets from the linen closet. I laid one on top of him and curled up inside mine while watching *Singing in the Rain.* I didn't know if Neil liked musicals or not, but it didn't matter since he was sound asleep. Not too soon after the first dance number, I could feel my eyelids growing heavy.

* * *

Warm sun rays lightly caressed my face. My eyes flew open, and I looked over to see Neil was still sleeping. I slowly got up, trying not to wake him, then walked over to see if I could read the digital clock on the stove in the kitchen: 10:22 a.m. Crap, Mom's probably in her room which means she saw Neil and me on the couch. Great. Maybe she won't be mad like when I told her about the party. Doubt I'd be so lucky two days in a row, though. I walked into her room and closed the door behind me, delicately climbing onto her bed.

"You're finally awake," she said, her face half buried in her pillow.

"Yeah. How was your night?"

"It was a lot of fun. The food at the restaurant was excellent and we made fools of ourselves on the dance floor."

"Cool."

"I got carded at the club. Can you believe it?"

"Go you."

"I know, right? So now that we've gotten the small talk out of the way, are we going to discuss the boy in the living room sleeping on my couch now?"

"Oh, that."

"Yeah, that. Why do you have boys spending the night here, especially when I'm not home?"

"It's just the one."

She wasn't amused.

"Mom, you met Neil a couple times, remember?"

"I remember him, but why is he here? Was he here all night?"

"When I found out you weren't coming home, I asked him to come by just for a little while to hang out, but we fell asleep."

"What did you two do last night?" her tone was suspicious.

"We watched TV, then we watched *Singing in the Rain*—well I did, anyway. Neil was already asleep. I got scared and didn't want to be here alone."

"So nothing happened?"

"What?"

"Did you two…?"

"Mom! No!"

"I didn't think so, but I had to ask."

"Do you see what I'm wearing? No, nothing like that happened."

"Is he still asleep?"

"I guess."

We both got out of the bed and walked into the living room.

"You know he's really cute," my mom whispered.

"It's not like that. We're just friends."

"You don't think he's cute?"

"Mom, please stop."

"C'mon. I know you think he's cute. Just admit it."

"Fine, I guess he's mildly attractive."

"He's mildly attractive. What are you, a forty-four-year-old divorcée?"

"Okay. Yes, he's cute. I just might rear his children."

"Ha! I knew it."

I rolled my eyes.

"Oh, remind me to tell you about the guy who was totally chatting me up last night. Super cute, but I wasn't digging the goatee. I mean, I suppose that's doable, unlike flesh-eating disease guy."

"And you talk about me being dramatic."

"What?"

"You're totally overreacting. Remember that guy you met at Pottery Barn? He had a bad case of dry skin. What was his name again?"

"Not a clue. Anyway, back to cute bar guy. He had to have been in his mid to late-twenties—"

"No, no. Go back to the flesh-eating disease guy—was his name Phillip or Robert? Ugh, that's going to bug me now."

"Can we please get back to cute bar guy? He had to be around twenty-five, and he thought we were the same age." She giggled.

"That's great, Mom." I gestured toward Neil. "Can you please stay focused?"

"Oh right," she sighed. "So, what should we do?"

"We? You're asking me?"

"You invited him here."

"So?"

"He's your friend."

"You're the grown up."

"I know, but we've never been in this type of situation before. I'm not sure how I should be handling this."

"And you expect me to know?"

"Well, don't you? I know you learned something from watching all those Lifetime movies."

"I do not watch Lifetime Movie Network."

"The fact that you refer to it by the full name suggests otherwise. Oh, honey, it's okay. I won't tell anyone your dirty little secret."

I pulled away from her. "I don't know what it is with that channel. The movies are like three hours long, but you can't watch just one. They're addictive, like Doritos."

"I know. That's what I've heard, anyway. So?"

"If I've learned anything, it's that you shouldn't plot to ruin the life of the doctor who performed your recent hysterectomy, which inadvertently made you go crazy enough to kill your husband."

"Ooh! That's the one with Delta Burke, right?"

I gasped and pointed. "You saw it? I knew you loved their movies! Unbelievable."

"All right, let's flip for it. Heads, I handle it, tails, you do."

"Mom," I said, aggravated.

"I'm not sure if this will help, but I think there should be yelling involved," Neil said, opening his eyes.

"Hey, you're awake," I said, a little embarrassed that he overheard our conversation.

"Good morning, Ms. Kaplan," Neil said, running his hands through his curls. "I'm sorry about last night and this morning. I better go."

"Hi, Neil," my mother replied. "Can you have some pancakes before you go? Are you two hungry?"

"Yeah," we both said.

My mom made her way to the kitchen. She looked over her shoulder and mouthed the words "he's so cute," making kissing faces.

I sat down next to Neil on the couch, moving the sea of blankets out of my way. Luckily Neil's back was facing her so he couldn't see the spectacle she was making. I shot her a disapproving glare.

"You okay?" I asked Neil.

"Yeah."

"That was a little weird, wasn't it?"

"A little."

"Exactly how much of that did you hear?"

"Not much. However, I've never heard anyone use the word rear in a sentence before."

I was mortified and was sure it showed all over my face.

"Thank you for keeping me company last night," I said, staring down at my ring.

"Anytime." He nudged me.

9

The Aftermath

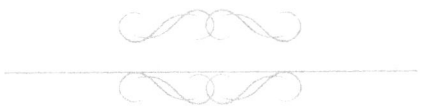

Monday was unbearable. My classes were awful, apart from having to take a career aptitude test in homeroom. It was exactly what I needed to help guide me in the right direction. Too bad it was overshadowed by a paper due in creative writing and a presentation for economics.

Word had spread like wildfire about my little performance Friday night. I received nothing but lecherous grins from many of the guys. Like the plague, I could sense the disgust and disapproval from the girls. Of course, they'd never come out and confront me because of Avery. That was my saving grace. Unfortunately, I wasn't so sure if her influence would benefit Emily and her friends.

I fully intended to find Emily and apologize, but to my surprise, she never showed up. Her closest friends were MIA, too. I'm sure they were trying to console her after my actions. Tomorrow would be another chance.

* * *

"Happy Valentine's Day!" Avery said as I slipped into her car.

"It's Valentine's Day?"

"Yeah. I can't wait to see what Rodney got me."

"I thought you told him exactly what you wanted. You said if he didn't get it, you wouldn't speak to him for weeks," Carmen said from the backseat.

"No one asked you, Carmen, okay? So, Kristen, did you talk to Tyler yesterday?"

"I didn't see him," I said, staring out the window.

"Really? He was looking for you all day."

"Oh, really?"

"Look, maybe you feel bad about the whole Emily's-heart-being-torn-out-and-stomped-on thing, but she'll get over it. It's all a part of the game. Plus, I heard her dad is some kind of psycho therapist or something, so you have nothing to worry about. He'll probably prescribe her some Prozac and she'll be back to normal in no time.... OMG!"

Avery pulled into her normal parking spot to see Rodney standing close by with half a dozen red and pink heart-shaped balloons. They were tied to a basket filled with Valentine's Day paraphernalia. She quickly got out of the car and ran over to retrieve them. "OMG, Rodney! I can't believe you did all this!"

The first bell rang, saving us from having to witness any more of Avery's performance. My stomach began to feel uneasy as I walked to class, wondering if Emily would be at school. I doubted it. Today would be particularly bad for her since it was Valentine's Day.

First period dragged. When I made it to Calculus, Avery was showing off her gift again. I just sat there, watching the show. This will probably have more reruns then RENT or Wicked.

"Hey."

I turned to Neil. He was seated at his desk, taking his notebook out of his backpack.

Thank God. The one person who wouldn't get sucked into the whole V-Day propaganda. He prided himself on being the total opposite of everyone else—a rebel.

"Thanks again for Saturday. I really appreciate it."

"No problem. Anytime." He smiled.

There was something different about his smile. Maybe he felt sorry for me. I'm sure the guys had been talking in the locker room. I cringed at the thought of being the topic of anyone's conversation, especially teenage boys'.

"What's going on over there?" He motioned toward Avery and the crowd.

"Oh, Avery's just showing off the Valentine's Day gift Rodney gave her."

"Wow, looks like he went all out."

"Doesn't it?"

Neil cleared his throat and leaned in. "So, I was wondering—"

"Class, let's settle down. Please take your seats," Ms. Marquardt said as she walked in.

Neil straightened up and turned to face the front.

"Natalie, would you read the bulletin for today?"

Natalie Tran walked to the front of the class to read all the upcoming activities, congratulatory mentions, and the menu for the school cafeteria. Like clockwork each day, Ms. Marquardt would appoint someone to read the school bulletin, and then she would start her lesson plan.

"Was wondering what?" I whispered to Neil, checking to see if Ms. Marquardt was looking in our direction.

"Um, well I was wondering. We had so much fun the other night...."

"Yeah?"

"I wanted to know if you—"

"I wonder when they're going to do the candy grams," Avery interrupted.

"Come again?" I whispered, irritated.

"The candy grams. I was just wondering when they're going to deliver them already."

"I'm sure they'll be here any minute."

Student council came up with selling candy grams to the student body as a way to raise money. When some major holiday came around, they would attach the sweets to a telegram from the sender. This quickly turned into a popularity contest to see who could collect the most. For Valentine's Day, they would be handing out heart-shaped suckers. Naturally, Avery was determined to collect the most. She would threaten all her followers, and whoever bought her the most would get to sit at the lunch table with us for a week. It was ridiculous—but then again, it was high school.

"What are you talking to Neil about?" she asked curiously.

"Nothing major, just class stuff."

"So he didn't mention me? Not that I'd care if he did."

"Avery, you're disrupting my class with your side chatter," Ms. Marquardt said. "Perhaps you can tell the class your answer to this problem: find an equation of the line which passes through the point 8, -2, and has y-intercept 5."

Avery scribbled the problem down on her paper, put her pencil down, and looked up at Ms. Marquardt. "Using the slope-intercept form, $y = mx + 5$ where $y = -2$ when $x = 8$, so $-2 = 8m + 5$ and therefore $m = -7/8$. So, the line has an equation $y = -7/8x + 5$."

"Right," Ms. Marquardt said in disappointment after consulting her teacher's guide.

A few members of student council entered the classroom. Ms. Marquardt stopped and let them hand out the candy grams. Some people received two or three—I received seven. One from Avery, Carmen, Lisa,

Charlotte, and the rest were from Avery's fans who probably hoped it would give them some sort of extra credit from Avery. Thankfully, none were from Tyler. Avery received a whopping twenty-five.

Connor Marshall—wide receiver and best friend of Tyler Reed—was carrying a bouquet of roses and a white Teddy bear holding a red heart.

"Um, excuse me," Connor said to Ms. Marquardt. "This is for...."

Don't say it, don't say it, I thought.

"Kristen Kaplan."

"Oh, how nice." Ms. Marquardt said, taking the gift from Connor. She examined both as she walked over and set them on my desk.

I've never been so embarrassed in my life. I sat there with my hands on either side of my face, staring at the bear in horror.

Ms. Marquardt walked back up to the front of the class to continue her lesson.

"OMG!" Avery whispered, making sure Ms. Marquardt was still facing the chalkboard. "That has to be from Tyler. He is so into you. You did it. He's yours."

"I don't want him, Avery," I whispered.

"Don't be silly; you won him fair and square. If he really loved her he wouldn't be so easily swayed."

She turned back to the front and started taking notes.

In between classes, I went straight to my locker to hide all evidence of Tyler's infatuation, grabbing my economic and chemistry books in the process.

"Hey," Neil said, looking a little gloomy.

"Hi, Neil."

"So was all that stuff from Tyler?"

"Yeah," I said halfheartedly.

"Are you guys dating now?"

"No. Why would you think that? Did he say something?"

"No, it's just the flowers and stuff," he pointed to the lovey-dovey explosion seeping out of my locker, visible for all to see.

"Oh, that," I shut my locker quickly. "I don't know what Tyler is thinking. I haven't seen or talked to him since that night."

Neil's expression was unreadable. "So, you're not dating him?"

"No."

"Do you want to?"

"I don't know."

Neil was the only person I could talk honestly to. I wanted to tell him so much more, but every time I tried, something held me back.

We wandered outside and grabbed a seat in front of the English building.

"I hate everything that happened with Emily, but he's the only guy who's showed any interest in me."

"Oh, come on. You've got to be kidding, right?" he said, frustrated. "There are plenty of guys here who would love to get a chance to talk to you." He sat back on the bench with his arms folded.

"Oh, you must be talking about this long line of guys right here," I said, gesturing at the empty space in front of me.

"They're intimidated by you. Your beauty alone is intimidating, but…."

"But what?"

"The way you look at people, it's like you can see right through them, and although you don't say much, it's written all over your face. Many guys figure why bother."

"I don't know about that."

"Well I do, and it's the truth."

"So…." I paused, working up the nerve to finish. "Do you ever feel that way? I mean, do I intimidate you?"

My face burned from the anticipation.

"I'm talking to you, aren't I?" He leaned in closer. "You don't scare me."

"Good," I smiled, unnerved by his proximity.

February 14

Dear Diary,

Today was Valentine's Day. I think that says it all, but I guess I will elaborate. The outward show of affection was extremely more prevalent today than any other. Tyler Reed had Connor Marshall deliver flowers, a Teddy bear, and a card that I still have not forced myself to read yet. How dare he do such a thing after I had done such a terrible thing? But still, I was flattered. Maybe I too was being sucked into the whole V-Day hoopla. I don't know. Would it be so bad to be with Tyler? I've never really heard Neil say anything bad about him. It was so strange today, I don't remember him ever being that close to me before. Actually, he seemed weird all day. He wanted to ask me something in calculus, but he never had the chance. I wonder if he was trying to ask me out. Neil? I mean, I do have to admit that I have noticed more recently that.... I don't know, I guess he's.... Oh crap, I think I might like him. After all, he is the one person I can be myself around. I wonder if he likes me, or maybe not. But what if he does? Tyler or Neil? I would have to give both parties full consideration before making a decision. So, pro-con list it is!

10

Breaking Point

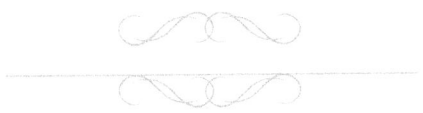

The next day, first period had gone by in a blur. Calculus was a bit awkward. Since my epiphany, I was unable to look at Neil the same way. He seemed so perfect now. His sparkling white teeth, his coiffed curly hair, his hypnotizing blue eyes—they were all distractions.

"Hey, Kristen," Neil whispered.

Crap. Try to play it off like you haven't been staring at him for most of the period.

"Uh…yeah," I said casually.

Gibberish is my forte. I reached into my backpack and pulled out an extra pencil. It got caught on the inner lining of my bag and broke the lead, so I just gave him mine. What's wrong with me? This is Neil we're talking about. I've spent enough time alone with him and everything was normal. Why are things so different between us?

"What's wrong with you?" Avery snapped.

"Nothing," I said quickly. I wondered if she caught me staring at him.

She gave me a befuddled look, then continued writing her notes. The bell finally rang, putting me out of my misery.

"Class, before you leave, please grab your results from the aptitude test off the table in the back."

Everyone rushed to find their results. Once the crowd subsided, I walked to the back of the classroom to find mine.

"Miss Kaplan, can you please come here?" Ms. Marquardt called.

I walked to the front of the classroom, wondering if I was in some kind of trouble. She held a piece of paper firmly between her fingers. She looked anxious, more so than usual.

"I held your results back because, well, we've been giving this aptitude test for quite some time now, and I'm not sure how this could have happened. This test shows you have no interest in anything."

"What? How could that be?"

"I don't understand it either, but you flatlined in every area. The test showed that you have no interest in anything," she said, handing me my results.

It was true. I showed no peak of interest in anything. I was going through the motions of life, never really living. And this test made it all clear: my future was hopeless, non-existent. The recurring images of me on the street suddenly began to feel more like a reality.

After class, Neil met me at my locker. "So, I was wondering if you possibly wanted to hang out sometime, with me."

"You really felt you needed to add the 'with me' part?"

"I just wanted to be clear. I had a fun time the other night and haven't been able to stop thinking about it. We could do something as friends."

"Uh, sure," I said, a bit confused.

"Great. I'll talk to you later."

"Okay," I said, disappointed as he walked away.

Why is he sending mixed signals? What does he mean? Does he really just want to be friends? If only I had someone to talk to about this.

For the rest of the day, I was in deep thought over my results and over what Neil said. I played it over in my head a thousand times, seeing the sadness in Ms. Marquardt's eyes, then trying to decipher Neil's body language when he suggested we hang out as friends.

"Kristen, Kristen!" Avery called. "Are you here or what? I called you like four times. We have to get this routine down before Friday's rally. Press play," she said, agitated.

"Sorry." I pushed play and tried to stay in the present. We were practicing in the school's dance studio.

Suddenly, Emily and three of her friends stormed in.

I stopped the music and stood up. I hadn't seen Emily all day, so I figured she ditched again. Wrong. She looked upset. This was my fault. After the pain I caused her, I was no better than my father.

Avery and the others stopped dancing once they spotted the girls. Avery walked over to my side. Carmen and Lisa followed suit. I had been practicing what I wanted to say, but every word vanished.

"How could you?" Emily choked.

"Shouldn't you be talking to Tyler about this? He practically took advantage of Kristen that night. She was totally wasted. Why are you mad at her?" Avery chimed in.

"Stay out of it, Avery," Emily warned.

"Or what? You should be talking to Tyler, not Kristen."

"He won't talk to me. He's been ignoring my phone calls." Emily stood directly in front of me.

"Why is that our problem? You're disrupting our practice time. So why don't you and your friends go find Tyler and leave Kristen alone."

"No, Avery, it's okay." I couldn't let Avery fight this battle for me. I was wrong, it didn't matter how much I'd had to drink. "I'm really sorry,

Emily. I never meant for all of this to happen. I never meant to hurt you or break up your relationship. I'm so sorry."

"You think I care if you're sorry? He was my boyfriend, you slore."

"Hey! She said she was sorry so you better pipe down with all that," Carmen said.

"People like you don't deserve to live," Emily spewed.

Carmen started putting her hair up in a bun. "Chick, you got one more time."

"Or what?" Emily said, poking me.

That's when everything got real. Screaming pierced my ears and the room spun. I heard voices, but I couldn't make out what was being said. When I regained focus, I found myself on top of Emily, my arms being restrained by Coach Logan and Avery.

"Get her off me! She's gone crazy! She's trying to kill me!" Emily shouted.

Just like the other night at Tyler's party, I had no idea what came over me.

Coach Logan pulled me off Emily and ordered the girls to leave. Emily's lip was busted, and I knew she'd be black and blue tomorrow. Even after she and her friends left, I was still shaking. She thought I deserved to die. Hearing it from someone else shook me to my core. I'm sure she was right; I could think of no objections. That was the second time today that my death had been brought to my attention. Emily was hoping for my demise, but little did she know I was already comatose.

That night I lay on my bed, staring at the ceiling, thinking about Emily confronting me. I was tired of replaying that scene in my mind, so I decided to hop on Facebook. I got up, went to my desk, and powered up my laptop. I had a new friend request from my father's wife. I guess she finally took the Facebook plunge. I accepted and creeped on her wall. Her profile picture looked like an older holiday photo. My dad, his wife, and the three girls dressed in reds and whites. A perfect family, I thought. The next series of pictures were from the eldest daughter, Michelle's birthday that had just passed. They went to Disney World. After seeing the picture of Michelle in Minnie Mouse ears with my dad wrapping his arms around her, embracing her as his daughter, I couldn't look anymore. I slammed my laptop shut and closed my eyes to hold back the tears. Too late. They came running down one after another. I crawled on my bed and curled up in the fetal position.

"Hopeless and without purpose."

I froze.

"They hate you."

I shot up, scanning the room. I knew I heard it this time. "Who are you?"

"Call me…. Kate."

This can't be real.

"They all think you deserve to die. You think anyone could ever really care about you or love you? How can they when your own father doesn't even care about you?"

I stood up and cautiously walked over to my door. I peeked down the hall to see my mother's closed door. I turned around and paced my bedroom.

"I'm not crazy, I'm not crazy," I said, wiping the tears from my face.

"The world would be such a better place without you. All you do is get in the way. There's no point to you being on this earth and the test proves it—a waste of space. But there is an escape for you. This life is hell, but I know a better place…."

That's when she materialized. She appeared out of nowhere by my bedroom door. I wiped more tears from my eyes to get a better look. Her back was facing me. Her long, beautiful golden waves reached the small of her back. They were gently blowing in a wind that I could not feel. But her presence felt like serenity. She wore a brilliant white dress that fastened at the shoulders. An elaborate golden band was cinched around her waist.

Even though she was translucent, I could see her. She was the most beautiful woman I had ever laid eyes on. She had to be some sort of goddess. I was in a daze, unable to look away. She smiled a comforting smile and motioned for me to follow her, then disappeared through my door. Still in a trance, I obeyed.

"Kristen? Kristen, honey? Can you hear Mommy?" my mom said in a shaky voice. Up until that moment, it was like everything had gone black. When I came out of whatever spell I was under, I was sitting on the edge of the balcony outside the kitchen, sixteen flights away from the ground. I didn't even remember coming out here. Mom grabbed me and pulled me back inside. We both sat on the kitchen floor with me in her arms, weeping.

That night I slept in my mother's bed. Every time I would get up to use the bathroom, she would ask me where I was going. Did she get any sleep? Before I knew it, the digital clock on the nightstand read 6:25 a.m.

"Did you get any sleep?" my mom asked in a raspy voice.

"No, not really."

"I sent Avery a text to let her know that I will be taking you to school today."

"Okay."

"Honey. What—"

"I better get ready for school," I said quickly. I got up and walked out of her bedroom.

Last night she just let me cry in her arms, but I knew today she would have questions—questions I was not ready to answer. What would I say? I had no idea how or even what happened last night.

I stood in front of my closet, trying to focus on picking out an outfit for school. I heard my mom talking to someone. Figuring she was on the phone, I walked over to my door so I could eavesdrop.

"It happened last night," my mom said, trying to whisper. "I don't know what else to do. Clearly what we've been doing is not working. I thought it was but…." She paused. "No, she's not delusional, Carol. How could you even say something like that? Look, I don't want to get into it right now. I just wanted to let you know what was going on. I'll call you later after I drop her off at school."

I couldn't believe it. My aunt thought I was crazy. It hurt me deeply to know that one of the people who I truly looked up to could write me off so easily. Didn't she have enough proof from the past that would say otherwise? Guess she didn't really know me. Hell, I wasn't sure if I even knew myself. I wiped the tears from my eyes and continued getting ready for school. I wasn't sure what I had started last night, but I knew I had to finish it. I thought about the spirit before my blackout. She was right. Anything else would be better than this. I was already dead anyway. I thought about my grandfather and how they must have found his unresponsive body hanging in that abandoned building. He had been successful in ending his misery, and soon I would be next. Is that why he appeared to me? He probably knew this moment was coming—the moment I would join him, wherever he was.

It was silent on the drive to school. No complaints. The minute I set foot on campus, I searched for the highest building and tried to figure how I could get up there. Just need to make it through the guidance counselor first. I made my way to her office.

"Have a seat, Kristen," Mrs. Wilson said with a smile.

I sat down and stared at the floor.

"Your mother notified us about what happened last night. She's worried about you. How are you feeling today?"

I shrugged.

115

"Have you thought about committing suicide before?"

"Yes."

"Are you are taking any anti-depressants?"

"Yes."

"So they're not helping you." It sounded more like a statement than a question.

"I guess not."

"Kristen, can you promise me that you will not try to hurt yourself again?"

"No," I answered as a single tear escaped.

Should've lied.

"Well, unfortunately by law we have to inform your doctor that you need to be hospitalized, at least until they can get you stable. I have to call for an ambulance, but I'll make sure they don't use the sirens."

The ambulance came, and as promised there were no sirens. The paramedics walked me to the truck. For everyone else, it was just another regular day. I could hear the birds chirping and the dogs barking. The sky was clear, and the sun was shining brightly. What a contrast to my current situation. I was sent to Woodruff Psychiatric Hospital, which was a freestanding psychiatric hospital. My guidance counselor said it was one of the nicer ones.

She's full of it.

Hospitals should be the one sterile place, but that didn't seem to be the case here. The smell alone made me queasy. I was almost certain that my mother had spoken with my aunt Carol, and they both concluded that hospitalization was the way to go. Never have I felt more alone.

The staff took all my possessions, including my shoelaces. I hated that it had come down to this. How embarrassing. After I was admitted, they took me to my room. There were two twin-sized beds and the closest one to the door looked occupied.

"Hi," a small squeaky voice chirped.

The girl was tiny, and she looked younger than me. She was probably about 95 lbs. She sat on her bed and began rubbing lotion on her cocoa colored skin.

"Oh, hello," I said, still standing in the same spot.

"This one's mine so you can take the other. I'm Tori. What's your name?"

"I'm Kristen."

"What are you in for?" she asked casually.

"Um, I tried to commit suicide." I walked over to the empty bed and sat down. "Why are you here?"

"Addiction. They busted me with meth."

"How old are you?" I asked.

"I'm fourteen. What high school do you go to?"

"Belmont."

"For real? I know some people who go to Belmont. Do you know Rodney Johnson?"

"Yeah. How do you know Rodney?"

"I've hung out with him and his friends a few times. It's been a while, though. Whenever you get out, tell him I said hi."

"Okay."

"But don't tell him where you saw me," she chuckled. "Maybe tell him we met at the mall. That sounds pretty normal."

"Right," I smiled back.

Talk about a prison and a summer camp all rolled into one. This place wasn't just for those with suicidal thoughts and actions, it was also for druggies.

Tori walked me through the facility, giving me the rundown.

"That's Jeremy." She pointed to a young guy wearing a black hoodie and khakis. "He's here because he stabbed his teacher. Oh, and that girl over there in the corner? She's delusional, so don't think anything of it if she asks you when her mom is coming to pick her up after school. She says that to everyone when she's not too busy talking to herself. See that guy over there on the couch?"

"Which one?" I asked.

"The one wearing sweats that looks like a statue. He had to go into time-out last week because he broke a light bulb and tried to cut another girl."

I looked at her, wide-eyed.

"Don't worry, you'll be fine. They detained him and adjusted his meds. See, he's totally chill now. He won't do it again."

"What about that girl over there, the one staring out the window."

"That's Chelsea. She's schizophrenic. The Looney Tune sees things," Tori said judgmentally.

"She sees things? Like what?" I asked curiously.

"Crazy things like monsters, I guess. She's always talking about the eyes watching her, or some man with a hood or something like that. She says she sees ghosts—talk about paranoid. She hears things that no one else can hear, too. Good thing she keeps to herself."

I was in complete shock at the things Tori was telling me, but I hoped it didn't show on my face. Chelsea was a diagnosed schizophrenic, and I had some of the same symptoms. Does this mean I'm also schizophrenic? Was I crazy after all? I was so consumed with that thought that I didn't realize how hard it had become to breathe.

"Are you all right?" Tori asked.

I couldn't answer. The walls were closing in on me, and everything went black. When I came to, some the nurses were hovering.

"Kristen, can you hear me?" my doctor asked.

My eyes were still adjusting to the fluorescent lights.

"I'm fine," I said, sitting up slowly. "My head hurts."

"You hit it when you collapsed. What happened?" Doctor Wilkins asked.

"Um." I thought quickly. I couldn't tell him what had led me to my fainting spell because that would reveal the commonalities I had with Chelsea. I couldn't bear the thought that I might be considered clinically insane. I didn't feel crazy. Then again, I guess most crazy people don't think of themselves as being crazy. Nevertheless, their diagnosis would only solidify my assumptions. My deepest fears would become a reality.

"I think she may still be a little dazed from the blow to her head." Doctor Wilkins said to one of the nurses. "Let's check her vitals."

One of the nurses ran and got her equipment. While still seated on the linoleum floor, she strapped the blood pressure band around my left arm to check my vitals. The doctor reached for a small flashlight, glancing at my pupils. He had me follow his finger side to side.

"Everything looks good. We'll give you some Tylenol for that headache, though," Doctor Wilkins said, helping me up. "Can you tell me what happened before you passed out?"

"I think I was hyperventilating. I guess I didn't realize until it was too late."

He nodded. "Do you sometimes feel anxious?"

"Sometimes. It's been more recent."

"All right. I think what I'll do is start giving you something for the anxiety. The medication you're already taking can cause anxiety, so we'll counteract that."

Great, I seemed to be getting worse every minute.

* * *

The next couple of days dragged at a snail's pace. My nights were filled with interrupted sleep patterns. Since my arrival, my dreams consisted of one thing in particular: me in two unknown locations, planting flowers. The hole I was digging was far too big for a plant.

During my sessions with Doctor Wilkins, I kept my mouth shut. I figured if I opened up, it would only prolong my stay here. Besides, if they couldn't help Chelsea, then they wouldn't be able to help me.

Doctor Wilkins changed my dosage, which they administered every morning after breakfast. In here, we had to stick to a strict schedule. Wake up, brush teeth, breakfast, take meds, group session, crafts time, lunch, take meds, free time, individual sessions, dinner, take meds, TV time, shower, lights out. This monotonous schedule went on for what felt like centuries. At least it was Saturday, which meant I'd get to see Mom. The hospital allowed visiting between 6:30 p.m. and 8:00 p.m.

"Hi, honey," my mom greeted me with open arms.

"Hi, Mom," I squeezed her back.

She kissed me on my forehead.

"How are you doing?" I asked.

I knew she was probably blaming herself for my actions.

"Me? Shouldn't I be asking you that?" She quickly wiped a tear.

"I'm fine."

We walked over to the '70s-style sofa in the common room and sat down.

"Are you feeling any better? Are they treating you well?"

"Yeah, I feel better, just ready to come home. Can I come home yet?"

"Hon, they want to keep you here a few more days to monitor the new meds."

I groaned.

"All your aunts and your uncle are sending their hugs and kisses. Your grandmother called. She says she loves you very much and wanted me to give you a hug and a kiss. She says she's praying for you."

"Tell her I said thanks." I wasn't sure how much help it would do.

"She said that the pastor of her church passed away this week. I guess she's been helping with the funeral arrangements."

"Oh, that's too bad."

"Yeah, so she said a new pastor is supposed to be taking over, but your Nana doesn't seem too happy about it. She says he's too young and he's not even Baptist."

"Does it matter?" I asked.

"I guess so. The whole town is talking about it."

"Well when you talk to her, tell her that I hope everything works out." I looked up to see Neil walking in. My mouth fell open.

"What?" She turned around. "Oh, that's right, I told him he could come by. I want you to continue to get better so you can come home soon, okay?" She kissed me on my forehead. "I'll go so you guys can talk, but I'll be back on Wednesday."

I nodded.

She left as Neil meandered toward me. I wondered what he was thinking. Does he think I'm crazy? My current situation doesn't exactly depict otherwise. I must admit I was a little upset with my mom for telling him where to find me, but I was also glad because I really wanted to see him. What if he came to tell me that we could no longer be friends? I didn't know if I'd be able to handle the rejection. We stood for what felt like an eternity before he finally spoke.

"Hello," he said softly.

"Hi."

"Are you ok?" he asked, moving closer.

"Yes. At least, I think so. What are you doing here?"

"When you didn't show up for economics and chemistry on Thursday, I looked for you. I went to your cheer practice after school but no one knew where you were. The next day I asked Avery if she had talked to you, and she gave some bogus story about you being out of town, so Friday night I called the bat line."

I could feel the sting of the tears trying to form, but I fought them back. "Ah, the bat line. I forgot about that."

"I talked to your mom. She told me what happened. I asked if I could call you and she said she was coming here to see you and that I could come by today, too, so I did."

"Oh."

"I wasn't sure if you wanted to see me, but I had to make sure you were okay."

I was relieved that he hadn't written me off. It would only be a matter of time, though.

"I can't believe you purposely spoke to Avery."

We both smiled. His face went serious, his eyes boring into mine. "Anything for you."

Suddenly, I needed to sit down.

He gently grabbed my arm and sat down next to me. "Are you okay?"

"I'm fine, just tired. They have us on a tight schedule here."

"Avery's telling everyone you've gone to a spa retreat. If you don't come back well-rested, everyone's going to think something's up."

"Avery," I sighed, shaking my head. "I guess she means well. What's been going on at school?"

"Oh, nothing. It's been pretty drama-free."

"Seriously?"

"Yeah."

"Are you lying?"

He hesitated, then let out a sigh. "Yeah."

"What's going on? You can tell me."

He studied my expression, unsure.

"Seriously, Neil, I'm fine. Now what is it?"

"Emily and her friends have been spreading pretty bad rumors around about you. And I guess they were writing things in the girls' bathroom about you, but the principal found out that they were the ones doing it and they got suspended for three days."

"And they probably got that punishment because I'm in here." I shook my head. "Neil, why are you here?"

"What do you mean? I was worried about you. I want to be here."

It was only a matter of time before he would abandon me like the others. My eyes welled with tears. "I don't need you to feel sorry for me or treat me like some charity case."

"I don't and I'm not. I'm here because I really like you. I care about you."

I shook my head and wiped my eyes. "That's impossible. Do you want to know why? It's because my own father doesn't even care if I'm dead or alive. My own family thinks I'm crazy."

"But—"

"Please, don't. Just go," I said, focusing on the checkered floor.

He sat there, gazing.

I stood and exited the common area, leaving him on the couch.

It was lights out at 9:00 p.m. like every other night, but I couldn't sleep. Sure Neil was convinced he cared for me, but once he got to know me better, he would see what a hot mess I really was.

Days began to blur. The next night, I fell into a deep sleep. I was in an unfamiliar house. The light from the rising sun had just begun to illuminate the sky. I walked down a short hallway and caught my reflection in an antique mirror that hung on the wall over a red Chinese Chippendale credenza. Was this me? It couldn't be. The reflection was of a young Caucasian male. I touched the right side of my face, and the reflection mimicked. I was so confused. I almost didn't notice that my hand was bleeding. I held it out in front of me and began to panic. I flipped it over a few times, trying to find the open wound. There was none. I held out my other hand and noticed I was holding a straight-edged butcher knife, completely covered in blood. I jumped, and the knife fell out of my hand, dropping to the floor.

I woke with a startle.

What just happened? I was in someone else's body. But how is that possible? I racked my brain, trying to figure out what the dream meant, but I came up short.

Later that evening, I sat in the common room, still replaying the dream in my mind, trying to make sense of it. The TV in the background kept distracting me. I glanced up at the screen. The news anchor was reporting on a gruesome killing that took place not too far away in one of the more prestigious neighborhoods. Apparently, a seventeen-year-old boy killed his mother and then killed himself. They were both found dead when his father returned home early this morning from a prolonged business trip. My jaw dropped. I recognized the boy immediately: Eugene Webber from Doctor Lewis' office. He was the reflection in my dream. I sat in horror. I couldn't believe he was dead. How was I able to see this in my dream? I only knew him in passing, I had never been to his house, yet I saw every detail of that hallway. In an effort to stay calm, I chalked it up as pure coincidence. After all, I wasn't certain that it was Eugene, as they never showed the boy's picture or gave his name. I had no way of knowing if the house matched the one in my dream. It's just a nightmare....

I noticed Chelsea was staring at me from across the room. I looked away, trying to ignore her. She started laughing hysterically, got up, and stood directly in front of me.

"I know your secret," she whispered. "It won't get better. It only gets worse."

"Chelsea, go and have a seat," one of the nurses called from the adjoining room.

Chelsea paid her no attention. Instead, she leaned forward, inches away from my face. Our eyes locked. I leaned back reflexively.

"The evil ones bring the cold with them. And no matter how hard you try to get away from them, you can't. Even when you can't see them, they're still there. You feel them."

"Chelsea, I mean it. Go back to your seat, or it's lights out," the nurse threatened.

"You can't run from them," Chelsea whispered with a menacing expression.

Two large male orderlies appeared on either side, pulling her back.

She jerked out of their grip and was back in my face. "They're everywhere. The eyes are everywhere, watching, always watching. And they know you see them, too. They won't stop watching you."

The orderlies grabbed Chelsea again, dragging her out of the common area as she fought back in protest.

"No, please don't. She sees them too. Just ask her. They told me. Tell them! Kristen, tell them! Please!"

I sat there in astonishment. My heart raced, hoping no one would believe her. How did she know? Did they really tell her? Why would they do that? Although Chelsea was average in size, the two large men struggled to contain her. Two more men came to help, while the nurse came with a syringe. I composed myself. The nurse injected Chelsea, and she quickly calmed down and was taken to her room.

"That was crazy," Tori said, taking a seat.

"Yeah."

"That's kind of weird how she singled you out. She's never done that before."

"I don't get it," I said, trying to sound convincing.

The whole thing with Chelsea freaked me out. Am I a magnet for crazy? Because she's crazy. It seems to be following me everywhere. I'm not insane; I can't be. I know right from wrong, I function just fine—well, most of the time. And what did she mean when she said a spirit had told her those things?

* * *

I had the dream about the little girl again. This time it was different. I can't put my finger on why. Maybe God was trying to tell me something. But what was the message? And was it even God?

Something was emerging; I could feel it. The encounters and incidents that had lead me here were proof. But my path seemed unclear. Turns out the answer was right in front of me with wide-set, dark brown eyes, penetrating mine. Was I schizophrenic? If so, the depression and delusions made sense. Was I destined to be like Chelsea, or worse? The only thing I knew for certain was I couldn't stop it. Was it evil or was it good? Only God knew what tomorrow would bring.

Intermission

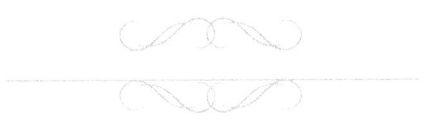

Transliteration of Discern:

Yada' (Hebrew)—"To know by seeing; learn to know; to perceive and see; find out and discern; to know by experience; to consider; to cause to know; to know how; be skillful in; to have knowledge; be wise." Ezekiel 44:23 (Hebrew Lexicon H3045).

"Now concerning spiritual gifts, brethren, I do not want you to be ignorant: You know that you were Gentiles, carried away to these dumb idols, however you were led. Therefore, I make known to you that no one speaking by the Spirit of God calls Jesus accursed, and no one can say that Jesus is Lord except by the Holy Spirit.

"There are diversities of gifts, but the same Spirit. There are differences of ministries, but the same Lord. And there are diversities of activities, but it is the same God who works all in all. But the manifestation of the Spirit is given to each one for the profit of all: for to one is given the word of wisdom through the Spirit, to another the word of knowledge through the same Spirit, to another faith by the same Spirit, to another gifts of healings by the same Spirit, to another the working of miracles, to another prophecy, to another discerning of spirits, to another different kinds of tongues, to another the interpretation of tongues. But one and the same Spirit works all these things, distributing to each one individually as He wills.

"For as the body is one and has many members, but all the members of that one body, being many, are one body, so also is Christ" (1 Corinthians 12:1–12).

PART II

11

Homecoming

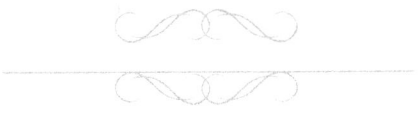

February 25

Dear Diary,

I was finally released yesterday. I never want to go back to that place ever again. I tried to commit suicide. Mom was worried about me, and Aunt Carol thinks I'm crazy now. I'm not sure where I go from here. Everything just seems so pointless. I have to see Dr. Lewis twice a week, and I hate it. I'm not looking forward to going back to school, either. I'm sick of pretending I'm someone I'm not. And I don't want to see Neil. I can't believe he came and visited me in the hospital. Naturally, I screwed everything up. I want to be happy, but sometimes it feels like I don't deserve happiness. He looked so genuine when he told me he cared about me, but I'm sure those feelings won't last. Especially if he discovers the truth. Then he'd probably feel the same way as everyone else. Why can't I be normal like other people?

My mom dropped me off at school on Monday. I half expected her to attend my classes from the way she'd been acting since my return. She wouldn't let me out of her sight. Even coming out of my bathroom a few times, I caught her lingering by the door. Although I wasn't happy about going back to school, I was glad to get away from being under constant watch.

"Hey, girlie," Carmen greeted as I approached our usual table.

"Hi," I replied.

"Oh, hey, Kristen. How was your spa week? Did you have fun?" Charlotte asked.

"Oh…ah," I said off guard.

"Charlotte, please don't bombard Kristen with your intrusive questions. Hey," Avery hugged me. "I told everyone you were in Colorado at the Broadmoor on vacation. 'Kay?" she whispered, releasing me as the first bell rang.

"Right."

"You know since your spa vacation, I've reevaluated myself and decided to turn over a new leaf. We're seniors now, and we'll be leaving high school soon, so I think it's time for a new Avery—a more mature Avery. This Avery is more in tune with other people's feelings. Of course, this Avery is still popular with a remarkable fashion sense, but she's more a beloved leader than a tyrant."

"Does this Avery always refer to herself in the third person?"

"Oh, Kristen, you're so witty," Avery chuckled. "Did that seem genuine to you?"

"Um…yeah. Wow, you have changed," I said sarcastically.

"Look, complete change doesn't happen overnight. Baby steps, right? I even said please to Charlotte. Did you catch that?"

"Baby steps? Good luck with that." I wiggled my way out from under her arm and headed off to class.

First period we had a writing assignment due, but because of my "situation," Mr. Swisher gave me an extension. Second period I tried not to make eye contact with Neil. I could see out my periphery that he was staring, however, I stayed focused on the board and on my notes. The bell finally rang, ending my torture. I rushed to put my things away.

"So, guess who was totally hooking up with Nathan Perry?"

"Who?" I asked, uninterested.

"None other than Emily Lewis."

"Really?" I immediately froze and looked at Avery.

"Apparently, they had been secretly hooking up while she and Tyler were together. Such whorish behavior. And she had the nerve to get mad at you. People in glass houses, right? I guess what goes around comes around," she said smugly.

"I guess," I said, still holding my notebook.

"Oh, and you'll never guess who's pregnant. Emily Finch. Crazy, huh? She's going to have to drop out of school and get a job at Del Taco or something. Your dream came true. Anyway, I'm off to find Rodney. He's supposed to be getting muffins for all my fans. The new Avery feeds her people. See you at the table?"

"Yeah, sure," I said in a daze.

"I'll save you a muffin," she said, walking out the door.

I couldn't believe it. After I had felt so badly about breaking Emily's heart, and she didn't even really care about him the way I thought she did. And then the whole thing about my dream coming true was so crazy. How could I have possibly known that she would become pregnant months before it happened?

"Hi, Kristen," Neil said, startling me.

"Oh, hi."

I put my notebook in my backpack and walked out the classroom with Neil right on my heels.

"Hey," he grabbed my arm. "I wanted to talk to you in class. How are you?"

"I'm great," I said sardonically.

He looked concerned.

I sighed. "I don't want to be here, but I'm fine."

"I've been worried about you. I wish you would have told me what was going on with you. Did Avery know?"

"No."

"I can't imagine having all of that pent up inside and not having anyone to talk to. I feel like such a jerk."

I made eye contact. "What? Why?"

"Because of all those times you let me just go on and on about my problems with Avery, all the while you were going through something so much more serious."

I paused, unsure of what I wanted to say. I had so many thoughts swirling around in my head.

"I wanted to tell you. I just…I don't know." I could feel the tears coming. The last thing I wanted to do was start crying in front of Neil again. "I have to…um, I have to go to the bathroom. I'll talk to you later."

I ran off to the nearest bathroom; it was vacant. I hid in the last stall, trying to stop the tears as the searing pain deep inside boiled up to the surface. This was no good. I was a mess. I was unmasked and in no shape to return to my classes for the day. I pulled myself together before forging a note from my mother, permitting me to leave early for a doctor's appointment.

I had to get away from everything and everyone, so I walked to the park. The geese scurried along as I sat on the plush green grass, facing the pond. A beautiful golden-winged butterfly perched itself on a blade of grass at arm's length, its body black with white spots. I reached out to touch it, but it fluttered away, no longer within my reach. I wondered how it would feel to be as free as that butterfly—so beautiful and uninhibited.

All the stress from being at school was now gone. I sat under a tall oak and laid down using my backpack as a pillow. Before I knew it, sleep found me. I wasn't sure how long I had been out when someone cleared their throat.

"Is this seat taken?"

I opened one eye to see Neil standing over me. I sat up slowly, still a little groggy. I tried to fix my hair.

"What are you doing here?" I asked.

"Do you mind?" he gestured toward the ground.

I shook my head.

He took a seat next to me. "I couldn't find you at lunch, and you weren't in economics or chemistry, so I figured you went home."

"Lunch?! Crap. What time is it?"

"After one."

"I didn't realize I had been sleeping that long." I thought for a moment. "So, if you figured I went home, then why are you here?"

"Well, that was my first thought, but when I started driving, I remembered you told me you like coming here. So I decided to try here first. Did you walk here?"

"Yeah. It's not that far on foot."

"It's nice here. I drive by all the time but I never actually stop. I didn't realize how big this park is. I'm just glad you can see the pond from the road or else I would have been driving around for a while."

"Neil, you didn't have to come looking for me. I'm fine."

"Are you? You looked like you were going to cry earlier."

I folded my arms across my chest. "I prefer to cry in the privacy of my bedroom. That way I don't have to worry about people asking me what's wrong."

"Then I won't ask you any questions. We can just sit here if you like."

I pulled my knees up to my chest and wrapped my arms around them tightly. We sat in silence for a moment, listening to the wind rustle through the leaves.

"I blacked out that night. I don't remember much. I remember that my mom found me out on the balcony. There was a woman in my room.

I must have followed her out there." I shook my head. "It's all kind of a blur."

"A woman?" Neil asked.

"Yeah. A spirit."

"A spirit?"

"Yes."

"Like a ghost?"

"I guess. I'm not really sure what they are."

"They?"

"It's not the first one I've seen."

"Are you serious?" His look changed to one of exhilaration.

"Are you excited to hear this or something?"

"I'm sorry. It's just that I've never met anyone who actually experienced these types of things." Then reality set in. "So all that stuff is real." It was more of a statement than a question.

"Yeah."

"Does it scare you?"

"Yes. It's not normal. I'm not normal."

"Being normal is overrated. You're unique. That's way better than being normal."

"You don't think I'm a freak?" I rested my face on my knees, looking over at him.

"No, not at all. I think you're amazing. I don't know what I would do if I saw what you see. Is…?"

"Is what?"

"Is that why to tried to…."

"Commit suicide?" I asked.

He nodded.

"I'm not sure. I don't think so. I mean, I've been sad long before I started seeing these things. I think it just added to everything I was already going through. I'm fine now, though. You don't have to worry about me. I will never go back to that place again."

I knew if another suicide attempt was made, I would have to make sure that this time it stuck.

"I am, however, starving."

"Oh, of course. Let's go get you something to eat," he said, getting up.

We left the park and went to In-N-Out. I devoured a cheeseburger, fries, and a vanilla shake. I told Neil about the spirit I had seen in Long Island, and the ones I had seen in my house. It felt good to finally have someone to talk to about what I had been keeping secret for so long. He listened attentively without any judgment.

By the time I got home, there was a message on our machine from school informing my mother that I had been absent today. I panicked and hit delete.

"You're not going to tell her you ditched?" Neil asked while taking a seat on the couch.

"I don't think that would be such a good idea. She'd freak out, plus she's already been acting weird since I've been back. It was just a one-time thing anyway."

The truth was I really wasn't sure what my mother would do if she found out, but at least this way I wouldn't have to explain why I did it. No use worrying her any more.

We watched TV for about an hour and then started on homework. I sat on the floor in front of the couch, using the ottoman as a table. Neil claimed the couch with his books. It looked like we were working—a good pretense for when my mother finally arrived. She would have no idea I skipped school today. I just hoped she wouldn't ask me any in-depth questions about my day because I knew I wouldn't be able to lie to her. At least not very well, anyway.

Around 5:30, Mom came rolling in.

"Hey, hon," she said, holding takeout bags.

"Hi, Mom."

"Hi, Ms. Kaplan," Neil said.

"Oh, hi, Neil. I didn't know you'd be here. How are you doing?"

"I'm good, thank you."

"Are you guys hungry? I brought home Chinese."

"Starving," I said, getting up to join my mother in the kitchen.

Neil followed suit. "This is a lot of food. This was just for the two of you?"

"We get enough for leftovers," my mother said, quickly stealing some chow mein. She disappeared into her bedroom with the container.

Neil and I made our plates and went back into the living room. A few minutes later, my mother came in, rifling through a gym bag.

"Do you have my pink sports bra?" she asked.

"Why would I have your pink sports bra?"

"Didn't you borrow it for cheer camp?"

"Mom, that was last June."

"Well, do you still have it?"

"No, I don't have it. I returned it to you like seven months ago."

"I can't find it."

"Don't you have other sports bras?" I asked.

"Yes, but I want that one because it matches my outfit," she said, pouting.

"Where are you going?"

"The girls and I are taking Zumba classes."

"Really? Like that infomercial?"

"They teach classes at the gym."

"Since when did you join the gym?"

"I've been a member for a few months now, remember? I wanted you to join so we could stay fit together while wearing matching outfits."

"Oh, right. But you never actually went, so I figured you canceled your membership."

"I went that one night, but I pulled my hamstring."

I looked at her incredulously. "I don't remember you pulling a hamstring."

"Well, I didn't actually pull a hamstring, but it was pretty darn close."

I glanced over at Neil. "I'm sorry you have to witness this."

"Will you be okay here while I'm at the gym?" she asked, concerned.

"Mom, I'm fine. Besides, I won't be here alone. Neil will be with me. We have a project to work on."

"I don't know. Maybe I should cancel."

"Mom, don't be silly. Really, I'm good."

"All right then. Shoot, look at the time." She seized her gym bag and disappeared into the kitchen, grabbing a bottled water from the fridge. "I'm leaving now. Oh, after Zumba we're going to Cheesecake Factory for dessert and drinks, so I may be home late, but I will be checking in on you periodically."

"Let me get this straight. You're going to go workout and then after you've worked out you're going to get dessert and drinks?" I deadpanned.

"You think you're so funny, don't you?"

"Isn't that kind of ridiculous to you, though? Why even go workout?"

"It's not that big a deal," my mother said.

"Isn't that ridiculous to you?" I asked Neil.

"I'm staying out of this one," he replied.

"I don't care what you think. I'm going to go workout, and then I'm going to reward myself with a tiny piece of cheesecake. I'll call to check in with you."

"Okay."

After Neil left, I received five calls and eight text messages from my mother. I laid on the couch in the living room, thinking about Chelsea. I wondered if she was still at Woodruff Psychiatric Hospital and if she had improved. Highly doubtful. The last words she spoke replayed in my head over and over. Was I schizophrenic? I decided to do some research on the matter. I went to my room and logged into my laptop. I Googled schizophrenia to see what would come up. Skimming through the first paragraph on WebMD, certain key phrases stood out: severe brain disorders, distorted reality, hallucinations, delusions—a chronic condition requiring lifelong treatment. The last words hit me the hardest. Complications associated with schizophrenia may include suicide, depression, or homelessness. It was all becoming clear. My fate was staring right back at me on my computer screen in black Times New Roman. Was I delusional like Aunt Carol had said? Were the things I was seeing and hearing only hallucinations? From what I read, all signs pointed to yes. I couldn't read any further. Tightness gripped my chest. I closed the web browser and stared at my desktop screen.

I suddenly felt irritable and agitated. Tears steadily streamed down my cheeks. My thoughts were jumbled as I tried to make sense of everything. Soon I was completely overwhelmed with fear and felt like the room was closing in on me as the panic set in. I crawled into bed and curled up, picturing myself on a beach somewhere. Then I tried regulating my breathing and focused on the surroundings. I fabricated a cool, calm, serene beach just as Doctor Lewis had taught me. But the image began to change.

Blue skies morphed into a stark white ceiling with generic fluorescent lights. My secluded beach had become an 8x10 room with white padded walls. The white sands of the beach were now linoleum floors. I sat up and looked around the empty room. That's when I saw a small square window with bars. It was sunny out, but I couldn't move. I yearned to break free from the room, but it seemed impossible. Oddly, it also felt comforting and safe. At least in here, I knew what to expect. And so I sat there, frozen in my own personal reformatory. I lay back down, resting my cheek on the cool, sterile floor. Soon I was lulled to sleep, comforted by the predictability of my safeguarded cognizance.

12

Subtle Rebellion

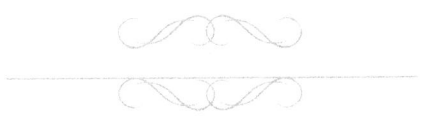

The next morning I stood in front of my closet, staring at the clothes. I was feeling a little better since my meltdown last night, but nowhere near normal.

"Kristen, you're not even dressed yet!" my mom yelled after bursting through my door.

"Is it okay if Neil takes me this morning? I don't want to make you late, I just can't figure out what I want to wear today."

She paused for a moment. "I'm not sure if that's such a good idea, hon."

"Mom, you can't possibly be with me every second of every day, so please stop being so worried."

"You do realize that's easier said than done?" Then she sighed. "All right, that's fine. Just hurry so you won't be late."

"Okay."

I heard the front door shut. I grabbed my cell phone off my nightstand and dialed Neil's number.

"Hello."

"Hi. You at school yet?"

"No, just about to leave my house. Why?"

"Do you feel like going to the beach today?"

"I thought you said it was a one-time thing?"

"I thought it was, but I guess not. Are you in?"

He sighed. "I'll be there in twenty."

We spent the day at Seal Beach making sand castles and swimming. He took me home so I could shower, change, and erase all messages from the answering machine before they could get to my mother. I let my mom know that Neil would be taking me to my appointment with Doctor Lewis, so all seemed well.

"How have you been doing since you've been back home?" Doctor Lewis asked.

"Everything has been much better," I lied.

"That's good. I'm glad to hear the new dosage is working." He scribbled on his notepad.

"Doctor Lewis?"

"Yes?"

"Did you hear about the boy who killed his mother and then himself?"

He hesitated for a moment. "Yes, it's terrible what happened to Eugene. But let's stay focused on you."

But I couldn't now. It was Eugene Webber. I couldn't believe it. It was true and I'd seen it. I could still smell the blood mixed with lilac air fresher.

"The knife," I whispered. I remember how the hard wood of the handle—still sticky from the blood—felt in my hand.

"Knife?" Doctor Lewis asked.

"Oh, sorry I was still thinking about Eugene. I thought I was thinking it."

"You mentioned a knife," Doctor Lewis said curiously.

"I just couldn't believe that he could stab someone with a butcher knife, much less his own mother."

"Did you know Eugene?"

"No. I would just see him waiting out front after my appointments."

"And you made no contact with him outside this office?"

"No," I said, wondering where he was going with this.

"Then how did you know the exact murder weapon?"

"What?" I asked confused.

"How did you know he stabbed his mother and then slit his throat with a butcher knife? No one else knows that. It was never mentioned on the news. Only I and the authorities know that."

I could feel the heat rising in my body, probably indicating that I was guilty of something. But it wouldn't be for what he thought. I could see no other way around this. I was going to have to tell the truth.... Or not.

"I don't know. I guess it was just a good guess."

He looked at me suspiciously, but continued the session, focusing his questions on me.

An hour later, I met up with Neil who was waiting for me outside in his car.

"How'd it go? You still crazy?" he asked.

"Appears so," I replied halfheartedly, looking out my window.

"You know I'm not serious when I say that, right?"

I nodded, still not making eye contact.

"I only make light of it because it's so ridiculous. Hey...."

I turned to look at him.

"You're not crazy."

I sighed. But I still wasn't 100% certain his words were true. "Thanks for doing this."

"Doing what?"

"You know, dropping me off and picking me up for my appointment, and for taking me to the beach today."

"Don't worry about it. I don't mind. I had fun."

"I know, but I still wanted to say it. You haven't been getting in trouble with your mom for ditching, have you?"

"No. I just tell her I'm not going."

"Really?"

"Yeah."

"I wish it were that easy with my mom."

Before long, we were merging in and out of traffic.

"So, what should we do tomorrow?" I smiled.

I rolled over on my bed and put my notebook on my nightstand just as my cell rang. It was Avery. I let out a strenuous groan.

"Hi, Avery," I said, mustering up a cheery tone.

"Oh, so you are alive. I was calling to check and make sure you weren't…oh. Sorry, I forgot."

"It's fine, Avery. I just haven't been feeling well."

"Really? Are you sick? Because you sound fine."

"It's actually my allergies. I'm going to rest up this weekend, so I should be good by Monday. You're holding everything down for me, right?"

"Of course. Who else is going to do it? Neil's been out, too."

"Oh, yeah?"

"Yeah. I've been thinking, and the new Avery realizes she has been kind of a jerk to Neil."

"Is that so?"

"Yep. I was thinking about it the other day during my mani-pedi. You know, he's pretty spicy. And who cares if he's not popular. I could make him popular by association."

"I don't know, Avery. It sounds like the plot of a cheesy teen movie. What about Rodney? I thought you two were in love?"

"I'm bored with Rodney, and I think the new Avery would be with someone more like Neil, you know?"

"No, I don't know." I sat up on my bed, fury running through my veins. "Neil is sweet, intelligent, and caring. He deserves someone who will care about him, not just toy with his emotions like you've done so many times."

"What's your problem? Why are you all Team Neil when you should be Team Avery?"

"I'm not on anyone's team. I'm just game for doing what's right, and if you're planning on hurting him yet again, then I don't want to be part of it."

"Fine, but don't think I won't get what I want. I know he's still in love with me."

"What?"

"Yup. Well, anyway, I've got to put my plan in motion. Feel better soon. Whatever it is you're sick with is making you crabby. Talk to you later, girlie."

I sat there, staring at my phone. Why did Avery's plans bother me so much? I mean, sure Neil and I are friends, but this was jealousy, which I had no right to be feeling; he wasn't mine. Even the thought of him being mine was funny, especially since he clearly saw me as a friend. I wondered if Avery's "charms" would work on him. The thought of losing Neil scared me more than anything. I went to my favorites in my phone and a picture of Neil popped up. I snapped it the other day when we were at Island Burger. I wanted to call him, but what would be my reasoning? I had no right to tell him who he should or shouldn't date. But as a friend, it was my duty to tell him when a snare was being set up. But would I be doing this for selfish reasons? Guess I still had a crush on him. I put my phone down. What now? I would have to tell him anyway. I cared too much not to. I reached for my phone again just as it began ringing. My face lit up, and I immediately pulled myself together.

"Hey, Neil," I said casually.

"Hey."

"What's up?"

"I had to call you and tell you. Guess who just called me? You'll never guess."

That's when my second line beeped. I looked at my phone it was my mom.

"Sorry, Neil, can you hold on a sec? That's my mom on the other line." I clicked over.

"Hello?"

"Hey, hon. I'm on my way."

"Okay," I said, anxiously waiting to get back to Neil.

"Hey, what do you think about sushi for dinner?"

"Sounds fine." I rushed.

"Okay. Oh, and did you buy Doritos?"

"What?"

Her phone was breaking up.

"I ate all the Doritos."

"I just bought a bag yesterday."

"You did?"

"Oh my gosh, Mom. You ate that whole bag?"

"So you did buy those?"

I sighed. "Look, I can't do this right now. I have Neil on the other line."

"All right, I guess I'll pick up another bag. See you in a little bit."

"Okay." I clicked back over.

"Neil, you still there?"

"Yeah, I'm here."

"I'm so sorry about that."

"Is everything all right?"

"Yeah, my mother is just crazy."

"So it runs in the family then."

"Very funny. Now, what were you saying?"

"Guess who just called me."

"Avery?"

"How did you know?"

"Because I got off the phone with her not too long ago. She said she was going to call you."

"Oh."

"She noticed you haven't been at school."

"Oh, really?"

"Yeah. I didn't tell her we've been hanging out this past week."

"No worries."

"Well, what did she say?" I asked.

"I don't know. I didn't answer my phone."

"Oh."

"She left me a message and asked me to call her back."

"Are you going to call her back?"

"I don't know. You think I should?"

I thought for a moment. I could try to beat Avery at her own game. After all, I was certain I cared more for Neil than she did. Why should the egomaniacal win in this situation? But then again, I was still me.

"I think you should do whatever you want to do. Just use your best judgment."

"Okay, I will. I'm sorry to put you in the middle of all this."

"It's fine. Avery does it all the time, but she doesn't apologize. Besides, I don't mind listening to you vent. If you don't let it out, you'll just explode."

We both laughed.

The call lasted until after midnight. The next morning, we went to IHOP for breakfast and hit the road. We decided to stop at Venice Beach to hang out for a little while before heading to Santa Monica Pier. There was always an eclectic gathering of people at Venice Beach. We stopped at a crab shack for lunch and then ended up seeing a movie at Santa Monica Plaza. I missed five calls from my mother while we were watching the movie. I slid into Neil's 2008 Challenger and listened to my voicemail messages as I buckled my seat belt. They were all from my mother; she was livid. The school had contacted her about me skipping school. I felt guilty and didn't want her calling the cops, so I sent her a text letting her know I was okay, then turned my phone off.

"Is she really upset?" Neil asked.

"Yeah. I'll probably be grounded for the rest of my life."

"Do you want me to take you home?"

"No! We haven't gone to the pier yet."

"Kristen."

I shook my head. "Today is my last day before I go back to my perpetual hell."

Neil's phone began to ring.

"Who is it? My mom?" I asked, a bit paranoid.

"No, it's Avery. Should I answer?"

"May as well get it over with," I said.

It didn't matter anyway. I would be grounded for the rest of life, so I doubted I'd be able to hang out with Neil. Avery would win—as if Neil were some prize to claim. I guess that's how she saw him. It'd only be a matter of time before she'd cast him off to the side. How can she hurt someone so easily and not feel any sense of guilt or remorse? I don't even think she apologized for what she had done to him in the past.

"I think we should get tattoos," I said, breaking the silence.

"What?!"

"Yeah, we should get tattoos. We can go back to Venice to that tattoo place we saw. You know, the one with the big skull and the fairies in the window."

"We are not getting tattoos. You are not getting a tattoo."

"Why not?!"

"Because it's stupid. You don't really want a tattoo."

"Yes, I do!"

"Since when have you had a desire to get a tattoo?"

I thought for a moment. "It's been more of a recent decision."

We were both quiet.

Neil turned and looked at me. "Are you sane now?"

I nodded.

"Where did this sudden urge to get a tattoo come from?"

"I don't know, I just want to do something different. I feel so trapped. I'm tired of the ordinary. Aren't you?"

"I guess, but a tattoo's not going to change anything. Your life will still be the same. Instead, you'll just have some stupid tribal marking or Chinese words on you that probably don't even mean what they're supposed to. And you'll have it on you for the rest of your life."

"I guess you're right. Plus, I don't really like needles. Speaking of sharp pains, how did the conversation with Avery go?"

Neil was quiet as he stared out the window.

"If you don't want to tell me, or you just don't want to talk about it, I understand."

I was dying to know what had transpired. He shook his head. My stomach knotted and my palms were instantly clammy.

"So…which one is it?" I murmured.

He sat unmoving as if I'd never spoken.

I cleared my throat. "Is it that you don't want to talk about it now, or you don't want to tell me at all?" I asked carefully.

He said nothing.

"I'm sorry, it's just that you shaking your head no was kind of vague. I'm not sure which one you were referring to."

Still nothing.

He started the car and we drove in silence. He finally turned the radio up and we continued the drive, not saying a word. I wondered if he was reconsidering being with Avery. Did he still love her? Was he ready to take another chance at getting his heart broken? Why go through all that? What was it about Avery that had him so bewitched he couldn't let her go, even when he knew she was all wrong for him? I secretly wished he could see me the way he saw Avery, but it was impossible for anyone to see me that way; I was sure of it.

He stared straight ahead, not once making eye contact, even though I purposely stared at him a couple times during the drive. He held a tight grip on the steering wheel with both hands, one at ten and the other two, his back as straight as a flagpole, which was not like his normal laid-back attitude. There'd never been this much silence between us. Not even when he came to visit me in the hospital. I wondered if it were something I had done or said, or maybe Avery said something about me to him.

The sun was setting over the horizon of the Pacific Ocean. We parked the car and walked along the wooden planks of the boardwalk, still silent. The temperature cooled off as the brine from the ocean was more evident in the breeze.

"Are you hungry? Do you want to get something to eat?" I said, finally trying to start up a conversation.

"No, not yet," he said, staring ahead.

"Okay. Do you want to go on the Merry-Go-Round or play one of those games? The skeet shooting's usually fun."

"No," he said, his hands shoved deep into his pockets.

"Okay. Well, is there something you want to do?"

He didn't answer.

"Look, Neil, if you want to go home…."

"No. I'm sorry. I just—"

"What? Is it something I did or said?"

"No." He stopped and turned to face me. "You think I'm mad at you?"

"Aren't you?"

"No. I'm not mad you, Kristen. Avery wants to get back with me."

"Yeah, she had mentioned that last night."

"Right, of course she would have called you first to gloat as if it would be so easy."

"So you didn't tell her yes?"

"No. I told her I was in love with someone else. But I didn't say who."

My heart stopped for a second and then restarted again, working harder than ever. How on earth did I miss him say that while we were in the car?

"What do you mean you're in love with someone else? How is that possible? I didn't even know you were dating anyone else. I mean, dating anyone. I'm not saying that we…I didn't mean to say that we were dating. I just…. This is a surprise."

I walked over to the edge of the boardwalk to steady myself against the iron railing.

Neil followed suit. "Kristen, I'm not dating or hanging out with anyone else."

"I don't understand. Then who is she?"

My hair whipped across my face. Goosebumps appeared on my arms and I rubbed them vigorously to warm myself up.

"Here, take my sweatshirt." He pulled off his hoodie and handed it over. It was way too big, but I put it on anyway and threw up the hood to help tame my hair.

"Thanks," I said, pulling the sleeves down over my hands.

"You're welcome." He helped me get the loose ends of my hair under the hood. "So you really don't know who I'm referring to? I've had a crush on her since middle school. I didn't have the nerve to talk to her until last year when we sat next to each other in history class. And she happens to be wearing my favorite Hurley sweatshirt."

Like a spaz, I quickly looked down to check the logo written across the sweatshirt. "You're talking about me?"

"Yes," he laughed.

My heart was racing a mile a minute.

"I don't understand."

He shrugged. "What's there to understand? It's just the way I feel. I don't think you can choose who you fall in love with. It just happens."

"But what about Avery?"

"I'm not in love with Avery."

"Okay, please stop saying the L word."

He rolled his eyes.

"Why wouldn't you talk to me in the car?"

"Because I knew I had to tell you how I felt, but I wasn't sure if it was reciprocated. I was scared to even bring it up."

"Oh."

"Well?"

"Well, what?" I asked, trying to avoid what was coming next.

"How do you feel about me?" he said, staring into my eyes. His baby blues were full of uncertainty, but they still smoldered in anticipation.

At that moment, it was almost impossible to breathe, let alone form a coherent response to his question. Despite the cooler temperature of our surroundings, a heat wave came over my body. I knew I should probably say something, but I was at a loss.

"Do you like me?"

I nodded.

"Do you just like me as a friend?"

I shook my head.

"So you like me as more than a friend?"

I nodded.

He flashed his perfect smile and took my hands. "Are you ever going to talk to me again?"

I thought for a second, then nodded, smiling.

"I guess that means that we're together? Or maybe we should make this more formal." He cleared his throat and ran his hand through his wild curls. "Kristen?"

"Yes?"

"I'm sorry if this might sound a bit cheesy, but would you be my girl-friend?"

I covered my mouth, hiding my glee. Then I shrugged. "Sure, why not."

"Good. You hungry?"

"Famished."

We went to a seafood restaurant on the pier for dinner, then headed home. I was ecstatic about what had transpired, and even though I knew what was awaiting me at home, I couldn't stop staring at Neil's hand, which was intertwined with mine as he steered with the other. He pulled up to the front of my building and parked. I quickly pulled off his sweat-shirt and grabbed my purse.

"Do you want me to come up with you?" he asked.

"No, it's best if I leave you out of this altogether if I ever want to see you again outside of school."

"All right. Call me later?"

"Um, I'm not sure if I'll have that privilege or not. Either way, though, I don't want to push my luck."

"Okay."

I jumped out the car and flew inside. Each floor I passed on the ele-vator brought me closer to my impending fate. Nerves got the best of me and I began concocting my web of lies. I couldn't tell her the whole truth because that would involve Neil...*Neil.* I thought about the feel of his hand in mine, and about what it would be like to run my fingers through his gorgeous curls. That beautiful boy was mine. I wonder how Avery would feel about that.

I reached my floor and slowly walked down the long corridor to prolong the inevitable. I unlocked the front door and walked in to see my mother sitting on the sofa in the living room, talking on the house phone.

"Okay, Mom, I got to go. She just walked in." She said her goodbyes and hung up. "Come in here, Kristen."

I walked into the living room and stood next to the couch.

"Have a seat."

I sat down slowly, not wanting to make any sudden moves. She was obviously past the yelling stage of her anger and had gone to another level, one which scared me even more.

"Do you know how worried I've been?"

Quick, is that a rhetorical question, or should I actually answer?

"Mrs. Wilson said you haven't been to school all week. I've been calling you all day to make sure you were okay. I get one text from you saying you're fine, but then you don't come home until hours later. You're ditching school and fighting. That's not like you, Kristen." She sniffed, wiping her nose with the back of her sleeve. "You've never done anything like this before. What is going on with you?"

Tears began to fall down her cheeks. I could tell she'd been crying all day. Puffiness and bloodshot eyes—dead giveaway.

"I don't know what to do anymore. We used to talk all the time. I thought we didn't keep secrets from one another. We're supposed to be a team, remember? I just don't know what I'm doing wrong with you. I don't know how to fix it. How do I fix this?" She grabbed a tissue and wiped her face, then closed her eyes to gather herself. "You'll be fine. You're just going through a thing right now, that's all. Yes, that's got to be it," she said, looking past me. "You'll be fine. Did you eat?"

"Uh, yeah," I said, bewildered by her drastic change in behavior.

"Good, I'm going to bed." A placid smile appeared on her face, replacing the weariness. She stood slowly, went into her room, and shut the door.

I sat there, unable to move. What just happened? Had she snapped now? Tears filled my eyes, dropping one by one on my shirt. I felt horrible about what my mother was going through, but she was right. There was nothing she could do or say to help. At this point, I wasn't sure if anyone could.

13

Big Changes

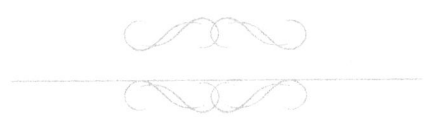

Over the weekend, I tried to avoid my mom as much as possible. She stayed in her room, but when she did come out for meals, we barely said two words. It was like she had turned into a catatonic zombie.

Monday morning was even more quiet. After my alarm woke me up, I got out of bed and peeked out my door, only to find the living room and kitchen empty. The blinds were closed and everything was dark. I walked over to my mother's door and listened; silence. I wondered if she was even awake yet. This was unlike her.

I knocked. "Mom?"

No answer. I cracked the door to see her still lying in her bed. "Mom?"

"Yeah?" Her voice was weak and muffled.

"Neil's going to take me to school today, for real this time."

"Fine," she said, uninterested.

I closed her door and texted Neil to pick me up, then got ready for school. When he arrived, I met him outside and slid into his car.

"Hi," he said quickly.

"Hey," I replied, fumbling with my seat belt.

"So?"

"She was mad, but it was a calm, scary mad. I think I would have preferred the yelling."

"She didn't yell at all?"

"No. It was so creepy. I think she may have snapped. She wasn't herself. You know how a sociopath can boil a live puppy and then host a dinner party like nothing happened? That's what it was like. And then for the rest of the weekend, she checked out or something. I don't even know if she's going to work today. She was still lying in bed when I left."

"That's crazy."

"I know."

Not that she needed to work. Our condo was paid for in full, along with her car. My father gave her child support and alimony each month, not to mention the division of assets. She probably never had to work another day in her life if she didn't want to, but she was always determined to make her own money. *"Get a good education so you never have to depend on a man,"* she'd say.

"So she didn't ground you or put you on punishment or anything?"

"No, but I won't be asking for anything anytime soon. I think things need to die down for a while, then I'm sure she'll be back to herself. I hope, anyway. Let's talk about something else, please."

"Okay. Well, we haven't spoken since Friday…."

"Yeah."

"So are you still…? I mean, do you still want to be…?"

I grabbed his free hand. "Yes. I haven't changed my mind. I'm just wondering how Avery will feel about it. I'm breaking girl code in a major way."

"How so?"

"Dating one of your best friend's exes is grounds for exile."

"Well, she's just going to have to deal with it."

"You really think it's going to be that easy? I wouldn't be surprised if she started a petition to have me stoned."

"All right, I think you're getting a little carried away. Just tell her that I have absolutely no interest and you can't help that I lo—that I'm into you and not her."

"Yeah, but my response to you should be that I don't care if you like me, you're Avery's ex."

"We don't have to tell anyone if you don't want to," he said, focusing on the road.

I could see where this thought pattern was going.

"I'm not ashamed to be with you. You know that, right?"

He pulled into the school parking lot and circled, looking for a spot.

"Sure."

"Neil, I mean it."

"Yeah, of course."

"That didn't sound very convincing."

He parked and turned off the engine.

"It's fine if you do. I know you don't gloat like Avery does, but you're just as popular as she is, if not more because everyone likes you. So I'm fine with whatever you want to do."

"That's absurd, Neil. I would never ask you to do something like that."

"I know you wouldn't want to ask, but—"

"But nothing. If any of that mattered to me, I would be with Tyler right now, not you. But I'm with you because you're the total opposite.

161

Plus, you're the only one who knows me—the real me—but somehow you think you're in love. I don't understand it, but I guess you do. All I ask is that you let me tell Avery before we go public. Okay?"

He smiled. "Of course, whatever you want."

The bell rang, and we headed off to class. I didn't get a chance to go to our table before first period, so I held off until later. When I walked into calculus, I scanned the room. Both Avery and Neil hadn't made it in yet. I took my seat and unpacked my textbook and notebook.

"You're a real piece of work, you know that?" Neil said to Avery, walking in ahead.

"I don't know what you're talking about," she said with a snide look on her face.

"I know it was you, Avery. Don't play dumb."

He made his way across the room to stand on the right side of my desk. Avery stood on my left. I looked back and forth, confused as to what was going on.

"Neil, I don't know who started that rumor about you, but it was bound to come out sooner or later. No pun intended," she said with a grin on her face.

"What's going on?" I asked.

"Tell her, Avery. Tell her the rumor you started."

She rolled her eyes and looked at me.

"Apparently, someone started a rumor that Neil bats for the other team." She shrugged. "I think it's awful, but it's nothing to be ashamed of, and it does make a lot of sense," she said, taking her seat.

The classroom was filled with students who were snickering among themselves. Neil was furious. I just hoped he wouldn't let Avery get under his skin to the point where he spilled our secret.

And that's when it happened.

Neil grabbed me and kissed me.

I almost forgot where I was, but as soon as I realized, he pulled away. I stood there, still in shock. I could hear the gasps throughout the room. I couldn't bring myself to look at Avery, so I just stood there, facing the front of the class. Ms. Marquardt finally arrived, and I gradually forced myself to sit down. I looked over at Avery. She wore a myriad of emotions, anger being the most prevalent.

"I cannot believe him!" Avery whispered. "He purposely did that in front of everyone to make himself look good. And I can't believe he kissed you. Of all people, he kisses my best friend. But if that's the way he wants to play it, that's fine with me."

"Avery," I whispered back.

"Yeah?"

"I need to talk to you about something at nutrition, 'kay?"

"Yeah, sure, whatever."

We caught Ms. Marquardt's attention, so we quickly began taking notes. The bell finally rang, and everyone dispersed. I grabbed my things and walked out. Neil followed closely behind.

"Are you mad at me," he asked.

I stopped and turned to face him. "What do you think?"

"I'm not really sure with all the scowling you're doing, but I'm guessing yes."

"Well, you'd be right. How could you do that after I asked you not to say anything about us to anyone, especially Avery?"

"Technically, I didn't say anything." He smiled.

"So you think this is funny? It's just all fun and games, right?"

"No, it's not." He held my arms and looked into my eyes. "I'm sorry, I shouldn't have done that. I was just so mad. She has no conscience. I wished I could have gotten a picture of her face, though," he laughed and then became serious. "Do you forgive me?"

"I don't know."

"Why not?"

163

"Because our first kiss should have been special and not done out of spite. Now I'll never get that back."

I broke free from his hands and walked up to my locker, opened it, and exchanged my books. Neil leaned up against the locker next to mine.

"What do I have to do to make that up to you?"

"You can't. It's gone forever."

"That's not at all dramatic." He paused. "I'm kind of curious, who is the better kisser, me or Tyler?"

"Can't say." I shrugged.

"Why not?"

"Because I don't really remember ever kissing Tyler, for all I know it was just an elaborate dream."

"What do you mean by that?"

"Ah, nothing. But from what I've heard about that night, it kind of seems as though Tyler's got you beat," I said with a mocking smile.

Neil scowled.

I rose to my tippy toes and leaned into him. "You smell good."

"It's soap. I'm sure Tyler smells better. I bet he wears expensive cologne or that toilet stuff."

"I can't believe you're jealous."

"I'm not jealous, just making an observation, that's all."

"Oh, okay," I said, not buying it. "Believe me, I've made my decision carefully. And a pro-con list never lies. It's a very objective way to make decisions."

"You did a pro-con list?"

"Yeah. And it was quite clear who I wanted to be with."

"Do you do those a lot?"

"Yeah, I love them. Or sometimes I'll do pie charts or…."

He was smiling at me in admiration.

"What?"

"You're such a weirdo. I love learning your little quirks."

Suddenly I didn't feel so ashamed.

"Well, if I really want to get crazy, I'll do some Excel spreadsheets. I like having inventory on all my makeup."

"You need to keep inventory on makeup? How much do you have?"

I looked away, but he caught my expression.

"Is it really that much?"

"I need help. It's a sickness," I said as I hid my face in his shirt.

We both laughed. He lifted my chin, gazed into my eyes, and for the first time, I truly felt loved—idiosyncrasies and all.

"So, are you going to kiss me or what?"

And he did. It felt like a swarm of butterflies. He began to fill the void my father left behind. I'd hoped that the more I filled the void with love, the less pain I'd feel.

Neil wrapped his arms around me, and for once, I was able to breathe a little easier. Maybe this was what I had been looking for all along.

"You got to be kidding me!" a voice came from behind. I broke free of Neil's embrace and spun around to see Tyler and his friends approaching us.

"Oh, hey, Tyler," I said, flustered.

"Are you seriously with him now? You chose him over me?"

"Tyler," I pleaded.

"I don't get it," he said, looking Neil up and down. "How can you choose him when I'm the one in love with you?"

"Tyler, you can't be in love with me, you don't even know me. Quick: What kind of lunch meat do I like in my sandwich?"

He shrugged. "I don't know, turkey?"

Neil scoffed under his breath.

"Do you know?" Tyler asked Neil, walking closer to us.

"It was a trick question. She doesn't like lunch meat sandwiches."

"It's such a waste, get a real meal already. It's fine for a snack or maybe for lunch, but for dinner? Who does that? A sandwich is not a real meal.

I guess a burger is filling, but that's different," I said, annoyed. "Anyway, you don't really love me, Tyler. It's just infatuation."

"But what about that night?" Tyler whispered, leaning into me.

"I was drunk. I don't remember any of it. I'm sorry."

Disappointed, he walked away, not saying another word. His friends followed. I wished there was something more encouraging to say, but I had nothing. Then I remembered I still needed to talk to Avery.

"Hey, girlie!" Carmen exclaimed when I reached their table. "Where have you been?"

"Oh, I've just been so sick."

"Kristen, tell them how Neil totally raped your face just to get back at me," Avery said, infuriated.

"Actually, I wanted to talk to you about something. Can we talk alone?"

"Okay."

She got up from the table and we walked far enough away so that the others wouldn't hear.

"I wasn't sick last week. I skipped school."

"What?! You skipped school and didn't include me? I totally would have ditched. We could've gone to the Beverly Center or The Grove. What'd you do all week?"

"Monday I left school and went to the park. Neil showed up and we hung out. The next day I didn't want to go to school, so I called Neil and we went to the beach. We've been hanging out a lot lately. He asked me to be his girlfriend."

"OMG! I cannot believe this! What a jerk!" she said, balling up her fists.

"Do you love him? Because if you love him, I'll tell him we can't be together."

Her face immediately softened. She looked away, seemingly torn.

"Do you care about him?"

166

Nothing.

"Do you even like him?" I asked.

She rolled her eyes.

"Do you know how many guys would kill to be with me? So what if Neil Schneider rejected me. It's not like his opinion matters."

"Then why were you trying to get back with him?" I asked, confused.

"I've seen the way he looks at you in class. He used to look at me the same way, you know." She paused and a deep pain was revealed in her eyes. "I just wanted him to look at me like that again. Rodney doesn't..." she scoffed and shrugged. "I kind of miss it, I guess." She quickly masked her vulnerability with a false confidence again. "Not that it matters, though."

"Are you mad at me?" I asked softly.

"For now. I'm not talking to you for the rest of the day."

"I'm sorry."

"Do you love him?" Avery asked.

"Yes," I said without hesitation. I hadn't realized it until now, but I was falling in love with Neil. Thank God I wouldn't have to give him up.

Suddenly the bell rang, and everyone made their way to class. Neil met me outside of our economics class. We walked in together, all eyes on us. Word must have spread during nutrition. It was uncanny how fast news got around a high school.

We took our seats just in time for the second bell.

"So, what did she say?"

"She's not talking to me for the rest of the day, but she'll be fine."

"It was that easy? See, everything worked out."

Mr. Coletti called the class to order, so we turned our attention to his lecture. But I couldn't pay attention; my mind began to wander like always. I thought about what Avery had said, about the way Neil looked at me. Why did I never notice before? I glanced over at him. He was taking notes, tapping his pen on the desk rhythmically. To my horror, I soon realized I wasn't the only one admiring him. A couple of girls across the room were giggling and whispering. This went on for most of the period. Chemistry was no different—just different girls. Neil sat unusually close while reading the worksheet Mrs. Marshall gave each lab partner.

"What's wrong?" he asked, still focused on the paper.

"Nothing."

"You're lying," he said, finally making eye contact. "You forget, I know you pretty well, and I know that something is bothering you. I let it go last period, but now you have to tell me."

I was about to make a smart comment when Veronica Green walked up to our lab table.

"Hey, Kristen. Hi, Neil," she cooed.

I rolled my eyes.

"Hi," Neil answered, seemingly unaware of his new admirer. I watched him out of the corner of my eye, then glanced back at Veronica.

"I'm Veronica Green. I recently started dating Kevin," she said to Neil. "You know Kevin, Kristen. He's on the basketball team with Rodney." She handed Neil a bright fuchsia invitation. I just stared, unresponsive. "Anyway, I'm having a party at my house this Friday night. It's invitation only, so you need to have that to get in. Do you think you two will come as a couple?"

"I don't know if we'll be able to make it. This is such short notice," I said sharply.

"Oh, well, it's four days away. I thought that would be enough time to let everyone know—"

"Like I said, I'm not sure if we'll be able to make it, but thanks." I grabbed the chemistry worksheet and pretended to read it.

"Okay, well I hope you guys can come. It's going to be lit." Veronica walked back to her table.

"What was that about?" Neil asked.

"What was what about?"

"You were pretty short with her. Since when do we have plans for Friday?"

"I just think it's hypocritical of them to invite you to their parties and pretend like they never used to ignore you. Now they gawk at you like you're Tyler Reed. It's disgusting."

He smiled. "Who was looking at me?"

I rolled my eyes and turned back to the worksheet.

"I only noticed one green-eyed beauty staring at me." He leaned in and gave me a kiss on the cheek. "I think it's cute that you're jealous," he whispered in my ear.

"I'm not jealous, it's just annoying."

He leaned back to study my face. "If you don't want to go, we can do something else Friday night."

"Did you want to go?" I asked, looking up at him.

"It would be nice to go at least once, you know, without being thrown out for crashing. But if you really don't want to go…."

I sighed. "No, it's fine, we can go. Seeing how I'm not jealous and all."

"Right."

And that was that.

* * *

The next few days became routine. Neil and I were almost inseparable, my mother was going to work again, but she still didn't seem like herself. She barely spoke, and I was unsure of how to fix things, so I didn't speak much either. I figured I'd stay out of her way as much as possible.

"Tomorrow night we're going out to dinner. I need you ready to go at seven. Maybe we can go to Chin Chin or The Ivy."

My eyes grew wide as I looked up from my dinner plate. It was the most she'd said to me all week.

"You want to go out to a restaurant on Sunset Blvd on a Friday night?"

"Yeah. I think it will be fun. It's been a while since the last time we hung out."

"I can't. I have plans with Neil tomorrow night."

"You've been spending a lot of time with Neil lately."

"Um, yeah."

"How come? Are you two dating or something?" she asked.

"Yeah."

"How long has this been going on?"

"Tomorrow will be a week."

"Is this something casual, or is it serious?"

"It's getting serious."

I wondered where all of this was coming from. Maybe she was finally getting back to her old self.

"Hon, I don't think right now is such a good time for you to get serious about one boy."

"I thought you liked Neil?"

"I do. I just think you should be focusing on getting better before you get into a serious relationship."

"Well, we've already made plans."

"You can do that after dinner. You'll have more than enough time to do whatever once we're done."

"Fine," I said, stabbing one of my meatballs.

We continued our dinner in silence.

The next day, I dreaded every moment leading up to dinner. Maybe Mom was trying to resolve what had been messed up the past week. Oddly enough, this is what she did whenever she wanted to talk. For years she would take me out to restaurants for mother/daughter talks.

The first few minutes of lunch, I had a meeting for dance team, so as soon as we were done, I went looking for Neil. I knew he would be with his friends. I felt kind of bad because I had been monopolizing most of his time. I found them in the cafeteria. As I approached their table, they abruptly stopped talking and their eyes widened.

"Hi," I said cautiously.

"Oh, hey. You're already done?" Neil said, getting up from his seat. He gave me a quick kiss.

"It was a quick meeting."

Someone cleared their throat loudly.

"Oh." Neil gave the guy a look of disapproval. "Kristen, these are my friends. This is Bryce, Jeff, and Mike."

The tall one that cleared his throat was Jeff. He had short, spiky brown hair with braces. Mike was shorter and a lot rounder with wavy blond hair—almost like a modern-day mullet. Bryce was brown skinned with dark hair.

"Nice to meet you," I said. "I'm sorry I've been monopolizing all of Neil's time."

"Don't worry about it," Bryce said. "So, you guys are really a couple?"

I looked at Neil with a smile, then back at Bryce.

"We didn't believe him at first. I mean, we knew you two were friends, but this is crazy." They began discussing the subject among themselves.

I turned to face Neil. "If you want to hang out with them for lunch, we can stay here."

"I don't think that's such a good idea."

"Well, I'm feeling kind of bad about keeping you away from your friends as much as I have."

"I understand that, but I don't mind hanging out with you and your friends. That doesn't include Avery."

"See, I know the Avery situation can't be easy for you. Am I right?"

"Well of course not."

"So either we can both hang out with your friends, or I can hang out with my friends and you hang out with yours."

"I don't like the second option, but a break from Avery would be nice."

"Then it's settled. We'll hang out with your friends."

"Really? Are you sure? You're willing to hang out with this?"

Neil and I looked at Mike, who was picking something white and flaky from his elbow. Mike glanced up at us. I must've had a look of disgust on my face.

"Oh, don't worry, I think it's just from when I got my elbow stuck in Jeff's honey bun." He peeled a piece off his elbow and stuck it in his mouth. "Yeah, it's just icing."

I turned back to Neil. "I'll see you later then?"

"Okay," he smiled. "Hey, you okay?"

"Yeah."

"Are you sure? You're not still worrying about tonight, are you?"

"No."

"Are you lying?"

"Maybe."

He walked out of the cafeteria with me.

"Don't be, it'll be fine. Do you want me to come with you?"

"Yes. But I think it will be best if it's just my mom and me."

"Where are you guys going, anyway?"

"The Stinking Rose—it's her fave. I figured I'd let her choose. Maybe it will cheer her up a little."

He hugged me and everything immediately felt right. In Neil's arms, I didn't have a care in the world. He soothed all the pain with one touch. I wished I could stay here for eternity and hold on to this feeling, but we couldn't be together all the time, and I didn't want him growing tired of me.

"You know, I don't have to hang out with my friends for lunch. We could just hang out by ourselves," Neil suggested.

"No, spend time with your friends. Have fun. I'm fine."

"Are you sure?"

"Yes."

"All right, I'll see you later." He kissed me goodbye.

The rest of the day flew by. I was now sitting in the passenger seat of my mother's car as we pulled up to the restaurant. The valet got both of our doors, and we stepped out of the vehicle. It was Friday night, so of course the restaurant was packed.

"Mom?"

She was headed for the door, but she stopped and turned to face me.

"I'm sorry for.... Well, for everything. I never meant to hurt you. Do you hate me now?"

"No, I don't hate you. I love you, hon. I'm just trying to figure things out, that's all. I could never hate you. Okay?"

I nodded and she gave me a hug.

"I know things have been weird between us lately, and I'm sick of it. We've both been going through a rough patch. I just want to fix things, especially between the two of us."

"Me too."

Out of my peripheral, I could see a car pull up to the valet—a white-on-white BMW 760Li. I broke free from my mother's embrace. The stranger got out of the vehicle, adjusting his suit jacket. With ease, he fastened the two buttons. A crisp, white collared dress shirt and a crimson tie finished the ensemble. It was no surprise because he had always preferred Brooks Brothers. He smiled at both of us as he approached. He wasn't exactly a stranger, but he might as well have been. It's been years since the last time I saw him. He gave my mother a hug and turned to me.

"Hello, Kristen." His familiar green eyes probed me.

"Hi, Daddy."

He gave me a shallow hug, not wanting to wrinkle his suit.

"It's been a while. You both look well. Sorry I'm late. I came straight from work, but there was traffic."

"No, you're actually right on time. We just got here, too," my mom replied.

"Good. Shall we?" He gestured toward the door.

We walked in and were seated immediately, despite what looked like at least an hour wait time. My father had no patience for such a thing. Rita, his secretary, must've called ahead on his behalf, ensuring we'd have a table waiting.

"So how have you been, Anna?" my dad asked my mom.

"I've been good."

"You look beautiful as always."

"Thank you, and you?"

"I'm good," he said while checking his BlackBerry.

"And the family?"

"They're good." He slid his phone back in the inner pocket and adjusted his tie. "Juliana is decorating yet another room in the house. She's like you in that regard. You know my motto, if it's not broke…. Anyway, she occupies her time well. The girls are good. Michelle just came in first place for her science fair."

"Wow, and you were actually present for that? Old age really seems to agree with you," my mom laughed.

"Yes, well I would have never heard the end of it from her mother if I hadn't."

Awkward silence.

One of the valets approached our table, giving my father a ticket. The waitress arrived shortly after.

"I'll have the Silence of the Lamb Shank with a Chianti glaze and fava beans," I said, closing my menu and handing it to the waitress. She jotted down my order down and glanced at my mother.

"I'll have one of your sizzling iron skillet combos. The mussels, shrimp, and crab, please."

Dad was still mulling over the menu.

"Do you want me to come back?" the waitress asked.

"No, that won't be necessary. I'll have the garlic-roasted prime rib, large."

The waitress took the menus and left. After an uncomfortable period of more small talk, our food finally arrived.

"So I called this family meeting together because there are some big changes that I wanted to announce. I've already spoken to your father about this, so I'm just going to come out and say it. I've decided that it would be best for us to move in with my mother—in Georgia."

It took me a while to process what she said.

"What?" I said, confused.

"Your mother thinks it would be a better environment for you to be in right now, what with everything that's been going on with you."

Everything that's been going on with me? How could he possibly know everything that has been going on with me? How dare he come here and try to be a parent after everything he had missed. But I could never express my true feelings. I felt the tears coming, but I fought them back. She really wanted us to move. I couldn't believe it. That was the last thing I wanted. I couldn't bear the thought of being away from Neil.

"No. I don't want to move," I protested. "Can't we stay here? I promise I'll be good."

"I'm sorry, sweetie. The decision has been made. We're leaving on the thirty-first," my mom said.

That was only a couple weeks away. Why would she do this to me? I would expect something like this from him, but not from my mother. It suddenly felt like the walls were closing in.

"I have to get out of here." I got up and walked out to the front of the restaurant. I quickly wiped the tears cascading down my cheeks. My mother came after me.

"Hon, are you okay?"

"No, I'm not okay, Mom. I don't want to leave. I've lived here my whole life. All my friends are here…Neil's here."

"I know, but I don't know what else to do. It won't be so bad, you'll see." She hugged me.

My father joined us.

I broke free from my mother, wiping all traces of tears.

"Is everything okay?" he handed the valet two tickets.

"It will be," my mother answered.

"Good. I've got to get going. I paid the bill and had the waitress box up the leftovers." He reached inside his jacket, pulled out an envelope, and handed it over. "It's a going away gift to make things a little easier."

I opened the envelope to see two car keys and a car title in my name.

"You got me a car?" I asked skeptically.

"I figured you'd need one to get around out there," he said, his face devoid of all emotion.

"Thanks…."

His car pulled up, and right behind his was a metallic grey Porsche Cayenne Turbo.

"I hope it suits you."

"That's the car you got me? You got me a Cayenne?"

"Do you like it?"

"It's great," I said indifferently.

"Good."

"Dad, couldn't I stay with you? I promise I won't be any trouble. You won't even know I'm there."

"Unfortunately, your mother feels strongly that this is what's best for you. If you came to live with me, it just wouldn't work." He hugged us both and we said our goodbyes.

My mom walked alongside the SUV and examined it. "Wow, you made out really well. Of course, Parenting 101: your child acts up so you buy them a $100,000 car," she said under her breath as she peeked inside. "I suppose you still have plans with Neil?"

"Um, yeah."

"I guess I'll see you later."

"Mom, are we really moving?" I asked somberly.

"I think it's for the best, hon."

I got my bag out of my mother's car and left for Neil's.

14

Not in the Light

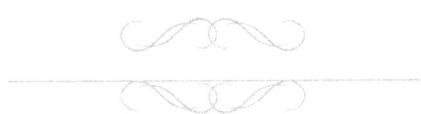

"Hi," he smiled and glanced over my shoulder. "Whose car is that?"

"It's mine," I said, walking inside.

He shut the door behind me. "When did you get a car?"

"About forty minutes ago. My dad made a trip down and had dinner with us. Didn't think I'd get a car out of the deal."

"He just shows up and gives you a car? Not just any car, a Porsche?"

"Pretty much. But it's not like he did it for me. These elaborate gifts are for show. He couldn't care less if I liked it. He does it because it makes him look good."

"What was his reasoning for giving it to you?"

"Can we talk about something else? I'm kind of over it right now."

"Yeah, sure. Are you ready to go?"

"No, I have to change first. Is your mom here?"

"She's working late at the hospital."

"Oh," I said, heading for the bathroom.

I quickly undressed and slipped on a yellow, short cap sleeve, French connection dress, complete with metallic Diane von Furstenberg wood wedges. I combed through my hair and touched up my makeup. Once I was done, I rejoined Neil in the living room.

"Wow. You look…."

"Thanks. You're not too shabby yourself."

He was wearing jeans and a crisp, white, button-down shirt with the sleeves rolled up his forearms. "Well you know I try," he smiled.

Neil was more excited about my car than I was, so I let him drive it to Veronica's. We pulled up right in front, and as soon as I stepped out, I could hear Lady Gaga blaring from the speakers. Neil grabbed my hand and we sauntered up the walkway. I could feel my uneasiness from dinner begin to subside. I knew I would have to tell Neil about my leaving, but that would only make it real. I decided tonight wasn't the night.

"You guys made it!" Veronica yelled as we walked in. "Make yourselves at home. There are drinks in the kitchen." Then she disappeared.

Neil wouldn't stop staring.

"What?"

"Have I told you how beautiful you look tonight?"

"Not since we left the car. Come on." I grabbed his hand and weaved through the crowd, eager to find my friends. Avery and a group of people were standing back by the patio doors.

"Hey! You're here!" She gave me a sloppy hug, spilling her drink on my shoes.

Neil grabbed a napkin from a nearby table and bent down to wipe it up.

"Sorry, Kristen," she said. "I'll give you the money for messing up your shoes. It's $300, right? I just have to find my purse."

"Are you drunk already?" I asked, grabbing her arm before she could walk away.

"No." She began laughing hysterically.

"Oh, okay." My tone was thick with sarcasm. "Did you drive here?"

"No, Charlotte brought us. But seriously, I'm not drunk." She took a sip of her drink and finally noticed Neil. "Ugh. I suppose you were invited this time. You're such a leech. Just because Kristen's popular and you're together now, suddenly you're popular, too? So stupid."

"Avery, be nice. You don't have to be best friends, but you have to be civil."

"Whatever," she said, rolling her eyes. "OMG! This is my song!" She grabbed some random guy and ran off.

"Sorry," I said to Neil.

"Don't worry about it. She hated me long before all this," he said, glancing down at my shoes. "Did you really pay $300 for those?"

"You're going to ask me that when we drove here in a Porsche?"

"Valid point." He scanned the room. "So this is what I've been missing."

The room was packed with teenagers drinking, laughing, dancing, and some cuddled up in dark corners.

"Do you want something to drink?" I asked.

"No. You?"

"Pass."

"Do you want to go outside?"

"Sure."

He led the way through the French doors and headed toward the pool. He sat down on one of the cabanas and motioned for me to join on his lap. I obliged. He slipped his arms around my waist and squeezed me tightly. I was going to miss this, but most of all, I would miss him. Neil was the only one I could talk freely to.

"What's wrong?" Neil asked.

"Everything. I'm moving to Georgia. That's why my mom wanted to have dinner tonight. She brought my dad as reinforcement. And that's why I got the Porsche. It's my consolation prize."

"What? Are you serious?"

"Yeah. We're leaving on the thirty-first."

"Of this month?"

"Yeah."

"That's only two weeks away."

"Yeah."

We were both quiet for a while. I tried to gauge his reaction. How long would it take for him to move on? Would I be able to move on? I shuddered at the thought.

"Are you cold?"

"A little."

"Do you want to go? We can go back to my place and watch a movie,"

"You've been dying to come to one of these parties, and now you want to leave? We just got here. Are you sure?"

He kissed me on my forehead. "I'm certain. These parties are over-rated."

"Okay."

We were both silent on the drive back. Once we got to his house, we sat on the living room couch—him on one end, me on the other. It was already starting. The distance between us would soon be permanent, and I couldn't bear it.

"What do you want to watch?" he asked.

"I don't care. Whatever's on." I glanced over at him. "Why are you sitting all the way over there?"

He shrugged his shoulders. "No reason."

"Meet me halfway?"

We both moved to the middle.

"There's nothing on," he said.

"Are you mad? It feels like you're mad at me."

"No. I'm not mad at you, I'm just frustrated with the situation."

I reached over and hugged him, pressing my cheek to his chest.

"Why is this happening? I don't want to lose you," he said, resting his chin on my head.

"We should run away together. We can move to Malibu and get jobs."

"And go to the beach every day after work," he added.

"Yeah, or maybe even work on the beach." I sat up and made eye contact. "Is your mom asleep? Is the TV too loud?"

"No, she's not here. She's been working double shifts."

"Oh. Is it okay if I stay here tonight?"

"What are you going to tell your mom?"

"I'm not sure. I can tell her that Avery got drunk and needs a ride home. But then she would know I went to another party. Maybe I'll tell her we went on a double date and I'm going to stay over at Avery's. What do you think?"

Neil shrugged.

"Great, thanks for the help."

I reached down and pulled my phone out of my purse. It was ten o'clock. I sent my mother a text asking if I could stay over Neil's—progress. She asked me if it was okay with his mother and I told her yes. Okay, *slight* progress. I excused myself to the bathroom and pulled my hair up in a pony. Neil let me borrow one of his T-shirts and some pajama pants. Once I was done changing, I rejoined him in the living room. He had changed into sweatpants and an old T-shirt and was lounging on the sofa, watching a movie. He glanced over and smiled.

"What?" I asked, looking down.

"Nothing." He beckoned me over.

I sat down and his arm slid around my waist.

"I'm going to miss you. I even asked my dad if I could stay with him. At least that way we wouldn't be too far away from each other. Santa Barbara's only an hour away. We could make time to see each other on the weekends. But of course, my dad rejected that idea. I don't even know why I asked. I guess I keep thinking he's going to realize what he's done and change—be the father I…. It's stupid," I said, shaking my head.

"No, it's not. It's perfectly natural to feel that way. I never even met my dad. He left when my mom was still pregnant with me. He didn't want to stick around to see what kind of person I would turn out to be. Believe me, I get it."

"Do you ever think about him? Or wonder what he looks like?"

"Sometimes. Sometimes, I wonder if he's a tech geek too, or if we like the same music. But I guess it doesn't really matter."

"Do you ever think about finding him?"

"No. If he really wanted to, he could find me."

I could see the pain he was trying to disguise. He did understand what I was going through.

"Well, it's his loss," I said as I gave him a kiss on his chin.

"Kristen, I think we can make this work. We can still be together, but just long distance."

"I don't know. It just feels like the odds are against us. You're going to USC out here next year and I don't know what I'm doing. Not that I was so sure before."

It was getting late, so we decided to go to bed. I crawled in Neil's bed, barely grazing the pillow that was on my side, then screamed and chucked it into the closet.

Neil stood in the doorway, staring.

"Was there a spider on it or something?" He walked over and inspected the pillow.

"What kind of pillow is that?"

"I don't know."

"It has feathers in it."

He squeezed. "Yeah, I guess it does."

"I can't sleep with that."

"Why not?"

"Well, I'm, um…kind of afraid of feathers."

Neil raised an eyebrow.

"I just don't like them, okay."

"My friend's mom is araguphobic, I think."

"What, she's afraid of meat sauce?"

"No. But that sounds absurd?"

"Very funny."

"She's afraid to go outside."

"I think you mean agoraphobia."

"Yeah, that's it. How can you be afraid of feathers?"

"Well, when you say it like that it sounds silly."

"It sounds silly because it is silly. Kristen, feathers can't attack you."

"See that's where you're wrong. They appear all innocent, so then you'll say, 'Oh, it's just a harmless feather,' and that's when it attacks…."

Neil dropped the pillow and crawled into bed next to me, his face full of amusement.

"Do you still love me, even though I'm crazy?"

"Yes, oddly enough, I do." He gave me a quick kiss and turned off the lamp.

I lied on his chest and scanned the room. It was clean for the most part—clean for a teenage boy's room, just one pile of clothes in the corner. He had a small desk that housed a computer and two laptops. Wires were everywhere. Piles and piles of CDs towered on every unused spot that was left on the desk, like a miniature city. Suddenly, I thought I saw movement in the shadows. My body stiffened and I shut my eyes.

"Are you okay?" Neil asked.

"Ah, yeah, I'm good. Neil?"

"Yeah?"

"I know I'm about to sound totally lame but...never mind."

"What? What were you going to say?"

"Never mind."

"Will you please tell me what you were going to say?"

"I don't think I can. It's way too embarrassing."

"It can't be as bad as being afraid of feathers."

"Clearly, you're not going to be serious about this."

"I'm sorry. Just tell me. I promise I won't laugh. And I won't make any more jokes."

"I don't know."

"C'mon you can tell me anything."

"I guess that's true."

"I want you to be able to tell me anything."

It was perfectly silent for a moment.

"Well?" he probed.

"I'm working up to it, okay?"

"All right, sorry."

"Neil?"

"Yes?"

"You don't happen to have a night light, do you?"

"A night light? Ah, no."

"Well, maybe you can turn the light on in the hallway and crack the door? Or maybe the closet?"

He sat up and turned the lamp back on.

"I.... I sleep with a night light," I said reluctantly. "I know I'm a total dork, but it helps. I can only see them when it's dark."

"Oh." By the look on his face, I was certain he knew exactly what I meant by them. "How long have you been using a night light?"

"A couple weeks now, and it really does work. I'm sure it's nothing, but the shadows are messing with my mind."

"Did you see something?"

"I'm not sure. I thought I saw something move in the corner. I'm sorry."

He glanced over in the direction I pointed and then gave me a swift kiss on my forehead.

"You have nothing to be sorry for."

He got up, turned the light on in his closet, and cracked the door. Then he crawled back in bed and turned off the lamp.

"Thank you. The light isn't going to bother you, is it?"

"I'll be fine."

"You think I'm a weirdo."

"I love you because you're a weirdo," he smiled. He kissed the crown of my head.

"Thanks. I love you more."

"That's impossible."

I wanted to reply, but I was already drifting off.

The next thing I knew, the sun was peeking through the curtains. I rolled over. Neil was nowhere to be found. The smell of something burning wafted up my nostrils. I got out of bed and tripped over a pile of his CDs. I glanced at the chick flick movie cover art, and then quickly put them back. While making my way around his bed, I got a side view of my appearance in his dresser mirror. *Ugh!* My hair was a wild mess. I slipped into the bathroom and raked my fingers through it. Didn't help much. I found some mouthwash and helped myself. That's when I heard voices coming from the living room.

Time to investigate.

"Hey, I hope you don't mind I used some of your mouthwash," I said as I walked into the living room. Neil was standing in the middle of the doorway with one hand on each side of the frame as if to block something or someone.

Neil's friends froze when they saw me. Neil turned to see what they were gawking at.

"Hi," I waved, unsure of what should be said in these types of situations. I folded my arms in front of my chest protectively. Neil wasn't wearing a shirt, making this scene look a thousand times worse.

"Hey, Kristen," they both said in unison.

"What's going on, guys?" Mike asked with a grin.

"Now we know why you've been so evasive. Are you going let us in, or what?" Jeff chimed, glancing back and forth between Neil and me.

"No," Neil insisted.

"But we were supposed to hang out today, remember? I know you're Mr. Popular and all, but you said you'd tell us all about the party," Jeff said.

"Did you take pictures?" Mike asked.

"Um, no," Neil said sharply.

"Not cool, man," Mike replied.

"I brought Wizards and Dragons. We were going to watch it, remember?" Jeff reminded.

"Look, guys, we'll have to do it another time. I'll call you." Neil slammed the door.

"Not cool, man!" Mike screeched.

Neil turned to face me. "Sorry about that."

"Wizards and Dragons? That's a movie, right?"

He nodded.

"You don't actually believe in that stuff—witches and warlocks casting spells on people," I said, giggling.

"It's a solid trilogy. The cinematography is incredible and special effects are insane," he said, shoving his hands in his pockets.

"Hey, no judgment here."

He reached out and hugged me.

"Well, maybe a little bit," I laughed. "I can't imagine what they must've thought."

"I'll tell them nothing happened later."

"You not wearing a shirt couldn't have helped matters much."

"True."

"So where is your shirt?"

"Oh. It caught on fire."

"What?!"

"I was too close to one of the gas burners. Tried to make you breakfast."

"Really?" I said with a grin. I made my way into the kitchen, which was a mess.

He followed. "You know, you're kind of violent when you sleep."

"What do you mean?"

"You were tossing and turning, and you hit me a few times."

"Oh," I giggled. "I'm sorry, I had no idea."

"What were you dreaming about?"

"It's kind of a recurring dream. I told you about it—the one with that little girl who pushes me into a deep hole. I hadn't had it for a while, but I had it again last night. I was trying to fight back, but she was too strong. Anyway, what did you make for breakfast?"

"Toast, eggs, bacon."

I peeked over at the stove. The bacon in the frying pan was burnt and hardly recognizable. The toast wasn't much better. I held up a slice up, examining it. "How did you burn toast?"

"I tried to speed up the process by putting the bread in the toaster oven, but its heat rivals the sun. I wasn't aware of that."

"Well, at least the eggs look edible." I grabbed a clean fork and tried some. After a few chews, I spat it out into a paper napkin and threw it in the trash.

"It wasn't good?"

"Let's just say scrambled eggs shouldn't be crunchy. But it's the thought that counts," I said, smiling. He looked so defeated, so I gave him a hug and a kiss on the cheek. "Thank you. You got any cereal?"

"Yeah."

I sat down at the kitchen table, watching his biceps flex as he grabbed a couple boxes from the top of the refrigerator.

"We have Frosted Flakes and Froot Loops."

"Froot Loops, please. So, what's with all the chick flick movies?"

"It's kind of a side job. I burn movies and sell them."

"Oh."

He grabbed the milk, two bowls, and two spoons. "I don't make much, but it's better than nothing. Voilà, breakfast is served."

"Thanks. Now, let's talk about your workouts," I said, fighting back my smile.

15

Goodbye

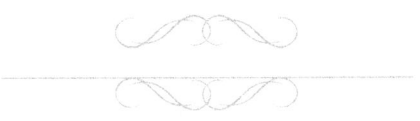

In the days that followed, Neil and I were inseparable. I wondered if he was getting tired of me, but his actions proved otherwise. What was I going to do? Soon I would be thousands of miles away. He promised we would remain together and make it work somehow. It would involve tons of phone calls, texts messages, and Skype sessions, which helped put me at ease, but I wondered if things would change once I left. I was almost certain that Katie Miller was waiting for the opportunity to pounce. All the more reason to keep a close eye out.

"So, this is the last weekend before you leave," Neil said, lingering in the hall after class.

"Yeah, don't remind me."

"We should do something big," Avery added. "We should spend the weekend at my dad's beach house in Malibu. What do you think?" She glared at Neil. "I guess you can come, too."

"I'll think about," I replied.

"Okay, well, let me know soon." Avery turned and left.

Neil and I walked to my locker.

"If you're not comfortable with that, we can think of something else," I suggested.

"No, it's not that. I just wanted you all to myself." He wrapped his arms around me and kissed me as if it were our last. He had been doing that a lot lately. I pulled away, slightly out of breath.

"Okay, what's up?"

"What?"

"You've been kissing me like you're fresh out of prison."

He laughed.

"Sorry. I just know our time together is limited, so I want to make sure every moment I'm with you, I treat it like it's our last. Must make sure I leave a lasting impression. I don't want you to forget about me."

"That would be impossible. So, what do you want to do this weekend?"

"I guess we can do the Avery thing."

"And you won't be uncomfortable?"

"Don't worry about me; I'll be fine."

* * *

That weekend, we all drove up to Avery's beach house. It wasn't a large gathering, just some close friends. Neil and I drove together and arrived around eight o'clock. He grabbed our bags and we walked up the cobblestone driveway. Avery buzzed us in. We followed the flagstone tiles of the courtyard to large, iron doors. The house seemed a bit sterile from all the white walls but was decorated in warm nudes with minimal accents.

Avery came around a sharp corner wearing a Juicy sweat suit, margarita glass in hand. The irony.

"Hola! Welcome to your going away weekend extravaganza. You want a drink? I can have Roberto make you one."

"Who is Roberto?" I asked.

She glanced over her shoulder, then leaned in, whispering, "He's my neighbor. He's going to hang out with us this weekend."

"Where's Rodney?"

"Oh, he and his friends are going to try out their new fake ID's at some strip club in Inglewood tonight, but I'm not sure what he's doing the rest of the weekend," she said, rolling her eyes. She slipped her arm around my shoulders and led me to the kitchen. "Roberto, this is my best friend, Kristen, and her lame-o boyfriend. She's the one who's going away."

"Nice to meet you guys."

We both shook hands.

"Babe, I have to get some more tequila from my house. I'll be right back." And with that, he walked out the back door.

"How old is he?" I asked.

"Twenty-one."

I gawk at her in disbelief.

"What? I'm eighteen, so it's perfectly legal."

"Does he know you're still in high school?"

"That is a minor technicality. He assumed I was a freshman at Pepperdine, so I went with it."

"Unbelievable. Where's everyone else?"

"They'll be here tomorrow. I figured you guys would want some alone time," she said, rolling her eyes.

"Thanks, Avery."

She showed us to one of the master suits where we'd be staying. The room had vaulted French oak ceilings and sick views of the Pacific Ocean. A queen-sized bed graced the center, along with two mahogany side tables, and a seating area beneath the bay windows. Mounted above the fireplace was a flat screen TV.

Avery left us to get settled in.

I started unpacking when I felt Neil's arms envelop me from behind. I craned my neck and quickly kissed the underside of his chin.

"What am I going to do without you?" he asked.

"I was thinking the same thing."

He turned me around to face him. "Promise me you won't forget me. Maybe even keep a place for me in your future."

"You have to do the same." I sighed. "But I know it's only a matter of time."

"For what?"

"Before you start to notice all the girls who have already noticed you. They're such vultures, just waiting for me to make my exit."

"It doesn't matter. I only want to be with you. I always have, and now that I know that it can be a reality, I have no intention of losing this."

I wished that could be true, but the fact was, I really didn't know where our relationship would go from here, or if I would ever see him again once I was gone. No matter the outcome, I decided that I, too, would just take it one day at a time. I got one solid kiss in, then he gently pulled away.

"Geesh, prison break," Neil said, laughing. "What's gotten into you?"

"I guess I want to live each moment with you to the fullest," I smiled.

He brushed his hand against my cheek and kissed me softly. I kissed him back with everything I had, then he stopped and took two steps back, looking a bit concerned.

"Is everything okay?" I asked.

"I can't believe I'm about to say this, but I think we should go back out there with Avery and What's His Face," he said.

"Okay," I said softly.

I couldn't hide the disappointment. What was he thinking? And what brought on this sudden urge to hang out with Avery and her new friends? I decided not to verbalize any of this. No point in killing the vibe. At this point, I probably would have done whatever he asked. I was so in love; Taylor Swift could write a song about it. But seriously, how could I possibly be away from him? How would I manage not seeing him anymore, not holding him anymore, not being able to get lost in his eyes anymore? *Must stop thinking about these things and focus on what's going on right now.*

We rejoined the party in the living room. Avery and Roberto sat on one of the full-sized couches, conversing quietly. We occupied the other. Bad Teacher was playing on the screen, but it didn't seem to be holding anyone's attention. I looked away from the film. Neil was staring at me.

"What?" I asked softly.

"Nothing," he shook his head. "You're just so beautiful."

Oh, God. I wished he would cut it out. He was only making it that much harder to leave.

"You don't have anything to worry about, I'm totally hooked," he whispered in my ear.

I closed my eyes, basking in every syllable. I felt like butter, and he was the flame. A heat wave came over my body, and I could feel a weird tingling sensation in the pit of my stomach. My hands were suddenly clammy. I rubbed them on my jeans and tried to focus on the movie, but my eyes wandered over to Neil's hand, which just so happened to be gently caressing my right arm. I began to fidget in my seat. What was wrong with me? Why was I acting this way?

I'm not sure when, but the mood shifted. I glanced at him periodically out the corner of my eye. He was watching the movie. Now I understood why he was so adamant about joining Avery and Roberto. But what did all this mean? I had never even thought about anything like *this* before, so I was unsure how to proceed. I decided to focus on the movie, which helped lessen my desires.

Later that night, I took my sweet time getting ready for bed. My shower was twice as long, and afterward, I must have combed through my wet hair forty times until I finally just let it be. The simple white tank I packed suddenly felt more risqué, even though it was paired with stripped, pink pajama bottoms. I didn't want to send the wrong message. I stood there—nerves and all—desperately trying to compose myself. When I entered the bedroom, Neil was already in bed. I took a deep breath, unsure of what to expect.

"Did you remember to bring your nightlight, or are we going to have to crack the bathroom door?" he asked, oblivious to what I was thinking.

"What? Oh, um, right."

I turned the light back on in the bathroom and cracked the door. My feet were rooted in place.

"Are you okay?" he asked.

"I'm great."

"Oh, okay. You don't have to worry, these aren't feather pillows. I already tested them," he smirked.

"I don't think we should have sex," I blurted.

Confusion washed over his features. "Okay…."

Now I was confused.

"Okay?"

"Yeah."

"You don't want to?" I asked, inching closer to the bed.

"Well, I'd be lying if I said no, but what I mean is, not yet. Did I make you feel like we had to?"

"No. I just, well, I was feeling like…. I wasn't sure if it was implied or not. It never even came to mind until tonight," I said, sitting on the far edge of the bed.

"Really?"

"Yeah. Do you ever think about it?"

"Yes. But I think it's different because, well, I'm a guy, and I'm not a virgin."

"Oh. Neil?"

"Yeah."

"Earlier when we were in here, why did you want to leave and hang out with Avery and Roberto?"

"Well, I wasn't expecting you to kiss me like that. I wasn't sure if I would be able to control myself. Once you get going, it's kind of hard to stop, from what I've experienced, anyway. And I wanted to make sure that your first time would be special."

I crawled across the bed and sat next to him. "Thanks. I never really thought about it before, but I think I might want to wait until I get married before, you know."

He kissed my forehead.

"Whatever you want to do, I'm perfectly fine with."

"Good." I got up and turned off the light, then snuggled underneath the covers and laid my head on his chest. "I love you."

"I love you more," he replied, kissing the top of my head.

The next day, everyone else arrived around noon. We all changed into our swimsuits and hit up the beach. Neil and I secured a spot on the private white sand. He was lying on his back with my head resting on his chest. I kissed him, then pushed myself up and grabbed one of his hands.

"Come on, let's go in the water."

Without waiting, I made a run for it. Before my bare feet hit the ocean, he scooped me up in his arms and kissed me senseless.

"Will you two get a room?!" Avery yelled from the deck. Roberto and his friends were up there, firing up the Viking grill.

"Leave them alone, Avery!" Carmen yelled, laughing.

She and the girls were lying out on the sand, but I paid them no attention.

Neil hoisted me up onto his back and walked farther out to sea. When he could no longer touch the bottom, he threw us both into a large wave. I swam back to the surface and splashed him in retaliation. He reached out and pulled me in, his eyes alight with mischief. His left hand cradled the right side of my face as he leaned in and kissed me.

Later that night, some members of the group split off to play drinking games, while Neil and I settled in for a movie marathon. Somewhere in the middle, Roberto's friends had convinced Neil to play a couple rounds of penny can. He seemed to fit in with Roberto's college friends. I began to picture Neil attending college parties next year, hanging out with plenty of eager girls who might not be as prudent.

That evening when we pulled up to Neil's house, the images in my head were as prevalent as ever.

"No matter what, I want you to be happy, even if it's not with me," I said.

"Why would you say something like that?"

"It's just reality. Who knows where we'll be a year from now, and if we'll even still want the same things."

"I will always want you. You have to know that. I will never love anyone the way I love you."

I made no comment, which seemed to ignite flames of fury inside me. Our relationship, and all the special moments that had brought us here, seemed pointless.

We sat in silence before he finally caved and exited the car. As I drove home, I could feel the hole in my chest burrowing. Pain and revelation hit me like a ton of bricks: I thought I had been filling the abyss, but I was only building a barricade over it. I thought Neil and I would be together forever—that his love would be the supplement to help me get me through each day. What am I supposed to do now? This newly reopened wound was festering and raw to the touch. Holding back tears was a small miracle, but this was far from over. First thing on the agenda when I got home? Meltdown.

*   *   *

My last week in Cali flew by, even though I tried desperately to make the days last. I decided to put my revelation on the back burner while I still had time with Neil. There would be plenty of time to lose it. I stayed up late, talking to Neil on the phone, and rose early every morning so we could meet up at school.

My last night, Neil took me to the Santa Monica Pier where he had first confessed his feelings. I had said goodbye to everyone else earlier that day at school. He took me to the same restaurant. After dinner, we rode the Ferris wheel and played some of the carnival games. Neil played a skeet shooting game and won me a weird-looking frog. It was green with bright blue polka dots that matched the color of the frog's eyes, so I named him Neil. Afterward, we walked aimlessly along the boardwalk. We reached the end of the pier and glanced up at the moon, its light reflecting off the ocean waves. This was it. He would no longer be only a twenty-minute drive away. I looked at him and ran my hand through his dark curly tresses. I wondered when or if I would ever be able to do that again. He gazed deeply into my eyes and ran his thumb across my cheek. It was suddenly hard to breathe. He leaned in and kissed me softly. Tears had already formed and were now gliding down my cheeks.

16

The Slow Life

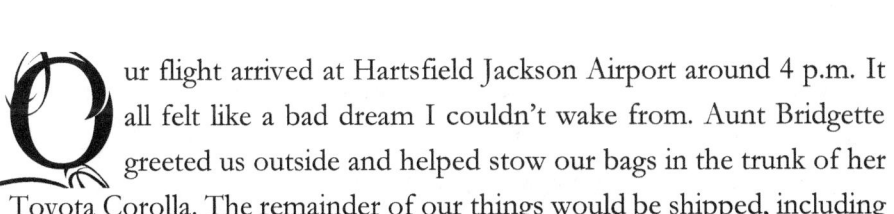

Our flight arrived at Hartsfield Jackson Airport around 4 p.m. It all felt like a bad dream I couldn't wake from. Aunt Bridgette greeted us outside and helped stow our bags in the trunk of her Toyota Corolla. The remainder of our things would be shipped, including our vehicles.

Aunt Bridgette had her own business where she baked and sold a variety of pastries straight out of Nana's kitchen. She made the best strawberry cheesecake I've ever tasted, but she was too flighty to open a bakery. She had often begged my mom to go into business with her, but my mother declined, partially because we lived so far away. Maybe now that would change.

As we rode on the interstate, I glanced around at the scenery—a vast difference from Los Angeles. I sat in the backseat, rereading the text I received from Neil earlier this morning.

Neil: *Have a safe slight. Miss you already, luv u always.*

Reading his text only made me more depressed, so I popped in earbuds and went back to staring out the window, trying to get my mind off him. I hated Georgia, and I'd only been here for a whopping five seconds.

"Is she okay?" Aunt Bridgette asked my mom.

"She's probably upset because she had to leave her boyfriend."

"She looks awful," Aunt Bridgette observed. "I don't think I've ever seen her look like this before."

"You know the music isn't that loud, I can hear you two," I said, still staring out the window.

They quickly changed the subject. This was my fate—a sentencing of who knows how long in Lower Slobbovia. At least I would be eighteen soon. I would be able to move out on my own, head back to California. I could attend USC and live off my trust until I found a stable job. Neil and I would be together again. I closed my eyes to picture it: me going to school by day, hanging out with Neil by night. Now if only I could nail down a major.

Suddenly, a pungent smell assaulted my senses. I yanked out my earphones. "Ugh! What is that smell?"

"Oh, that's the Yellow River, we're passing by Conyers. It smells sometimes," Aunt Bridgette explained.

I watched the cars creep along the interstate. This was the total opposite of driving in Cali where everyone seemed to be in a hurry. Not here, though. Apparently, Georgia residents had unlimited time on their hands. *Must be nice....*

We were no longer on the freeway but driving around the historic district of Covington. There was an art gallery on one corner, and an ice cream parlor on perched the other—*Scoops*. How fitting.

"This is downtown Covington. This is the town square," Aunt Bridgette said, pointing.

"This is downtown?" I said, astonished. It didn't hold a candle to Long Beach. "Our condo building was bigger than this."

Families were out, walking along the small shops and eateries.

"That's Ace Hardware. You can get anything from there. I bought my purse from there," Aunt Bridgette said with a sense of pride.

"You bought a purse from Ace Hardware?" my mother asked.

"Yeah. Like I said, they have everything. We can go and you can see for yourself."

"All right," my mother said skeptically. "So, where's Mom? Why didn't she come with to pick us up?"

"She's on a retreat with the seniors from her church. They went up Ellijay and should be back Thursday."

"Ellijay?" my mom asked.

"It's in northern Georgia."

"Is there a beach close by?" I asked.

"The closest beach is in Savannah," Aunt Bridgette answered.

"How far is that?"

"It's about four hours away."

"Four hours? Great," I said, annoyed.

We finally pulled onto a winding dirt road with woodlands on either side, which merged into a clearing of expansive green lawns lined with large oak trees. They reminded me of the twelve oaks in Gone with the Wind—one of my favorite movies. On the end of the driveway stood an enormous, white, classic revival-style house with a columned front porch.

Just like in my dream.

I was in shock, staring out my window, mouth all agape. It was the house in my dreams. Furthermore, the Corinthian, tetra-style portico was surrounded by an array of shrubs and hedges, intermittent with colorful hydrangeas. How could I have possibly dreamt of a place I'd never seen before? All I knew was Nana bought this place a few years back for her retirement. This was beyond eerie.

Aunt Bridgette stopped the car and turned around to face me. "What's wrong, Krissy? You look like you've seen a ghost."

"Nothing. I'm fine," I said, getting out.

Raindrops fell from the sky even though it was sunny and eighty degrees out—a sun shower. I had never seen such a thing before. I sighed and retrieved my bags from the trunk. We entered through the double doors and were met with a beautiful foyer. A round, antique, Queen Anne tea table sat in the middle with a tall trumpet vase full of blue and white hydrangeas. An exquisite crystal chandelier hung directly overhead, illuminating the pinewood floors that ran throughout the bottom level. And just like in my dream, the foyer was flanked by the living room and a library.

Aunt Bridgette showed me to the room I would be staying in. It was the same exact room in the dream that had caught fire from the plane crash. I put my things down and walked over to the large bay window, passing a small antique writing table that held a crystal lamp and potted pink orchid. A tall oak tree stood just outside the window, also like in the dream.

"This is impossible," I said quietly, shaking my head. "How could this be?"

"What did you say?" Aunt Bridgette asked.

"Oh, nothing."

"Do you like it?"

"Yeah, it's nice."

"Good." And with that, she spun on a heel and walked out.

I grabbed my phone and went to my recent contacts, searching for Neil's number. Let's see it was now 5:30 here so it would be 2:30 in California. I could already tell I would have to get used to the time difference. I held up my phone searching for service. I could only get all four bars by the bay window. I held the phone up to my ear pacing back and forth in front of the window. The phone only rang once before Neil answered.

"Hello?"

"Hi. I'm here. Are you busy?"

"Nope." It was quiet for a moment. "So how is Georgia?"

"Very green."

"Huh."

Again, silence.

"You know, it's like eighty degrees outside, but it's raining."

"I guess that's Georgia weather."

"Yeah, I guess. It's nice out here, minus the rain."

"Oh."

I sighed defeatedly. "I can't believe this, it's not even been a full day and we're already resorting to talking about the weather. I hate this. I hate being away from you."

"I know. I miss you more than words can express, but everything happens for a reason."

"That's not what I want to hear right now," I said, plopping down on the bed. "Hey, guess what? You know that dream I told you about with that huge plantation-looking house?"

"Yeah. What about it?"

"Well, I kid you not, it's exactly like the one I saw in my dreams. Isn't that crazy?"

"Are you sure?"

"Positive. Same type of trees, same dirt road, everything. It's kind of creepy."

"That is creepy. See? I told you everything happens for a reason."

"Since when did you become all Dalai Lama-ish?"

"I have to believe that something will help bring us back together again. Speaking of—do you have your laptop handy? I want to see you."

"Um, I think it's still downstairs. Besides, I look like a hot mess right now," I said, scanning the room for my luggage.

"I highly doubt that. Are we still on for our Skype date tonight?"

"Nine p.m. Eastern sharp."

"All right, well, I gotta go. The guys are waiting on me."

"Where are you?"

"I'm at home in my room. Everyone else is in the living room."

"Oh, well I don't want to keep you. I'll see you later. Love you."

"Love you more."

And just like that, he was gone. I crawled on the bed and curled up in the fetal position. I took my phone out, put my earphones in, and turned on Bruno Mars. I focused on the words and tried to imagine I was anywhere else but here.

Suddenly, an eerie feeling came over me, like someone was hovering over my shoulder. I sat up and searched the room, finding nothing out of the ordinary. I lay back down, thinking about the little girl in my dream. I wondered if the woodlands behind the house were the same ones I saw her in. If that was the case, she couldn't be too far away. But does she exist? Before, this was all just a bad dream. Now this was tangible, real.

Why did I let my thoughts run wild? I was doing nothing but scaring myself. Despite my best efforts, my imagination continued to spiral out of control. Even thoughts of cute, cuddly kittens morphed into rabid demonic guardians of the underworld, ready to attack.

Then I felt something grab my shoulder.

"Ahhh!" I screamed, pulling the earphones out of my ears. Once I realized it was my mom, my shoulders relaxed. "Oh."

"Are you okay?" she asked.

"Yeah."

She sat down next to me. "Sorry, honey. Didn't mean to scare you. I wanted to talk. Do you know why I decided to uproot us?"

"Yes, you want to make my life even more miserable. I never thought that would be possible, but look at you, overachieving."

"Can you please sit up and look at me?" my mom said.

I slowly did as she asked.

"So, I've been talking with your Nana a lot since…the incident."

"Are you talking about when I tried to kill myself? Because it's unclear which incident you're referring to."

My mother gave me a look of disapproval, so I let her finish without any further interruptions.

"Yes. Anyway, since then I have been trying to figure out what else could help. You've been to counselors, psychologists, and psychiatrists and you seem to be getting worse. I feel so helpless. I don't know what else to do," she said as the tears began to flow. "I feel like I'm failing you as a mother. It seems like every decision I've made has brought you to this point. If only I had better judgment when it came to men, or maybe if I was a better cook, or was more strict…. I don't know. I just think we needed a change of scenery. Start over fresh someplace new. Clear our heads a bit. Please don't hate me. I'm trying my best here."

"I don't hate you, Mom. I'm just not happy with my current situation. Please stop crying." I rubbed her arm, trying to console her. I hated seeing her cry, especially when I was the cause.

"Well, I'm glad to hear that. I'll try to pull myself together," she said, wiping the last of her tears. "You being unhappy wouldn't have anything to do with Neil, would it?"

I sighed. "Yes."

She adjusted her position and inched closer. "We never got to talk about the whole boyfriend thing," she said, now overly excited. "He's your first one. That's a big deal. You were a little bit of a late bloomer, but there's nothing wrong with that. You obviously didn't get that from me. But anyway, tell me all about him."

"What do you want to know?"

"Well, he doesn't look like the preppy type. Is he a jock? Does he play any sports?"

I shrugged my shoulders. "Do video games count?"

"I guess that answers my question," she said as she fixed a stray curl on my head. "Well, come on. Details, details."

"Umm, he likes almonds in milk chocolate bars, but not in Almond Joys. He prefers Mounds, but he doesn't like coconut in anything else. He loathes organized sports, except for baseball. He's a tech nerd who can tell you all about the newest iPhone before it's released to the public. He's such a dork in that way." I smiled to myself. "Oh, and he's really into Queen and Journey."

"The bands?"

"Yeah, he's not really into pop music."

"Okay. That's something."

"He's a good guy. I miss him already."

"Have you guys kissed yet?"

"Mom!" I said, embarrassed.

"What? Wasn't he any good at it?"

"I know what you're doing, and I'm not going to kiss and tell."

"Fine. I'm going to go see what's for dinner. You hungry yet?"

"Yes."

With that said, she gave me a kiss on the head and left.

I began unpacking when I realized I couldn't find my phone charger. I hoped I didn't leave it in California. I ran downstairs to the foyer and froze.

"Mom?"

"Yeah?"

"Where are you?"

"In the kitchen!"

"Where is the kitchen?" I asked, annoyed.

"Walk straight through the hallway and you'll see the kitchen door on the right."

I followed her directions. When I entered, three things stood out: maple cabinets, dark countertops, stainless steel appliances.

"You found us," my mom laughed.

"Have you seen my phone charger?"

"Did you pack it, or did the moving people pack it?"

"I think I did, but I can't remember. Where are the rest of my bags?"

"In my room, I believe." She turned to face my aunt. "Did you put some bags in my room, Bridgette?"

"Yeah," she said from inside the butler's pantry. "Well, guys, we may have to pick something up for dinner. There's nothing here to eat. We can kill two birds with one stone and pick something up from Shop-A-Lot."

"What's that?" I asked.

"It's only one of the biggest chains in the country."

"What do they sell?"

"What don't they sell? You can get groceries, toiletries, clothes, and electronics. You can even get tires and an oil change. Have you heard of Target?"

"Yeah, of course."

"Well, it's similar to Target."

We loaded up in Aunt Bridgette's car and headed off. When we arrived at the Shop-A-Lot, I quickly discovered it was nothing like Target.

Liars.

Aunt Bridgette grabbed a shopping cart and led the way. In the produce section, there was a woman who was wearing a shower cap and a family of four all dressed in camouflage. Talk about an eclectic bunch of people. Rivals L.A.

And with that thought, I was once again conned into thinking of home and everything I was missing.

17

Spirit of Heaviness

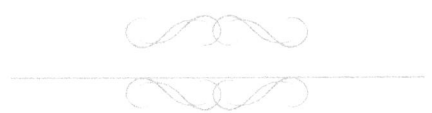

That night after dinner, I unpacked most of my things and settled in. This whole experience felt like a vacation—one that consisted of me being held captive against my will, insane asylum-style. My only solace? Neil. I fished out my laptop and laid on the bed, waiting impatiently for nine o'clock to roll around.

A knock sounded at the door.

"Kristen?" My mom entered and shut the door behind her.

"Yes?"

She walked over and turned down the volume on my laptop. "Are you really going to play this same song over and over?"

I shrugged.

She took a seat on the bed and made eye contact. "What do you think so far?"

"Do you want the truth?"

She nodded.

"There's no shower in the bathroom."

"There's no shower?" she repeated, genuinely surprised.

"You didn't know? There's only a bathtub. It's like we're back in the Dark Ages. Next thing I know, you're going to tell me we'll have to bake our own bread and churn our own butter."

"Oh, don't be so dramatic. Not being able to take a shower is trivial. Aside from that, what do you think?"

"I guess it's fine. I just miss all my friends," I whined.

"Tell you what, I'll make a deal. If you stick it out until your birthday, and you still feel like you want to go back to California, then you can go back to the condo."

"Really? You're not just saying that?"

"No. I mean it. You'll be eighteen by then anyway. But you have to give this a fair shot. Do we have a deal?"

"Fine."

We both shook on it.

She kissed my forehead and left the room. I grabbed my laptop and was eagerly awaiting my Skype date with Neil when my phone rang.

"Hello?"

"Hi."

"What's up? Why didn't you just Skype me?"

"I'm so sorry, but I can't make our date tonight. I feel awful."

"Why not?" I said, trying not to sound too disappointed.

"I got a job today and they need me to come in right away. They're short-staffed."

"Wow, Neil, that's awesome. I'm really happy for you. I don't remember you saying anything about wanting to get a job."

"I know, I just figured I'm going to need more money if I plan on coming out there to see you."

"Aww, that's so sweet, but you don't have to do that."

"I want to."

"So where are you working?"

"At the Best Buy close to school."

"That totally suits you."

"Yeah, so anyway, I have to work tonight. As a matter of fact, I should get going."

"Oh. Okay. I guess I'll talk to you later then."

I glanced at my screen as the call ended and suddenly felt isolated. I'd not even been here a full day, and I was already losing him—losing my sense of normalcy, losing my old life—but most importantly, I was losing the last of my invisible wall. I'd never felt so alone. I pressed play on my new theme song, turning it up as loud as it could go. I curled up in my bed, wishing I could escape reality. I would go someplace happy and safe—free from my emotions, free from the thoughts that ran rampant through my head. I yearned for my utopian society, but I settled for sleep instead.

* * *

The next few days seemed to drag. It was spring break, so I didn't have to worry about starting my new school yet. I slept most of the day away, but never felt rested. Neil had become very busy with work. Coupled with the time difference, it was almost impossible to get in touch. We'd been playing phone tag with one another nonstop. I had thought about emailing him, but as I stared at my laptop screen, I could feel my eyelids growing heavy.

It mirrored the heaviness I felt suppressing me—a heaviness that seemed to wrap me tightly in its grip, pulling me deeper into a sea of misery that was slowly consuming me from the inside out. Depression has a way of strangling the life right out of its victims. I was drowning in darkness, letting it ravish every part of my mind, body, and soul. It was the only constant I could count on.

In the back of my mind, I wanted the pain to stop, but it was an addiction. After all, pain was all I knew; my loyal companion. Maybe this is what I deserved. I longed for an escape, but suicide was out of the question. I couldn't bear the thought of how it would affect my mother. Maybe I would get lucky and my life would end early. What a nice thought. The fleeting glimpse to be free from its hold, to be free from the darkness, was what I wanted more than anything, but I had no idea how to pull myself out of it. Was it even possible? Before hopelessness suffocated me completely, sleep came to the rescue.

"Kristen? Kristen?" my mom called, shaking my arm.

I felt lethargic.

"Hmm?"

"Kristen, I can't allow this anymore. You need to get up. It's spring break. You should be out discovering new places, meeting new people, or at least getting out of bed to brush your teeth. When was the last time you took a bath?"

"I don't know," I mumbled into my pillow, slowly drifting back into my dream state.

"Kristen!"

"Yes," I whispered.

She grabbed my arm. "Come on, get up. I'm tired of you hiding up in this room all the time. When you're not sleeping, you're moping around and listening to that same sad song over and over—"

Aunt Bridgette was in the hallway singing the infamous Bruno Mars song.

"Bridgette!" My mom yelled.

Aunt Bridgette waltzed in, curious as to what she had done wrong.

"Can you please stop singing that song?"

"Sorry. Kristen's been playing it so much, it stuck in my head. I like it. It's catchy."

"You're not helping," my mother said, annoyed.

Aunt Bridgette shrugged her shoulders and disappeared.

My mother turned to face me again. "Anyway, like I was saying, it's not healthy for you to be up here all day. Have you been taking your meds?"

"Yes," I said, still groggy. "But I don't see the point. I still feel numb."

"I think some fresh air will do you some good. Do you want to come to the Grower's Outlet with us?"

"What's that?"

"It's a place where Bridgette and Mom get all their plants. What do you say?"

"No."

"Fine, but I want you out of this bed with your teeth brushed and smelling fresh by the time we get back."

She left in a huff. Once I heard the front door open and close, I rolled over, wondering what time it was. Heck, I didn't even know what day it was. I had no desire to leave my bed, despite the recurring dreams. They started out pleasant, then quickly turned into something else—something dark and unpredictable. I would be dreaming about Neil one minute, then the next it would drastically change. These dreams were almost impossible to wake from. No matter how hard I tried, something would overpower me.

I rolled out of bed, brushed my teeth, took a bath, then wandered downstairs to grab a bite to eat. I forced down a few bites of leftover macaroni salad and decided to do some exploring outside. I strolled along the weathered path, off to the side of the house. The trail led to another courtyard that was a bit larger, anchored by a water fountain in the center. Four stone benches surrounded it. I dusted one off with my hand and sat down. Feeling relaxed, I closed my eyes and relished the light breeze tousling my curls. At least here I didn't have to worry about always looking perfect. Here, I didn't care about anything.

Before I knew it, the sun was starting to set. I'd survived another day in Georgia. Since it would be dark soon, I decided to make my way back to the house.

I walked into the living room, which was filled with antiques that Nana had collected over the years. The highlight piece was the vintage red sofa with ornate wood trim that sat in front of one of the large windows. The second seating area was positioned in front of the floor-to-ceiling fireplace, which anchored the room and was flanked with two red and cream wingback chairs. I wondered how long Nana had had them, and who possibly owned them prior. I ran my fingertips across the fabric, tracing the design along the backrest. A small, delicate chandelier hung from above, highlighting a grand piano. A beautiful arrangement of pink roses, tulips, white peonies, and lilies sat atop.

I crossed through the foyer, stepping into the library. Above the fireplace hung a large painting—four men and a woman. The woman looked as though she were falling to the ground in distress. There was one man behind her, trying to hold her up, but he was shielding his eyes with part of his garment—a deep crimson—as if not wanting to witness the confrontation between the three other men, two of whom were gripping a dagger. The painting seemed oddly familiar, but I didn't give it much thought.

Another painting showcased the crucifixion of Jesus Christ. I stood there a moment, taking in the scene. Did He really die that way and then rise from the dead? It seemed so far-fetched, like all the other elaborate stories found in the Bible. Why would someone, who was supposed to be

God's son, allow that to happen? Couldn't He just kill everyone if He wanted to? What would compel Him to be tortured? I didn't get it.

The next thing that caught my eye was a large desk sitting directly behind the sofa. I took a seat and turned on the light next to a small limestone figurine. Located on the other side was a picture of my mother and me. I recalled that day perfectly. It was a few years ago, Fourth of July weekend in Long Island. I looked happy, peaceful. If only I knew then what I know now....

Later that night, I woke up in the wee hours of the morning to find my nightlight had given out.

"Crap," I muttered, too tired to get up and crack open a door.

Maybe I won't see anything. After all, it's been weeks since the last time I saw a spirit.

I rolled over and tried to get comfortable. Right then, a floorboard creaked. My heart stopped. I could feel the hairs on my body rise. The sound had come from behind, but I was terrified to turn over and see what awaited me. I laid completely still, pretending to be asleep. Anything was better than facing my fear head-on.

Another creak sounded, as if supporting someone's weight. I finally mustered up the courage to check behind me. No one was there. However, I noticed my door was ajar. Maybe my mother came in to check on me and forgot to close it. I got out of bed and slowly walked over, then stood there, unsure of what to do next. I peeked out into the hallway and saw that everyone's door was shut. Since I was up, I decided to go to the bathroom. When I swung the door open, I nearly jumped out of my skin. There was a man standing right in front of me. I quickly reached out to turn on the bathroom light, and just like that, he was gone. My heart was pounding, but thankfully, I didn't pee myself. After emptying my bladder, I went back to my room and shut the door. I turned on the small lamp and crawled into bed.

Somewhere in the midst of my panic, I was able to calm down enough to fall back asleep. Once again, I dreamed of the woodlands and that little girl. Only instead of darkness, there was light. My surroundings were more clear. How could that be? Before the sun's appearance, I had been looking at the world through dimly lit eyes. They had adjusted to the darkness, creating an illusion. Now my eyes were wide open and the comprehension was a cold jolt that reverberated through me like an ice bath: I wasn't just dabbling in depression, I was fully immersed in it—so much that it affected how I viewed the world around me. But now as the marvelous light broke through my incessant midnight, morning came, and it was swift and strong as it cut through the atmosphere. My new sight, fighting to process all that I saw, finally adjusted to a crisp point of view. Everything was vivid and real. I couldn't look away.

I forgot about the little girl entirely until I heard her childish voice beckoning me from behind. But I paid her no attention—it was all a lie. I'd had this dream enough to know what was coming next. Instead, I was in pursuit to find the source of this light somewhere far off in the distance. I began to run, knocking branches out of the way and plowing over ferns until I finally made it out into a clearing. The light was only a few feet away. It was so bright, so beautiful, that I had to shield my eyes from its intensity. I looked down at the ground and noticed I was back on the path I had veered off of. My bare feet weren't the only ones here.

That's when I saw Him.

The Man was standing directly in front of me, and the light seemed to radiate from Him as if He and the light were one. It was the most magnificent thing I had ever seen, and no matter how much my eyes burned, I couldn't look away; I was in awe. I tried to get a good look at His face, but it was no use. The light shone the brightest there. He held out His hand and I felt a gravitational pull. Peace and serenity enveloped me. I held my hand out, and without taking a single step, I drew closer to Him.

That's when I realized I was crying. But they weren't tears of heartache or pain. They were tears of joy. The happiness I had been yearning for all along was immersed throughout my body to the point that it was almost unbearable, but I craved it all the more. I closed my eyes in rapture, praying that this feeling would never end. When I opened them again, I was lying in bed with my arm stretched out, reaching.

Now that I was conscious, I slowly lowered my hand to my side. Was it a dream? The warmth of the rays still lingered as I tried to remember every detail. It felt so real. I wondered who the Man was and why I would even have such a dream. What did it mean? Somehow it felt as though I knew Him, but that was impossible. I never did get a look at his face.

Sometime later, the sound of muffled voices woke me up for good.

Nana came bursting through the door. "Krissy! It's eleven and you're still in that bed." She walked over to the bay window and opened the curtains. Light flooded the room. "It's time to wake up. You're gonna sleep your whole life away."

"Hi, Nana," I said, wiping my eyes. "When did you get back?"

"I just walked through the door and your mom told me you were still asleep. Half the day is gone and you're still in bed. Get up and get dressed. We're going out," she said, exiting the room. That was the one thing about Nana; no one would be able to sleep past nine when she was around.

I threw the covers off and got ready.

We all piled into Aunt Bridgette's car and rode to the square.

"You haven't been flat ironing your hair," my mom observed, touching my curls.

"I haven't felt like strengthening it."

She looked at me with concern.

"Don't worry, I brushed my teeth," I said, rolling my eyes.

I had always made it a ritual to flat iron my hair and apply makeup before joining society, but I no longer wanted to live under false pretenses. Who cares if I look put together? Makeup or not, I still felt the same inside. Avery had said once that guys don't like girls with curly, unruly hair, but rather they wanted a girl with sleek hair they could run their fingers through. It all sounded so stupid now. Why should my hair or the way I look be the deciding factor on whether someone will love me or not? Neil said he preferred my curly hair because it was more me. *Neil.* The thought of him made the pain reemerge. Thankfully, that feeling halted the moment we set foot in Ace Hardware. And like Aunt Bridgette had promised, they had everything.

We stopped at an outdoor fruit stand. That's when I saw a man staring at me. He looked like he was in his late thirties. I casually looked over my shoulder to see if there was someone else he could be staring at, but no one was there. Everyone else had made their way over to the strawberries. Feeling uncomfortable, I turned my back to him and folded my arms across my chest, waiting for my family to finish up.

"Excuse me," a husky voice said.

I spun around.

"I'm sorry, I hope I didn't startle you. Hello, I'm John Reid."

I stared blankly.

"I just wanted to come over here and tell you that the Lord is calling you. You have a calling on your life."

"What?"

"The Lord told me to tell you that He is calling you."

"As in…God?"

"Yes." His face was pleasant.

"Um, okay, thanks," I said sarcastically, turning away.

"Hello, Pastor Reid!" Nana called out.

I looked over at Nana. She was waving at the man in front of me. How is that possible? He didn't look like a pastor. He wore a button-down, short sleeve shirt with jeans and white Air Force Ones. I looked back at him. Huh. He was wearing a chain around his neck with a cross pendant. Why didn't he say he was a pastor? Maybe then I would have taken him more seriously. Probably not. But in any case, I thought that was customary.

Nana walked over. Pastor John Reid reached out and give her a hug.

"Pastor Reid, this is my granddaughter, Kristen. She and her mother just moved here to Georgia."

"It's nice to meet you, Kristen. I was just telling her that the Lord has a calling on her life."

"Oh, definitely," Nana agreed, nodding.

A petite, fair-skinned woman joined our circle.

"Kristen, this is my wife, Brynelle."

I was about to reach my hand out, but she stepped forward and hugged me.

"Um...."

"Hello, Kristen. You can call me Bryn," she said after pulling away, her smile warm and welcoming.

"Hi."

Well, I guess he wasn't trying to hit on me. What a relief. I couldn't believe that such a stylish woman could be a pastor's wife. She wore a plum-colored, sleeveless blouse with skinny jeans, and bright yellow flats that coordinated with her purse. She looked like she was in her early thirties and was drop-dead gorgeous.

"So, will you be coming Sunday to service?" Bryn asked me.

"Oh, I don't know. I'm not really sure. I mean, we don't usually go."

"Well I think you should come. I think you'll enjoy it and meet some new people."

"I'll think about it," I said, even though I had already made up my mind. It would be more wasted time, like in Long Island and some odd years back when I visited my father and his family; we all went to church together. I got nothing out of it.

"Pastor Reid is new to Georgia. He took over for Pastor Williams after he passed," Nana informed us on our way home.

"That's right, I remember you telling me about that," my mother responded.

"They seem like nice people, but I don't know," Nana continued. "You know he dresses like that during service sometimes. Honestly, I don't know why the man can't just follow the order of the way things have always been done. It just seems like ever since he came to this town, he's been trying to turn everything upside down."

"Really?" my mom asked, intrigued.

"He certainly has an unorthodox way of leading the church. He's great with the youth, though. Since he began pastoring, we've had more young people attending. I don't know, they seem to listen to him…."

There went Nana, dropping her not-so-subtle hints again. Seed planted.

That night I spoke to Neil for a little while he was on his break. He had nothing new to report, except for hordes of girls flocking to him to console him in my absence. He thought it was funny. I was not amused.

When bedtime came around, I tossed and turned like crazy. Too frustrated to deal with it, I headed for the bathroom. It was dark in the hallway, but I could see someone standing by the staircase.

"Avery?" I whispered. "What are you doing here?"

Her back was facing me. She took the stairs one at a time.

"Avery!" I said, following after her.

I tried to catch up but she was too fast. "Avery, stop."

She never slowed her pace. I continued to follow her outside.

"Avery?"

She came to an abrupt halt and slowly turned to face me, but she looked different. Her clothes were filthy and tattered. Her hair was limp and greasy; she looked gaunt and tired.

And then it was clear.

"You're not Avery," I said, backing up.

She opened her mouth and an unnatural screech came out. I made a run for it with the thing disguised as Avery hot on my trail—her movements lithe and precise. I made it up the stairs to the terrace and into the kitchen just in time to shut the door on the monster.

Suddenly, my eyes flew open.

I was lying in bed, drenched in sweat. My heart was pounding so hard it hurt.

"It was just a dream, it was only a dream," I whispered, trying to catch my breath.

I had a feeling that I wasn't the only one in the room. My eyes darted over to the corner where the bay window was. I slowly rose on my elbows and squinted so I could see clearly. The thing from my dream standing there. I wanted to scream, but nothing came out. She waited in the shadows, glaring.

My body began to tremble. These creatures had always been contained in my dreams, but now she stood only a few feet away. Maybe I was still asleep. I rubbed my eyes in hopes that I was just seeing things, but when I reopened them, she was still there. I frantically searched the room, plotting my next move. I noticed a bright white light coming from the top of my door frame. It was an alternate route. Clearly this thing wasn't planning on going anywhere, so I got out of bed and sprinted to my mother's room, shutting the door behind me.

"What is it, Kristen?" she mumbled, turning on her side lamp.

"Oh, I just a bad dream. Can I sleep with you tonight?" I hopped in the bed, not waiting for her response. My eyes were glued to her bedroom door.

She threw back the covers and rolled out of bed.

"Where are you going?" I asked, panicked.

"Calm down. I'm just going downstairs to get some water," she replied.

And then she was gone.

She left the door open. I sat up, anxiously waiting for her to return. Goosebumps appeared on my arms—that's when I heard the floorboards creak. I craned my neck to see past the doorframe, but no one was there. The creaks continued to inch closer to the foot of the bed. I ducked under the covers, trying to disappear. I listened, waiting for more creaks. My whole body remained acutely alert. Just as I was entertaining the notion of peeking over the covers, something grabbed my shoulder. I screamed and thrashed.

"WHAT?!" my mom screamed, jumping back. "What is the matter with you? You scared me half to death," she panted, hand over her heart.

"I'm sorry, but you scared me," I said, my own heart pounding violently.

"My goodness, Kristen, you'd think you saw a ghost or something," she said, sitting on the edge of the bed, reaching for the water she brought up. She froze and twisted her head in my direction as if it finally clicked. We glanced at one another for a moment, then slowly surveyed the bedroom, not saying a word.

18

Resurrection

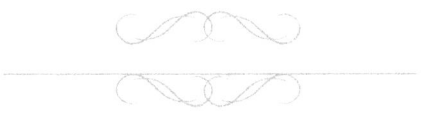

The following morning, Mom insisted on rummaging through her closet.

"What time is it?" I asked.

"Eight o'clock," she said, assessing two dresses in hand. "Which one is more churchy?"

I sat up and rubbed my eyes to get a better look. "Um, neither. You should burn both of them."

"What?! Why?"

"Because anyone over the age of thirty shouldn't be wearing spandex in public if they aren't on their way to the gym. Plus, they're both low cut."

She hung them back up.

"Are you going to church?"

"Yeah, Nana wants me to go. It's Easter Sunday," she added with reluctance.

"We've never gone before."

"I'm trying something new. I'm afraid I haven't been a good example for you in certain areas. Maybe church will help ground me."

"Well, I guess if you're going, I'll go."

"See, it's already working," she smiled.

I rolled my eyes and got out of bed.

We got to the building around 10:45 a.m. and they were already in the middle of praise and worship. We slipped in and found seats in the fourth row. The congregation consisted of thirty people, at best. I didn't know the songs, but they didn't seem like the types of songs you'd sing in church. The times I'd been before, I only heard slow, boring songs. These were lively. There was even a rap song that didn't sound cheesy. Everyone seemed to get into it, especially Pastor Reid. He was jumping around, shouting, and singing the loudest—and he wasn't even using the microphone yet. He wore a black button-down shirt that was tucked into his jeans with black, red, and gray Nike sneakers to match his baseball hat. After seeing his ensemble, I didn't feel so bad about wearing jeans. I guess that was the unorthodox part Nana was referring to, but I didn't see anything wrong with it.

After the songs ended, we were all seated, and Pastor Reid welcomed everyone. Then he had us pray. I think it held the record for the longest prayer. Every time I thought he was wrapping it up, he started thanking God for something else. After he finished, he went right into preaching. There were a lot of things I didn't understand, but one of the things that stood out was when he said that Jesus Christ is light and the darkness doesn't understand that light. Jesus died for our sins so that we may be made pure and be the light in this world. My thoughts drifted to the painting of the crucifixion that hung in Nana's library. The scene made more sense now. We can be made pure and be the light in this world because Jesus laid down His life for us.

Was the Man from my dream supposed to be Jesus? Pastor Reid's words about Jesus being the light resonated. Then I remembered what he said to me about the Lord calling me. I didn't give much thought to it then, but now it consumed my mind. In my dream, the Man—Jesus, was motioning for me to come to him. Was it all true? I mean, what are the odds of that happening? Is that even possible? My head was spinning. I closed my eyes and ran my hands through my hair. There had to be a logical explanation for everything, but I couldn't think of one.

After church, Pastor Reid and his wife came up to us to greet us with hugs.

"It's good to see you, Kristen. We're glad you could make it," Bryn said, giving me a side hug.

"Yes, it was a blessing to see all of you this morning," Pastor Reid chimed in.

"Pastor Reid, this is my other daughter, Anna, Kristen's mother.

"Nice to meet you," he said.

"Did you enjoy the service?" Bryn asked my mom.

"Oh, yes."

"Did you enjoy the word, Sister Edith?" Pastor Reid asked my grandmother.

"I enjoyed it, I just wished it would have been more about His resurrection since it is Easter Sunday, but other than that, it was a good message."

"That's understandable, but I have to do and say what the Holy Spirit leads me to preach. He knows exactly what His people need to hear. If He was only concerned about what people want to hear, then we'd all be in trouble."

My Grandmother looked at him, her eyes wide with shock, although I wasn't sure why.

Pastor Reid turned to me. "So did you learn anything from the word, Kristen?"

"Yeah, actually I did."

"Good. I won't put you on the spot and ask you…this time," he said, smiling.

And I was grateful for that, even though it was the first time I had learned anything from church. This place was different. I couldn't exactly put my finger on how yet.

"So I noticed that you and your mother didn't come up for the altar call. Are you two saved?" he asked, looking back and forth between my mother and me.

"No," we both said in unison.

"Do you want to be?"

"I figure that day will come after I get myself together," my mother said confidently.

"If we were able to save ourselves, there would've been no need for Jesus to be crucified. He wants us to come as we are, and then together, with help from the Holy Spirit, He makes us into a new creation."

I didn't say it, but I was thinking the same thing as my mom. I wasn't sold on being "saved." Regardless, I continued to listen.

"It's impossible to do it on your own. And guess what? He doesn't expect us to do it on our own. So, would you like to invite the Lord into your life?"

We both nodded.

Why not? I mean, it couldn't hurt. Right?

He put his hands out for me and my mother to take.

"Repeat after me. Lord."

"Lord," we said in unison.

"Come into my life."

"Come into my life."

"Save me, Lord."

228

"Save me, Lord."

"Forgive me for my sins."

"Forgive me for my sins."

"Cleanse me, Lord."

"Cleanse me, Lord."

"Purify me, Lord."

"Purify me, Lord."

"Sanctify me, Lord."

"Sanctify me, Lord."

"Holy Spirit, take residence in me to guide and counsel me."

"Holy Spirit, take residence in me to guide and counsel me."

"In Jesus' name, I pray."

"In Jesus' name, I pray."

"Amen."

"Amen."

"Now, do you two have Bibles?"

"Yes," my mother answered quickly.

"Um, yeah," I answered hesitantly.

They all looked at me.

"I have one, it's just really old. I've had it since the third grade. I guess I'll have to find it."

Pastor Reid lowered his hands from our shoulders and backed up.

"Okay, if you can't find yours, we have extras. I want both of you to start reading your Bibles. I want you to start with John, then read Matthew, Mark, Luke, and then go back and read John again. It will introduce you to who the Lord is."

Pastor Reid stopped talking and glanced at the floor for a moment, then looked at me sternly.

"The Lord says that He has always been there with you all those nights you cried into your pillow. And even the times you hid alone in your closet. He said He knows your secret thoughts regarding your father and the longing in your heart for him to be the father you've always imagined, but the Lord desires that place in you."

The room was still, silent. I looked at my mom and then over to Nana. They wore the same expression: shock, disbelief, and more than anything else, wonder.

"How did you…?" my voice trailed off.

How did he know these things that I had never even expressed to my mother or even spoke out of my mouth? Not even my mother knew I would hide to get away.

"The Lord says I am your Father, and I love you. I will never leave you or forsake you."

I couldn't take it anymore; the tears streamed down my face. I felt as though a weight had been lifted off me. An incredible feeling of joy flooded my chest. God wanted to be my father. I couldn't comprehend how someone so great and powerful would volunteer for that job when my own biological father wanted nothing to do with me.

Bryn brought me some tissues. I wiped my face and blew my nose. Bryn rubbed my back and pulled me in close to comfort me. Pastor Reid started talking to my mother, but I was such a mess I don't even know what he said. The only thing I could focus on was the fact that God loved me and I was His daughter.

Before we left, Pastor Reid and his wife gave me and my mom cards with their numbers on it. He said if we ever needed to talk, to feel free to call any time, it didn't matter how late or early. I took the card and put it in my back pocket since I didn't have my purse. After a round of goodbye hugs, we all left. On the ride home, I thought about everything that had taken place today. It was so amazing, I couldn't believe it.

The next morning was my first day at Eastside High. I could feel the nerves building up inside. Our cars hadn't arrived yet, so Aunt Bridgette dropped me off. Based on the looks of the town square, I was imagining a tiny schoolhouse like on Little House on the Prairie. But to my surprise, the campus didn't seem much smaller than Belmont. The only difference: concrete was replaced with foliage.

I entered the building and made my way to the office. I checked in at the front desk and waited for my guidance counselor. She was a young, bubbly brunette, wearing a white short-sleeved shirt tucked into her black pencil skirt, a black vest, and black slingback pumps.

"Hi, Kristen?"

"Yes."

"Hello, I'm Miss Taft." She motioned for me to follow.

I walked into a tiny office and sat down in the chair in front of her desk.

"Welcome to Eastside. How are you this morning?"

"I'm fine, thanks."

"Good, good. I was looking over your transcripts. You seem to be a well-rounded student. A's and B's in your advanced placement classes...." she said, flipping through my file. "You were involved in dance and cheer. Cool. Go eagles!"

"Um, right," I said after the awkward pause.

"Well, it appears you only need to complete a few classes to graduate." Her smile faltered. "Oh. I also see that you had to be hospitalized at the end of February into the first week of March. Is that correct?"

"Yes."

"So it's been over a month. How are you feeling?" She looked genuinely concerned.

"I'm a lot better."

She didn't seem convinced.

I sighed. "I'm not going to try and kill myself if that's what you're thinking," I said bluntly.

"Oh, no," she flustered, letting out a nervous laugh. "I'm glad you're feeling better."

"Thanks," I said, not making eye contact.

"If you ever need to talk about anything, my door is always open."

I looked up. Her bright smile was back. I nodded in response, although I knew I would not be taking her up on that offer. She handed me my schedule and a map of the school, then sent me on my way.

Before my last class of the day, I called Mom to let her know I'd be getting out early. When I exited the building, she was waiting for me in the parking lot. The heat was unbearable.

"So how was your first day, hon?"

"It was okay. I see our cars came."

"Yeah, this morning after Bridgette dropped you off."

I opened the door and threw my bag in the backseat, then hopped in the front.

"So, we didn't really get a chance to talk yesterday after church, but wasn't that something?"

"Yeah, it was pretty crazy," I said, recalling yesterday's events.

"I can't believe he knew all that stuff. I'm not sure I know what to make of it."

I stared at her in disbelief. "I do. It was God. Had to be. No way could it be anything else. He knew my innermost thoughts—things I've never voiced out loud. There's no other explanation."

I know that for a fact, I thought to myself.

Mom chose not to press the issue. We didn't talk the rest of the way home.

* * *

The next few days of school were bearable. Nothing exciting or noteworthy happened, aside from everyone's reaction to my car, which was the most expensive one in the lot. Talk about embarrassing. In California, my car blended in nicely, but in Covington, it stuck out like a sore thumb.

Wednesday night, we all went to Bible study. Pastor Reid was there, but Bryn was the one in charge. I prepared myself for all the hugs. Just like on Sunday, everyone was very welcoming. I learned something new and didn't feel too awkward being there this time. Afterward, everyone headed off to the recreation center to eat and socialize. I was about to follow my family when Pastor Reid stopped me.

"How have you been since Sunday?"

"Good."

"I heard you started a new school."

"Yeah."

"How's it going so far?"

"Fine."

He smiled. "You know, one of these days you're going to have to stop talking my ear off."

"Well, I haven't really met anyone. I've just been keeping to myself. My schedule has me leaving for lunch, so I'm not there very long anyway."

"You know, a few of the teens here attend the same school. I could introduce you guys."

"Oh, I don't know. That would be awkward. Maybe another time."

"All right, just let me know. I spoke with your mother this morning on the phone. She's pretty concerned about you."

"I know. She has been for a while."

"What's going on?"

Normally at this point, I would close up, but for whatever reason, a mood struck.

"She doesn't know how to help. Personally, I don't think anyone can. I've been depressed for a while and tried to kill myself, I guess."

"You guess?"

"I say that because I blacked out and when I came to, I was out on our balcony, prepared to jump, but I don't even remember walking out there. I…" I trailed off, deciding on whether I should tell him about the woman.

"You know you have power over depression."

I frowned.

"We can do nothing, but the Spirit within us has power."

As he spoke, I began to see a white glow emitting from the top of his head. I tried to stay focused on his face, but the more I did, the brighter it shined. And then it was gone.

"You said the Holy Spirit lives inside of you? Like, literally inside of you?" I asked.

"Yes."

"Have you ever seen it?"

"Him?"

"Huh?"

"Him, not It," he corrected.

"Oh, sorry. So have you ever seen Him?"

"No, I haven't. But I've seen angels."

"You have?"

"A couple of times. But there are plenty of people who have had angelic visitations. Numerous stories in the Bible describe angels coming down to help man and delivering messages from God."

"What about ghosts?"

He shook his head. "There are evil spirits and demons, but no ghosts."

"Hypothetically speaking, what if someone were to see something that resembled a ghost? What is that?"

"They're called familiar spirits. But even some evil spirits can resemble people. They look like us, but they're no different from demons that try to gain access to someone's life. It's more unsuspecting if they come disguised as people."

"Seriously?"

He nodded. "Have I answered your question?"

I nodded.

"Well, your mother was thinking that maybe we could do some counseling sessions to talk and see if we can get to the root of the problem. What do you think? Is that something you might be interested in?"

I pondered that. I knew where counseling sessions had gotten me in the past, and that made me hesitant. But this man seemed like he knew what he was talking about, so I kept an open mind.

"Okay."

"Good. It would have to be after my wife and I get off work. Is tomorrow night around five thirty all right?"

"That's fine."

"Good. We'll see you here at five thirty."

19

It's Not My Depression

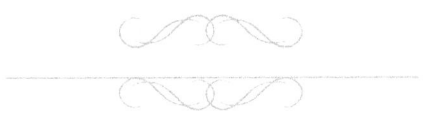

The next day at school dragged. I had an hour scheduled to talk with Neil before his shift started, so I raced home and fired up my laptop.

"Hi."

"Hi. It's good to see you," he said.

"I miss you. Is that a new shirt?"

"Yeah. I bought some new ones, the old ones had holes." He laughed.

"What have you been up to on your spring break?"

"Working, mostly. Shawn McKee had a party Monday night."

"Oh yeah?"

"Yeah, I was invited, but I didn't go."

"Why not?"

"It just didn't seem fair without you. You're right, they would never have invited me before. I just hung out with my friends instead. They were pretty upset. They wanted to go."

I wanted to find the perfect moment to share my news, but I wasn't sure how he would react. I figured now was as good a time as any. "I got saved."

"From what?"

"Are you trying to be funny?"

"I'm not, I just don't know what you're referring to."

"I'm saved from going to hell."

"It's not like you were such a horrible person before. I doubt you were going to hell."

"I learned from the Bible that you must be born again to go to heaven. It doesn't matter how nice of a person you are."

"Really?"

"Yup."

"Are you going to change now?" he asked, hesitantly.

"I hope so. I'm tired of being miserable. And I don't have you around anymore to distract me. But, my mom said I can come back out there when I turn eighteen."

"That's great, but—"

"But what?"

"You look really happy. Do you like it out there?"

"Do I?" I paused. "I've definitely learned a lot. And I feel happy. The world just seems more peaceful, I guess. Sorry if that sounds kind of cheesy."

"No, that's great. I'm glad you're feeling better. Maybe one day I'll get to meet this miracle-working pastor myself."

"Can you please be serious?"

"I am."

"I think you'd like him. He's not at all like most preachers. He wears Air Force Ones, and he explains things about God and the Bible so clearly."

"That's cool. I'm glad you're happy. Well, I hate to go but...."

"Oh, right."

We said our goodbyes.

I reclined on my bed and stared up at the ceiling, humming "Fall Afresh." The clock ticked as I waited impatiently for 5:30 to roll around. Who knew I'd be excited for a counseling session? Then my phone rang.

"Hello?"

"So, you are still alive."

"Hi, Avery. Yes, I'm doing great. How are you?"

"Who are you and what have you done with my friend?"

"You called me. What's new?" I said, surprisingly chipper.

"I'm missing you like crazy. Emily and her friends are out to make my life a living hell. Thank God I've been busy with dance practices and prom preparations."

"I totally forgot about prom. You and Rodney going together?"

"Of course. My dad's getting us a limo and a restaurant before."

"What do you mean he's getting you a restaurant?"

"He rented out Koi so a group of us can eat privately before prom."

"Oh, okay."

"You know, almost every girl at school wants to go with Neil."

"I'm not really surprised."

"Are you two still together?"

"Technically, but I don't know if it's working out too well. I feel bad he's missing out on so many things because of me."

"Well, he seems to be devoted. I haven't seen him flirting with any other girls. I've been keeping an eye on him, of course. He's back to hanging with his loser friends. I was expecting him to be at Shawn's party, but he was MIA."

I had to admit I was pleased to hear that, but I also felt bad for making him put his life on hold. I glanced over at the clock. "Listen, Avery, I gotta go. Can I text you later?"

"You better."

I hung up the phone and hustled to get ready.

I pulled into the church parking lot at exactly 5:30 p.m. There was another car, which I assumed was Pastor Reid's. I stepped outside and he greeted me; Bryn was not too far behind.

"How are you doing today?" he asked.

"Good, thanks."

"Let's go into my office."

Once inside, he turned on the overhead light and sat behind his oak desk. Bryn and I sat next to one another on the opposite side. Pastor Reid prayed, then focused his attention on me.

"So you've been battling with depression for how long now?"

"Um, I'm not sure, maybe it's been years, but more recently the thoughts of suicide came. I just didn't see the point in being here, on this earth, I mean. I just wanted to escape."

"Escape?"

"I can't seem to get away from the pain. It's always there."

"So where is your father?"

"Santa Barbara, with his family. He and my mother divorced almost ten years ago." Why was I telling him all this?

"You don't consider yourself part of his family?"

"No. We share the same hair and eye color, but that's it."

"How often do you talk?"

"The last time I saw or spoke to him was a few weeks ago when he and my mom told me we were moving here. Before that, it had been a few years. He's a very busy man and his free time doesn't involve me. He's a real estate developer, so he travels a lot."

"I see. I can understand how that would make you feel abandoned. When something traumatic like divorce happens, it makes a person vulnerable to demonic attacks. When most people think of demonic attacks, they think of things like *The* Exorcist. However, these attacks can also come in the form of depression, abandonment, anxiety, and rejection. It's not always someone's head spinning around or vomiting up pea soup."

"So, you're saying a spirit is making me feel depressed?"

"That's right," Bryn chimed in.

"Many times, these spirits can gain access to a person's life through sin, or through abandonment and rejection from others, but they can also be inherited through the bloodline," Pastor Reid continued.

"My grandfather committed suicide," I said.

"So that spirit was assigned to your grandfather and remained dormant until it was passed down to you."

"It's not me," I whispered, relieved. The layers of truth were finally unraveling. "So if it's not me, how do I get rid of it?"

"We'll pray and cast it out."

"Like an exorcism?"

"Not necessarily. Movies exaggerate. Most of the time a person may just cry. Sometimes people vomit, but there may be no other evidence until you realize you feel differently than you did before. In the Bible, Jesus cast demons out of people all the time. His disciples even cast out demons in His name, and because we have the power of the Holy Spirit in us, we can do the same. That means you can have that power as well."

"Me?"

"Yes. You are just a vessel the Lord uses. The enemy is a counterfeit, so whatever the Lord does, the enemy takes it and perverts it. The Holy Spirit is meant to dwell in man, so evil spirits want to do the same. And when they do gain access, they must be cast out."

"So when you cast this spirit out, is that it? I won't be depressed anymore? I mean, it sounds a little too good to be true. And if it's that easy, why doesn't everyone do it?"

"That's a good question. Unfortunately, not everyone's eyes are opened to the truth, and some pretend the truth doesn't exist. Once it's gone, you won't be depressed anymore, but it's up to you whether you stay free from that spirit."

"What do you mean?"

"The Bible says when a spirit is cast out of a person, it roams the dry places, seeking refuge. If it finds none, it goes back to the place where it was cast out. It finds the house—the house refers to your body—and if that home is empty, it will try to return with seven demons worse than the first. Your body is considered God's temple, and the demon will always try to come back. That's why I tell you to read your Bible. Reading the word of God will help you grow closer to the Lord. That way, when that spirit does try to come back, your temple will be filled with the Spirit of the Lord. But you have to know that you are delivered. If there is any doubt whatsoever, that demon can talk you right back into what you've been delivered from. As believers, we must rely on the word of God. If the word of God says you are free from depression, then why should you listen to the enemy who says you are not? Believe the word of God. That spirit is not your friend."

A spirit of depression was to blame for all this? Unbelievable. I could see it all much clearer now. I was in an abusive love-hate relationship with depression that I thought I'd always have to deal with—being hated was better than being ignored.

"What do I do when the demon tries to come back?"

"You tell depression to go in Jesus's name," he said, matter-of-factly.

"That's it?"

"Yeah. And watch what happens."

"Okay," I said, skeptically. "It all seems so easy."

"Well, it's as easy as you make it. It's your choice to believe what God says, or believe what the enemy says. That is why so many Christians struggle—they don't completely believe what God says. They may believe that Jesus died for their sins, but they don't believe that Jesus also gave them power over the enemy. But even believing in God is not enough. Even the demons believe and tremble. It all boils down to choice. The Bible says choose you this day life or death, blessing or curse. Every day we must choose to know God's word is true, and every day we must resist the Devil."

It was a lot of information to process, but the more he spoke, the more everything began to make sense. The spirit of depression was not mine. It was merely something that had attached itself to me by my permission. I never understood why I was depressed because I had no reason to be. I mean, sure, my father was never around, but I did have a mom who loved and cared for me. I had a roof over my head and never went hungry. But even if all those things weren't true, I still had a Father in heaven that I would be with one day. It's like my eyes were being opened for the first time, *Matrix*-style.

At the end of my session, Pastor Reid prayed and rebuked the spirit of depression and canceled every assignment that was transferred through my bloodline. And he was right, I felt great. It was as if a weight had been lifted off me.

* * *

The next day, I volunteered to help my mom and Nana in the garden, and later joined them in preparing dinner. In the midst of chopping onions, an ominous feeling came over me like a dark cloud. I remembered what Pastor Reid had said. I told the evil spirit to go in Jesus's name. Within seconds, the negative feelings went away. It was like flipping a switch. I had finally found someone who helped me. From now on, nothing could bring me down.

20

Purpose Revealed

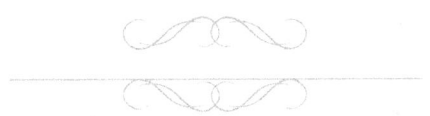

Although the depression was handled, I still had some unfinished business with another demonic spirit. It was early Saturday morning and the aroma of freshly made pancakes filled the air. I was so comfortable in my mother's bed that I deliberated over whether to get up at all, but I couldn't resist the sweet smell any longer. I rolled over and stretched, then faced my mother's dresser. In the mirror, I saw a spirit looking back at me. He reminded me of the joker; the corners of his mouth lifted in a Cheshire-like smile. I glanced away for a second, then looked back. He winked.

I scurried out of bed and ran downstairs to the kitchen. Still out of breath, I sat down and wondered how it was possible. Before, I could only see them in the dark. So why was I able to see him in the daylight? Panic began to set in.

"What's wrong? You don't like it?" Aunt Bridgette asked.

"Hmm?" I had been staring at my plate for God knows how long.

"You don't like the pancakes? I can make you something else," she offered.

"Oh, no, they're good. I just have a lot on my mind." I took a bite to appease her.

"How was the counseling session?" my mom asked.

"It was good. It really helped, and I learned a lot. I had no idea so much useful information was in the Bible."

"It's basically the roadmap for our lives," Nana interjected. "Oh, will you look at that!" She jumped up out of her seat and shot out the back door. She stopped in the middle of her garden with her back to us and started waving her arms violently.

"I think she's gone crazy," Aunt Bridgette said, walking toward the back door. "Mom, what are you doing?"

"These damn rabbits!" she yelled. "When I find you, I'm gonna skin you and cook you! Bridgette, go get me a stick from the garage."

I looked back at my mom. "Well, the session was definitely helpful."

"Good, I'm so glad. You seem better. I was happy to see you helping us in the garden yesterday."

I was full of surprises lately. Somehow, the Lord was changing me into a new Kristen.

After breakfast, I went upstairs and got dressed, still in deep thought. I was hoping the incident this morning was only a one-time thing. To help get my mind off it, I went strawberry picking with my family. The direct sunlight and humidity made it feel like a sauna outside. We laughed and joked with each other. At that moment, I realized I was finally living my life. I was no longer merely existing. Then I was reminded of this morning with flashbacks of that demon grinning at me. Would he be waiting for me back at the house? I couldn't take it anymore. I marched through the dust of the dirt road back to the car so I could be alone. I pulled my cell phone out, found Pastor Reid's number, and stared at the screen for a few minutes. He did say I could call anytime.... But what if he were just saying that to be polite? I shouldn't bother him on a Saturday, but the face of the spirit flashing through my mind was making me uneasy. His leering grin and wink was all I could see. I finally worked up the nerve to call.

"Hello?" a woman answered.

"Hello...is this Pastor Reid's number? This is Kristen Kaplan."

"Oh, hi, sweetie. It's Bryn."

"Hi, Mrs. Reid. I thought I was calling Pastor Reid's cell. I'm a little confused."

"Please call me Bryn. You called our house phone."

"I'm sorry, I hope I'm not bothering you."

"No, not at all. Let me get him."

"Thank you." I waited in silence, thinking about what I might confess first and how he might react to what I was about to say.

"Hello?"

"Hi, Pastor Reid. I hope this isn't a bad time. If it is, I can talk to you tomorrow after church."

"No, not at all, what's going on? You doing okay?"

"Um, yes and no. The spirit of depression tried to come back. I did what you said and it left."

"Well, praise God!"

"Yeah, but there's something else we haven't talked about yet, and I'm kind of afraid to bring it up because I don't want you to think I'm...well...I don't want you to think I'm crazy, but it's really bothering me now."

"Well, if it's something you need handled right away you are more than welcome to come by and we can talk."

We agreed to meet up that evening.

Nervousness filled me as I drove to the church. I told my mom I had another counseling session, and, of course, she was all for it. When I walked into the office, we all hugged and greeted each other, the gesture no longer odd to me.

"What's going on?" Pastor Reid asked, taking his seat.

Bryn and I followed suit.

"Well," I paused for a moment, working up the nerve to continue. "From time to time...I see things."

"Like what?"

"Um, well, spirits."

His expression was unreadable. He shook his head as though something had been confirmed.

"Before, I would only see them in the dark, and now, as of this morning, I saw one in broad daylight. It's just really messing with my mind. I haven't been able to shake the image all day. Do you believe me?"

"Yes, of course." He leaned forward, resting his arms on the desk.

"Do you think I'm crazy?"

"Absolutely not!" Bryn exclaimed. "We've heard of people being able to see into the supernatural realm."

"The supernatural realm?"

"Yes. You see, there's a natural realm, which is this tangible earth that we can see, feel, taste, and smell," Pastor Reid said. "Then there's the supernatural realm, which is beyond what most human eyes can see. A lot of witches, warlocks, and Voodoo priests operate in this realm."

My eyes widened. "You mean all that stuff is real? Like real witches casting spells?"

"Absolutely. Then there's also the spirit realm. A spirit is conjured up out of the spirit realm by a medium or witch, and it is given access to the supernatural realm. This is where you see them. In some cases, they can appear in the natural realm whenever they want to be seen by man. Your enhanced sight is part of the gift that God's given you."

This felt more like a curse.

"In the Bible, these people were referred to as seers or prophets. You are a prophetess."

"Okay, so, I'm sorry, I'm just trying to process what you said. You're telling me there's an actual name for this other than insanity? A prophetess?"

"Yes. The Bible says that God gave some to be apostles, some to be prophets, some to be pastors, some to be evangelists, and some to be teachers all for the equipping of the saints. This is known as the fivefold ministry gifts. These people are gifts from Christ. My wife is called to be a teacher, and I'm called to be an apostle."

"Apostle," I repeated.

"An apostle is one who builds and sets things in order in the church, but is not limited by that function."

"Oh. Why does Nana call you pastor if you're really an apostle? Is there a difference?"

"Yes, many people are called by God, but some are chosen to be apostles, prophets, pastors, evangelists, or teachers. An apostle can function in any role of the fivefold ministry, however, a pastor cannot. It all has to do with delegated authority from God. There are some people who believe the office of the apostle and prophet don't have a place in our world today. So, if someone calls me pastor, I don't correct them. As the word of God says, we are all called to be preachers of the gospel. But if someone were to ask, I would tell them I'm an apostle."

"Oh."

"And God made you a seer prophetess. Now He is equipping you with discernment."

"What's discernment?"

"The gift of discerning of spirits is just that—a gift from God. This gift is essential for a seer and will not only help you judge if a spirit is good or evil, but will also help you determine the type of spirit. You've always been a prophet, that's why you were able to see into the supernatural realm before being saved. The Bible says gifts are without repentance, meaning you can function as a prophet without ever giving your life to the Lord. That's how false prophets come into play. So, when you tap into the prophetic before salvation, you're likely following a spirit other than the Holy Spirit. This is also true of Christians who veer away from the word of God. That is why exercising the gifts of the Holy Spirit are so important. The gift of discerning of spirits is one of the gifts of the Holy Spirit given after salvation. Look at a medium, for instance. Maybe he or she is a seer prophet, but is letting demonic spirits operate through them. This is the opposite of the Lord's plan, which results in allowing evil spirits to empower. They think they're contacting the dead, when they're actually entertaining familiar spirits who disguise themselves as deceased loved ones."

"Maybe?"

"What was that?"

"You said maybe. So, people can see these spirits even if they're not a seer ?"

"Yes. It's called a third eye. You have to realize that this is all spiritual, so the person doesn't actually have a third eye that is being opened. The evil spirit is just simply counterfeiting the Holy Spirit's natural function by empowering the person to see beyond their natural eyes."

"Wow, I had no idea. I guess they don't, either," I chuckled. "That's crazy. So I could've easily become like them? A psychic or a medium, I mean."

"Yes. They have different spirit guides they use, usually indigenous people or children."

I immediately thought of the Native American man I saw in Long Island and the little girl from my dreams. "I've seen both."

"Really?"

"Yeah, I saw a Native American man in Long Island when I was out there visiting family. It scared the crap out of me. And I keep having the same dream about this little girl. But she's not a little girl. She always goes crazy and pushes me down this hole."

"Do you mind telling me about the dream?"

"It's always the same. I'm in the woods and I'm barefoot, standing on this dirt road. It's like a pathway. I see this little girl. She runs away and I run after her, but I lose her and stop when I hit this deep hole in the ground. That's when she appears behind me and pushes me in."

"It's a familiar spirit. Now, when you chase her, are you still on that dirt road?"

"No, I end up in the forest somewhere."

"The dirt road represents the path the Lord has predestined for you, but that spirit wants you to deviate from it so you'll end up lost and depressed. That's what the hole represents."

"Wow. It all makes so much sense now."

"You said you saw something this morning?"

"Yes, he was in my mother's mirror. He didn't exactly look like a person. He reminded me of the joker. It really freaked me out because I saw him in the daylight."

As he sat deep in thought, a glow of light emerged, shinning outward from his body.

"The spirit you saw is a mocking spirit. He's just trying to scare you."

My eyes quickly darted to Pastor Reid's face. I forced myself not to look away from his gaze.

"Well, it's working," I said, half-distracted.

"It definitely sounds as though the Lord is opening up your gift. It could be that He will allow you to see them in the daytime now, or it could have been a one-time thing." He paused and the light instantly sucked itself back into his body. "I've heard of seer prophets, but I don't know too much about their gifting. I'll pray about it and see what the Lord says. But you shouldn't be fearful. God has not given you a spirit of fear; he has given you a spirit of power, love, and a sound mind. If you see it again, tell it to go in Jesus's name. Okay?"

"Okay," I said, unsure it would be that easy. "You said there are people like me in the Bible?"

"Daniel, Samuel, Abraham, Moses, Ezekiel…. They were all prophets."

"What exactly does it mean to be a prophet?"

"A prophet is someone who hears directly from the Lord to give encouragement, correction, and admonishment to the people of God. You have been a prophetess before the foundation of the world. He was just waiting for the day you were born. You were always predestined to be a prophetess, but you must first be disciplined in the things of God. You must be taught the foundations before you can operate in the office of the prophet."

"And I'm a seer?"

"Yes. A seer is a type of prophet. They mostly refer to seer prophets in the Old Testament. Although a seer operates in the gift of discernment, not all people who see in other realms are seers. Are you understanding what I'm saying?"

"Um, kind of, it's just a lot. To hear you say these things—that I'm anything remotely close to being like those guys in the Bible—well, it's just crazy. I've always seen myself on the street, being homeless."

"That was the enemy's plan for you. But the Lord has a greater plan. There's greatness in you."

I just stared at him in disbelief as I tried to process exactly what all this meant. I came up short.

"I know it's a lot to take in right now, but don't worry, you'll get it. Just keep reading your Bible. That's what you need to focus on right now. Have you been reading what I told you to?"

I shook my head. "I forgot."

"You've got to read your Bible. You're a babe in Christ now, so it's like being a newborn again. You have to relearn everything, naturally and spiritually. The word of God is your sustenance. A baby can't survive without milk, right?"

"Yeah."

"The Bible will give you nutrients and help you grow to be healthy. Remember to read your Bible."

21

Tormenting Spirits

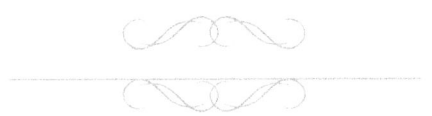

That night, I did like Apostle Reid said and read my Bible. I started in John and read about all the miracles Jesus preformed—healing the sick, the lame, and the blind. After reading about His love and compassion, I felt comfortable enough to sleep in my own bed with my nightlight on, although, I wasn't sure how much help it would be. As I was drifting off, I felt the presence of someone else in the room. I opened my eyes to see a large creature in the shadows. My heart jumped out of my chest. It was on all fours and reminded me of a reptile, but ram-like horns protruded from its forehead. Its wings were a thick layer of skin, like a bat's, spanning the length of my wall. I gasped and he darted up, disappearing into my ceiling. The last thing I saw was his long reptilian tail, swaying back and forth.

I got out of bed slowly and walked over to the wall. I examined my ceiling. There was nothing. I looked around. My room was exactly as it should have been. Once my heart rate returned to normal, I climbed back into bed. Every few minutes, I opened my eyes to scan the room.

The next day after church, I spoke privately with Apostle Reid. He said the creature I saw in my room was a gargoyle. Apparently, they are watching spirits and this one has taken notice of me. That was a little unnerving, to say the least. Why would this gargoyle want to watch me? I was no one special, definitely not important enough to warrant this type of attention. As if I didn't already have enough to deal with. Why not add a stalker gargoyle to the mix? Apostle Reid encouraged me to write down all the activity happening in my room.

Tuesday, April 17

I woke up at 3:15 a.m. to use the bathroom. Before I even made it out of bed, I saw script handwriting filling my room. I tried to make out what it said, but couldn't. It looked like it was in another language. Then after a few minutes, it was gone.

Later, I was sitting in the sunroom reading my Bible after school when I saw Kate, the spirit I saw before I blacked out on the balcony. She wore the same white linen and stood by the gazebo out back, just past the garden. I put my Bible down and stood up to get a better look, but in the blink of an eye, she was gone.

I was a bit worried, especially because of what happened last time she appeared. I couldn't even remember how or when I fell into the trance. That scared me more than anything. It was like going to a magic show and being hypnotized. I never gave it much thought before, but now I wonder if hypnosis was also demonic. I wonder if spirits like her were lurking behind the scenes, putting all those people under trances. Before, it would've been crazy to think something like that could happen, but nothing seems far-fetched anymore.

Wednesday, April 18

I was sitting on my bed around 7:00 p.m. when I saw Kate standing in my doorway. Her back was facing me and all I could see was her long, flowing hair. I was so afraid I might fall under her trance again that I called Apostle Reid. I put my phone on speaker and he began praying. She turned around to face me. I remembered the first time I saw this spirit and how unbelievably beautiful she was. She looked like a goddess. Her garments were radiant and glorious, depicting majesty and goodness. Even now, they looked the same. Her face, however, was comprised of large wrinkles, and she had the nose of an elephant's trunk. I jumped in horror. She was hideous old woman. It seems as if I'm now able to see these spirits as they really are, not how they want to be seen. Apostle Reid continued to pray until she vanished into thin air.

Thursday, April 19

Around 5 a.m. this morning I woke up and opened my eyes to see a flounder fish swimming up my wall like an animated stencil drawing. Instant amazement hit me. I watched him intently. Immediately after, another flounder followed and then a school of tiny fish followed after that. I just laid there watching fish swim up my wall. I thought about Chelsea and wondered if she'd seen anything like this before.

Tonight I was sitting on my bed doing homework. Thirty minutes in, boredom took hold and I decided to play with some new eye shadow colors. Through the reflection, I noticed my door was ajar. A spirit wearing a bright white cloak stood in the doorway, his face obscured by a hood. I didn't know what to make of him. The hairs on my arms suddenly rose and an odd feeling took over my body. That's when I realized he wasn't good. It wasn't until I reached for my cell phone that I noticed I was shaking. I called Apostle Reid. He prayed and the demon finally disappeared.

Saturday, April 21

Around 3:00 a.m. this morning, I was awakened by these small creatures wreaking havoc in my bedroom. They were bouncing off my walls. They looked like hairless Chihuahuas, but they could walk on their hind legs. One jumped up to my ceiling and began rattling my light fixtures. It was so early and I was too drowsy, so I just rolled over and went back to sleep. Later, Apostle Reid told me they were Nymphs, lower-ranking demons.

I'd had enough of the craziness. I wanted to get away from it all. So I was more than happy when my family and I took a road trip up to the Fields of the Wood Bible Park up in northern Georgia. The park had replicas of some of the major landmarks Jesus visited in Jerusalem. Mom rented a minivan so we would have room to stretch out in back.

"Did you read the instructions?" my mom asked Aunt Bridgette.

"It should work like any other GPS," Aunt Bridgette answered. "Maybe it just needs to charge for a little bit."

"Do you want me to start driving?" Mom asked.

"Yeah, we can head toward Hwy 20." Aunt Bridgette examined the GPS. "I don't get it, you'd think it would light up or something."

"Let Kristen look at it, maybe she can figure it out," my mom suggested.

Aunt Bridgette unplugged the GPS and handed it back to me.

I pressed the power button and it turned on in a matter of seconds.

Nana started laughing hysterically.

"You mean to tell me you didn't turn the darn thing on?" Nana asked Aunt Bridgette.

"I didn't know you had to turn it on."

"You know what, I think I'll stay here where it's safe."

"Nonsense, Mom. It will be smooth sailing from now on," Aunt Bridgette said. "Now, how do you put the address in this thing?"

I ended up putting the address in the GPS, but at least we were finally on our way. I was exhausted from the night before, so I promptly fell asleep. An hour or so later, jostling woke me. I figured we had reached our destination, as we were no longer on the freeway. Three U-turns quickly put me in check.

"Where are we?" I asked.

"We're lost, thanks to frick and frack up there," Nana answered.

"We are not lost, we're just a bit turned around," Aunt Bridgette was driving now.

"That's what people say when they're lost," Nana replied.

"Hey, Aunt Bridgette, the car sounds a little weird. Are you sure you have it in the right gear?" I asked.

"Of course, it's in drive. Wait…why are there two drives?"

"Lord Jesus help us," Nana replied.

After another thirty minutes of being turned around—but driving in the correct gear—we finally made it to our destination. We walked to the top of one of the highest mountains in the park. As I stood looking over the horizon, I couldn't believe that my Father in heaven had created all of what I was staring at now. His spirit was living inside of me. The beautiful scenery made me feel close to Him. It was exactly what I needed. But I still couldn't get away from my thoughts. How could the Lord expect me to live up to the prophets in the Bible? I know Jesus said that we would do greater works than He did on this earth because He was going to be with the Father. I couldn't see how that would be possible since He did some amazing things. I wished I could see myself as Apostle Reid saw me, but all I could see was little old me.

We walked the small park and ate lunch at one of the empty benches. Now all we had to do was find our way home.

* * *

Sunday, April 22

Early this morning, something appeared in my room. I sat up in my bed, watching it move fluidly. Then it was right in front of me. No matter how much I wanted to look away, I couldn't. The spirit was clear as water, rippling as it moved. It began spinning clockwise. Was I really seeing this? It held me captive for a moment, but then it was gone. I crawled out of bed and went to use the bathroom. While washing my hands, I looked in the mirror and noticed my eye sockets were a deep crimson, like they had been burned. I went back to sleep and when I woke up, they were back to normal. Had I imaged the whole thing?

After church, I was in my room listening to Maroon 5 when all of a sudden the hairs on the back of my neck stood up. I spun around and came face-to-face with an army of demons. I was able to see into another dimension, as if the wall was no longer there. Their faces resembled a raccoon's, but their bodies were birdlike. The biggest one was perched on top of my chest of drawers. I could feel their hatred radiating through the room, which terrified me. I was grossly outnumbered. There had to be at least a hundred of these creatures. I tried to rebuke them, but it wasn't working. I sunk to the floor and curled up into a ball, crying hysterically with my hands on either side of my head, rocking back and forth. I finally called Apostle Reid. After a few minutes of him praying, the attacks ceased.

Tuesday, April 24

Around 3:15 a.m. I woke up from a nightmare to see a huge hole in my wall. I stared at it for a while as the inside spun counterclockwise. Too freaked out to deal with any more of this, I threw back the covers and slept in Mom's room.

* * *

I had to get some clarity, so I called Apostle Reid.

"Any thoughts on what the spinning circle in my wall might be?" I asked.

"It sounds like a portal," Apostle Reid said.

"A portal?"

"It's like a door for spirits to travel from one realm to another."

"Why would there be a portal in my room?"

"I'm not sure, but I'll definitely be praying for the Lord to reveal exactly what's going on. But there does seem to be some consistency here."

"Consistency?"

"A lot of your experiences have been happening during the three o'clock hour—the witching hour."

"The witching hour?"

"It's the time of night that a lot of witches and warlocks practice their craft, but they're not limited to that one hour."

"That's interesting, I had no idea." Not to mention creepy.

"Like I said, I'll have to pray about it and see what the Lord reveals."

Thursday, April 26

Last night I was woken up to find the hooded demon spirit in my room. This time I could see his eyes. They reminded me of a Siberian husky's—piercing. He didn't stay long, but the look he gave scared me to death. And then early this morning, I saw another portal after I woke up from yet another nightmare.

Also:

Octopus spirits spewing microscopic germs at the doctor's office

Giant sitting in my room playing with my nightlight

I'm so sick of this crap.

22

Speaking in What?

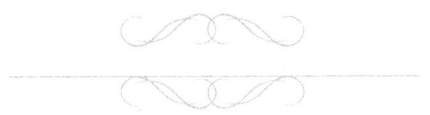

"Have you heard anything from the Lord about what all this might be yet?" I asked Apostle Reid.

"No, not yet, but as soon as I get something, I will definitely let you know. Have you been writing everything down that's been happening?"

"Not everything, but only because it's too much. Something's happening every night, sometimes multiple times. I thought everything was supposed to be happy and sunny after giving your life to the Lord."

"Not everyone's walk is the same. But the Lord gave you joy, and you can't let the enemy steal that."

All I could think about was all those sleepless nights, waking up to chaos in my room, and all the stupid spirits that were to blame.

"So, you gonna let the enemy steal your joy?"

I shrugged. "I don't know." I tried to hold it together as best as I could, but I couldn't help but wonder if this was how it would be from now on.

"Don't let the enemy steal your peace. You hear me?"

A lump clogged my throat and the tears began to flow. The feeling of defeat took over. I was exhausted from sleep deprivation.

"I can't do this anymore! It's too much. I mean, it wouldn't be so bad if I could just sleep through all of this, but I can't. Every time I fall asleep, something wakes me. If it's not a spirit, it's a nightmare. I feel like I'm going crazy. I don't know if I'm really seeing what I'm seeing because it's so bizarre." I tried to calm myself down, but it was no use. "I don't want this gift anymore! I want Him to take it away."

Bryn handed me some tissues.

"Thank you. I'm just so tired. I just…I can't do this anymore," I said softly, looking at the floor.

"The Lord will never give you more than you can handle. Everything you go through is a lesson. And right now, He is teaching you that you are stronger than you think."

I shook my head, wondering why he couldn't see how tired I was. Clearly, I was not strong enough to do this. It had to be a mistake. Maybe the Lord had gotten me confused with another Kristen. "But I'm not. I can't do this."

"Yes you can. And I don't want you using that word anymore."

"What word?" I sniffed.

"Can't. I don't want to hear you say it again. You can. The Lord has made you who you are because He knows you can handle everything the enemy tries to throw at you. He's just letting this happen so you'll see you can handle it. Jesus said that we have the power to trample the enemy under our feet, and that includes you."

As he spoke, the bright glow that shone out of him grew brighter and brighter.

"But I'm just little old me. Maybe He's getting me confused with someone else?"

"The Bible says that the Lord knows the numbers of hairs on your head, so no, He is not confusing you with someone else. But it's not about you. That's what you have to realize. It has nothing to do with you and your abilities. It's the Holy Spirit inside that does all the work. It doesn't matter how tall, short, skinny, pretty, or smart you are. None of that matters to God. What He cares about is your willingness to do His will. It's about obedience. Have you been reading your Bible?"

"Yes." I wiped the last of my tears away.

"Have you read about when Jesus was baptized?"

"Um, yeah. That's when the dove came and God said He was pleased with Jesus, right?"

"Right. It was actually the Holy Spirit in the form of a dove. Many believers—leaders in particular—teach about being baptized with water, but few teach about being baptized with the Holy Spirit. Being baptized with the Holy Spirit gives you power, the same power that raised Jesus from the grave. It's essential to this walk. Have you ever heard about people speaking in tongues?"

"Yeah, but I never really thought any of that was real. I don't really see how that's possible."

"That's because it's not something you can figure out with your mind. Let me ask you a question. Are you saved?"

"Yes."

"How do you know?"

I shrugged. "I dunno."

"You know because of your faith. Your faith tells you you're saved. It's the same faith you use to speak in the tongues of angels or to rebuke demons and heal the sick."

"Tongues of angels?"

"Yes. When you speak in this heavenly language, although we may not know what we're saying, the angels do. And the Bible says the angels harken unto our words. Speaking in tongues also helps build our inner-most faith, and I think that's what you need. It's also evidence that you've been baptized with the Holy Spirit."

"Oh."

"Would you like to be baptized with the Holy Spirit?"

I thought carefully for a moment. If this was going to help me get a good night's sleep, I would try anything.

"Okay. Yes, I want to."

Both Apostle Reid and Bryn stood up and laid their hands on me. I saw the same white light shining out of Bryn. They began praying in a language that I'd never heard before.

"Raise your hands," Apostle Reid said.

I had no idea what they were saying, but as their praying intensified, I could feel something in my stomach churning. That's when Bryn put one hand on my torso.

"Holy Spirit, fill her with your power," Apostle Reid said.

At this point, my whole body felt foreign. Something was trying to escape from my stomach up my esophagus and out my mouth. I held it back, unsure of what it might be.

"It's there, just let it out."

How did he know? I held on to it. How was any of this possible? Why was this happening?

"Just let it go. It doesn't matter how it sounds. Stop letting your mind get in the way."

This time, I listened. Very quietly, the words came out. I had no idea what I had said, but I did it. They finally stopped praying and had me try it a couple more times.

"Praise God!" they both exclaimed.

"Make sure you continue to pray in your heavenly language. Try doing it for a little while before you go to bed."

"Okay."

"Is everything all right?" Bryn asked.

"Yes, it's just that I keep seeing this bright white light. It's shinning out of you two."

They both looked at each other.

"Can you see it?" I asked.

They shook their heads.

"Do you know what it might be?" Apostle Reid asked.

I shrugged.

"Describe what you see," he urged with growing curiosity.

I stood back and focused on Apostle Reid. The light grew brighter until it came out completely and stood next to him. Upon closer inspection, I could see it was made up of multiple colors like a prism. Although the light was in Apostle Reid's form, it had no defining features like eyes, a nose, or a mouth. It was only a figure in the shape of his silhouette, but it was beautiful. Then the light disappeared back into Apostle Reid.

"The light is in the shape of you and was standing by your side."

"Was?"

"It went back inside you. I don't think it's evil." I glanced down at my arms. No chills. "I don't feel weird, either."

"What do you mean?"

"When a spirit is evil, I get the same feeling that comes over my body and the hair on my arms rise."

"Just like in the book of Job. The same thing happens when a demonic spirit is present. One of Job's friends describes that very same thing while being in the presence of an evil spirit."

"Seriously? That's so crazy."

"Do you think you're seeing the Holy Spirit?"

At that moment, I saw the light shining once again. "I can see the Holy Spirit."

That night, I didn't get home until after ten o'clock. When I walked through the front door, my mom was standing at the top of the staircase.

"Hi," she whispered.

"Hey. How long have you been standing there?"

"A few minutes. I had a feeling you'd be home soon."

"That's not creepy."

"Can you do me a favor, please? Can you go into the kitchen and get me one of those handy snacks? I'll be in my room."

She was waiting for me, sitting on her bed. I climbed in and handed her the snack. She opened the package and began applying cheese to one of the four crackers. "So, what's been going on? I feel like we've only seen each other in passing for the last couple weeks."

"Mom, I saw you at dinner last night."

"Yeah, but we haven't really talked in a while. I have no idea what's going on with you these days. How's Neil doing?" She stuck a cracker in her mouth.

"I wouldn't really know."

"I can't hear you. I keep missing every other word. I think it's my chewing."

"Well, stop eating for a few seconds. It's after ten and you're eating cheese and crackers."

"What crawled up your butt and died?"

"Sorry. It's just that I'm tired and confused and frustrated because I'm not sure what I should do. It's not right for me to have him put his life on hold. And I don't know if I can handle the added stress right now. It's just too much."

"Maybe you two should take a break from each other if it's stressing you out. You look awful, like you haven't been getting any sleep. You must really be cramming for your finals."

Well, she was halfway right.

"I'll be fine, Mom," I said, getting up. "Goodnight."

"Night, Krissy Wissy. Oh, hon, can you please throw this away?" She dangled her trash.

I took it downstairs and tossed it in the garbage can. Suddenly, I heard a faint giggle behind me. I turned to see who it was, but saw nothing. I searched the kitchen for anything out of the ordinary. Maybe I was just hearing things. I turned the kitchen light off and walked through the hallway to the stairs. I was about to take the first step when I looked up and saw a little girl standing at the top. I gasped. She ducked down behind the banister as if she were playing hide and seek. I stood there, frozen. She skipped off toward my room. *Great.* I took the steps one by one and made it to the top. She was nowhere in sight. I walked into my room and turned on the light. My cell phone rang, scaring me half to death. I shut my door and headed for my bed, retrieving it from my purse.

"Hello?"

"Hi. You weren't asleep, were you?"

"Hi. No, I wasn't asleep." There was an awkward silence. "Neil?"

"Yeah?"

"I don't think this is going to work."

"Am I calling too late?"

"No, it's not that. It's just that we can't make this work long distance."

"I'm sorry if I've been working too much. I know we haven't spoken in a while, but we can figure something out."

I shook my head.

"Hello?" Neil said.

"No, Neil, I don't think we can fix this right now. I feel awful that you're missing out on things you should be enjoying, like going to parties and prom."

"I don't care about any of that stuff."

"Maybe not now, but you'll regret it one day. I don't want to be the reason you miss out on things. You're not even talking to other girls at school."

"Well, I mean, I wouldn't say that. Wait a minute, how did you know that?"

"Avery told me."

"I should have known. Well, what's the big deal with that? I thought you wanted me to stay away from the vultures."

"I changed my mind. It's not fair to you and I really can't handle the extra stress right now."

"Why, what's going on?"

"Neil, it's awful," I began crying. "Everything's heightened and sometimes I feel like I'm going crazy. I've been seeing demons and they torment me. It's not contained to nighttime, either. I see them during the day. I'm just so tired. I haven't slept well in weeks. I can't handle what I've been going through and our relationship at the same time. It's too much. I'm sorry."

"Kristen, no," he said adamantly.

"This isn't up for discussion. I really am sorry, but I just can't do this anymore. I think this will be better for both of us."

"Why do you get to choose what's good for both of us. What about what I want?"

"What do you want, Neil? Is this really working for you? We barely talk now."

"I'm sorry for that."

"Please, stop apologizing. It's not one-sided. It's me, too. If I weren't so…if only I were different, then…. It's just a lot right now." I didn't even know what I was trying to say.

"I wish I was there to help you somehow."

We both sat in silence.

"So this is what you want?" he finally asked.

I sighed. "Yes."

"All right then, I guess I'll have to let you go."

We sat there a few more minutes and said our goodbyes. After ending things, I lay in my bed for hours, wondering if I had done the right thing. One by one, the tears continued to roll. Somewhere along the way, I managed to fall asleep.

The next morning, I woke up at 5:30 a.m. from yet another nightmare. I sat up slowly in my bed, not taking my eyes off the demon in front of me. I was about to make a dash for the door when I saw another one. I froze. A third demon appeared by the bay window. I was surrounded; I had to think quickly.

My thoughts ran rampant, but I could hear Apostle Reid's voice telling me to pray in the tongues of angels. I decided I would give it a try. The demons came out of the walls and came straight for me, but I kept praying.

That's when it happened.

Bright white beams of light ran vertically down my walls and began turning into bars. At that moment, some kind of force pulled the demons back into the walls they came out of. They were now stuck behind the bars. I was so shocked I didn't even realize I had stopped praying. That's when the bars disappeared and once again, they were free. I immediately started praying and, like before, the bars materialized and sucked the demons behind them. I kept praying this time, focused on the demon in front of me. That's when I saw a huge wing appear behind the demon.

The angel's image was very faint. The demon turned to face it. The other demons were in a standoff with other angels as well. And then, just like that, they all disappeared. I didn't know what the heck I was saying, but the angels did. Apostle Reid was right. From that moment on, I made the decision to always pray in my prayer language.

Later that evening, Apostle Reid and his wife were hosting a movie night for the teens at their house. It was a way for us all to get to know one another. Everyone was in the family room with Apostle Reid while I was in the kitchen helping Bryn.

"What's wrong, dear?" she asked.

"Oh, nothing. I'm fine."

"It doesn't look like you're fine," Apostle Reid said, walking up behind me.

I jumped a little in my seat.

"Sorry," he smiled. "What's going on?"

"It's nothing, really, I'm fine." I tried to force a smile.

"You know, I may not be able to see things the way you do, but the Lord still reveals things to me. I know something is bothering you. What is it?"

"Well," I paused, "I broke up with my boyfriend last night. He's in California and I'm out here. I was feeling bad because it felt like he was putting his life on hold for me and it was stressing me out knowing that. With all the attacks that have been happening lately, it was just getting to be too much. But now I'm not sure I made the right decision. He was the only thing in my life that really made me feel complete, and now that's gone. I don't really know how to explain it."

"We understand what you're saying," Bryn said.

"Kristen, the Lord is removing everything that has been a distraction. That's why he moved you all the way out to Georgia away from everything and everyone that's been holding you back. You see, everyone thinks of

God as being full of grace and mercy—a loving God. He is all of those things, but He's also a jealous God. And He doesn't want anything to be put before Him. God wants you to give Him the part of your heart that you've given to—"

"Neil."

"Right. When you are ready, He will share that piece of your heart with whomever He's entrusted it to. Whether that's Neil or not, I don't know. But you have to trust that the Lord will work everything out for your good. Sometimes He has us do things that we don't understand, and it may seem unfair or unclear at times, but it's all for the betterment of ourselves. Right now, you should be focusing on getting to know Jesus. That is the relationship you should be developing. Okay?"

It was the total opposite of what I wanted to hear. Why couldn't he have just lied to make me feel good?

"Okay," I said, reluctantly.

Over the past few years, the void of happiness has become more prevalent. Yes, I was guilty of trying to fill it with things, but that never worked. It didn't matter how many pairs of Jimmy Choos I bought, it still couldn't fill that void. Even trying to fill it with Neil didn't work. Of course, I felt better when I was with him. But now that we were no longer together, it became clear that our relationship was still only a temporary fix. Maybe that's what the Lord has been trying to show me. Apostle Reid said I needed to give that part of my heart to the Lord and He would fill it. Maybe that was the key. True, I was the one who broke things off with Neil, but it didn't matter because we were still separated. He was 3,000 miles away and there was nothing I could do about it. No matter how much I resisted, no matter how much I ran from the Lord, He was always with me. He never left me, even though I rejected Him over and over. If I gave the Lord my heart, He would fill it. He'd never leave me or turn His back on me. I would be forever whole. I'd finally be happy. The thought made me smile.

"Have you met some of the other teens yet?"

My smile turned into a frown. "Um, no. Not yet."

"Let me introduce you."

"Ah, I don't think—"

He grabbed my hand and pulled me into the family room. "Everyone, this is Kristen."

"Hi," I said awkwardly.

Everyone greeted me.

"She moved here from California and is new to the ministry. Kristen, this is Jordan, Chris, Patrick, and Vanessa."

I looked at Apostle Reid and tried to make my way back to the kitchen. He grabbed my shoulders and spun me around toward the group. He gave me a firm push in their direction. I took the hint and sat down on the same couch as Jordan. She was a slender girl with dark brown hair as straight as corn silk. Her welcoming eyes were a deep chocolate brown.

"It's Kristen, right?"

"Yeah."

"So, you go to Eastside?"

"Um, yeah."

"I go there, too. I've seen you a couple times. I was looking for you Friday at lunch. I didn't know if you wanted to eat together."

"Oh, well, I leave at lunch, that's why you couldn't find me. I'm only taking a few classes in the morning."

"Wow, that's cool. Must be nice. So, you're from Cali? Which part?"

"Los Angeles. Well, Long Beach, actually."

"Do you know Snoop Dogg?" she asked.

"No."

"Do you know Usher?" Patrick butted in, asking Jordan.

He was apparently eavesdropping on our conversation. His skin was a deep cocoa, with chiseled facial features like an international model. His sense of style was like nothing I'd ever seen, but it totally worked for him.

He wore a forest green shirt with long faded camouflage shorts. His combat boots had bright yellow shoe laces that were left untied.

Jordan rolled her eyes.

"Please excuse her, she sometimes has problems conversatin' with people," he said, flashing a perfect smile.

"I hate it when you say that," she seethed.

"What?" Patrick asked.

"Conversate is not a word…it's converse."

"You're wrong."

"So why did you move out here?" Jordan asked, ignoring him.

"My mom. My grandmother lives out here. We're staying with her."

"How long have you been out here?" he asked.

"Not long. Almost a month."

"Do you like it?"

"It's different."

Patrick leaned forward, his eyes fixated on mine. "I just wanted you to know that you are the most beautiful girl I've ever seen in my life."

I was speechless.

Jordan rolled her eyes and gave him a look of pity.

"You might just be my wife," he said, slowly sitting back, not breaking his gaze.

I looked down at my ring, fidgeting with it, completely mortified.

"Ignore him. He thinks every pretty girl he meets may be his wife."

"That's not true," Patrick insisted.

"You can't even have a simple conversation with a pretty girl without declaring your love for her."

"I never did that with you."

"Yes you did, until I made it clear that it was never going to happen."

"Oh, right."

"Have you lived here long?" I asked.

"No. I moved here with my family from Michigan a few years ago. But Vanessa has." Jordan pointed toward the girl sitting on the far end of the same couch Patrick was on. "She's lived here her whole life."

"Oh."

"We should hang out sometime. Maybe go to Stonecrest or something."

"What's that?"

"It's the closest mall."

I wondered if she meant the mall we passed coming from the airport. It didn't even have a Nordstrom. What a waste. "Yeah, maybe."

We exchanged numbers, then joined in with the others.

Although I was physically present, my mind was still thinking about the conversation I had in the kitchen. I decided to follow Apostle Reid's instructions and focus on my relationship with the Lord. Why not? Everything else he's suggested up to this point has worked.

23

Knowing

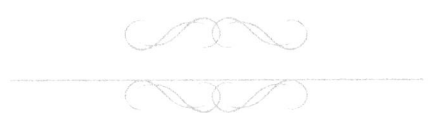

Monday, I picked Jordan and Patrick up from school and we went to the mall.

"I still can't believe that is your car," Jordan said. "I wish I could have a car like that."

"So, are you rich or something?" Patrick asked.

"My dad bought it for me. He has money."

"He must have an awful lot if he bought you a $100,000 car. I can't even get a Tic Tac from my parents," he mused.

"So this is the mall," I said.

"Yup."

"Do they have a Bloomingdale's here, or a Nordstrom?"

"No. You have to go to Lenox or Perimeter for those stores," Jordan responded.

"Oh."

"We should drive out there one day. In your car, though, 'cause that's a better look," Patrick suggested.

"How are you just going to offer up someone else's car to go somewhere?" Jordan asked.

"How far away is it?" I asked.

"About forty-five minutes without traffic," he said.

"That's not so bad."

We entered the cool confines of the mall, leisurely walking alongside the stores.

"So, have you guys been going to this church for long?"

"I have for about a year now," Patrick answered, distracted by his phone.

"What about you, Jordan?"

"Not too long, it's been a couple months." She suddenly smiled.

"What?"

"Nothing, I was just thinking to myself. I met Apostle and Mrs. Reid in Ingles. It's a grocery store. They just came up and started talking to me. I work there. They gave me their card and told me where the church was. I called them asking for prayers one day, and, the next thing you know, I started going to church. They're good people. You don't come across too many people like them. I'd been to that church before with my mom, but back then, a different pastor led the church. There were a lot more people who attended at the time, as well."

"So what happened?"

"The pastor died, and that's when Apostle Reid came along. I guess it was around the time I started attending again. Most of the older people left, along with some other families. I guess they were just used to the old pastor, I don't know. Patrick and his family have been at the church through the whole thing. He could probably tell you better than I can."

We both glanced back at Patrick, who was a few steps behind us, still preoccupied with his phone.

I was a little curious as to why so many people had left the church, but, then again, it didn't matter because I was seeing a change in my life.

"It's working for me. Hey, I haven't seen your mom at church the last couple Sundays."

"My grandmother found another church, so my mom and aunt have been going with her."

"Hey, pretty thang, you want some candy?"

Jordan and I both turned back to see Patrick chatting up some girl.

"Patrick, leave her alone," Jordan warned.

"What? I was just asking her a question."

The caramel-skinned girl giggled. Patrick jogged to catch up with us.

"Get saved, Patrick," Jordan teased.

"I am. Look, please don't take her seriously," he said. "I'm just admiring God's creation, that's all."

"So are you going to start going to the church your mom goes to?"

"I like where I am. It seems to be working for me, too." I smiled. "What else is there to do around here?"

For the rest of the day we shopped and talked. After dropping Jordan and Patrick off, I heard a quiet voice that told me to slow down. It was a small voice, but stern. I reduced my speed. Then a few minutes later, I passed a cop who was sitting on the side of the road with his radar gun out. *Wow, that's odd.*

Later that evening, I was searching for my cell phone that had somehow disappeared. I tore apart the house but came up short. That's when I heard that same voice tell me to go look in my car under the passenger seat. I was skeptical at first, but quickly remembered what happened earlier with the cop. I went outside to look in my car and, sure enough, there it was, sitting under the passenger seat. How did it get under there?

* * *

That Wednesday after Bible study, I told Apostle Reid and Bryn about what happened.

"That was the Holy Spirit talking to you," Apostle Reid said. "The Bible says He is there to lead, guide, and comfort us. And that's not just on spiritual matters, but in all things, even if it's something as small as a misplaced cell phone."

"Cool. I had no idea. I just wish I would have found out about all this a long time ago. My life would have been so much easier."

"Everything happens for a reason."

I froze in my seat. My mind went back to the conversation I had with Neil my first day in Georgia. He had said the same thing.

"We don't know why things happen the way they do, but God does. He knows everything from the beginning to the end. It wasn't by coincidence that everything happened to you the way it did. It was all in preparation for this moment. You now possess tools that you'll use later when you're ministering the word of God to others, just like I am to you right now."

My right eyebrow raised. "Me?"

"Yes, you. Soon you'll be able to talk to someone who was once where you were. You can show them you made it through, and they can, too. As believers, we are all called to be ministers of the Gospel of Jesus Christ. We all have the ministry of reconciliation—the ministry of bringing God's lost back to Him."

"I don't know if I can do that."

"Of course you can. It's part of who you are, whether you realize it or not. It won't happen overnight, of course, but you'll begin to see. I have an assignment for you. Sometime this week, I want you to tell one person that Jesus loves them."

A feeling of panic set in. I wasn't at all talkative or outgoing when it came to public speaking, or even speaking one on one.

"One person," he smiled. "I know it hasn't been easy for you, but, unfortunately, this walk isn't easy. You know I am extremely Godly proud of you and the growth you've shown in the short time you've given your life to the Lord. I just want to tell you to keep it up and keep moving forward."

"I don't know, they still laugh at me. And I still get really scared when they appear."

"You're not really fearful, you're just sensing that spirit's presence, and in its presence, there is fear. Next time you feel afraid rebuke that spirit of fear. But let me ask you this: Are you still depressed and thinking of committing suicide?"

"Well, no, but—"

"But nothing. That shows growth. You rebuke the spirit of depression and it leaves, right?"

"Yeah."

"Like I said before, it's the same faith you're using. You just have to go to that next level. You had faith in me telling you to rebuke the spirit of depression, but now you have to know that when you rebuke any spirit, they must go. Not because I said they will, but because the Lord gave you power over all the works of the enemy. Your trust has to be in the Lord, not me. You like fashion, right?"

"That's an understatement, but yeah."

"Your purse...I'm sure it cost a lot of money, right?"

I nodded.

"And you probably have multiple ones from the same designer?"

"Yes."

"If someone came up to you on the street and tried to sell you a purse claiming to be from the same designer, would you buy it?"

"No, of course not. I would be able to spot a fake a mile away."

"Exactly," he said.

"What does a satchel or clutch have to do with faith?"

"My point is that you would not be easily persuaded. The thief is betting that you'll believe what he's selling is real. But because you know beyond all doubt that the purse is a fake, you're not going to buy it. Paul said, 'I know in whom I have believed.' Paul had gone past just believing the word of God; he now knew what the Lord said was true. That's the place where the Lord is taking you."

I was silent for a while, processing all he had just said. It made sense. I suppose I needed to get to that next level in my faith, but I wasn't sure how to get there.

"And it's by choice," Apostle Reid said.

Unquestionably, the Holy Spirit was listening intently to my thoughts and was feeding Apostle Reid the answers to my questions.

"You know, it still kind of creeps me out when you do that," I said.

"You have to choose to know who you are in Christ and who He is in you. You are no different from Jesus when He walked on this earth because He was God in a man's body. You have the Spirit of God in you, and that same power dwells in you. It doesn't matter how long you've been saved. Do you know that there are plenty of believers who have been saved much longer than you who still battle with depression and have to take medication? The key is knowing what you already have. The Bible says if you believe there is one God, then you do well, but even the demons believe and tremble. It's one thing to believe that Jesus loves you because He died for you, but it's a totally different thing to know it. Because then, no one can persuade you otherwise."

Over the next few days, I reflected on everything Apostle Reid told me about believing and knowing. A shiver ran up my spine as I was brought back to the present.

"You know, the contents of that ice box won't change, no matter how long you stand there staring at it."

"Uh? Oh, sorry," I shut the door and walked over to the counter and grabbed an apple from the fruit bowl.

"How are you doing today, Nana?"

"I'm good, despite these old knees of mine."

"Are you going to be working out in the garden today?"

"Yup. I'm headed out there now."

"Can I help?"

"Sure," she said as she examined my face closely. "Humph."

"What is it, Nana?"

"You look different."

"Do I?"

She nodded. "I can't explain it, but you don't look the same to me. Your face seems brighter somehow." She pinched my cheek and we headed outside.

* * *

The days seemed to fly by, and I still hadn't completed my assignment. I was just about to leave school when I saw a girl sitting by herself, probably waiting for her ride. I was so nervous that I almost chickened out. It took me a while before I finally made my way over.

"Hi," I said timidly.

She looked up from the book she was reading and quickly removed her red oval-shaped glasses. "Hello."

"Um, I saw you sitting over here by yourself and I just wanted...um...." My heart was pounding in my chest and my palms were clammy. "I, uh, wanted to come over here and tell you that Jesus loves you."

There, I got it out.

She just stared up at me, bewildered.

"Okay, well, that was all, so…" I turned to leave.

"Wait."

I turned back around.

"Thanks," she said. I could see the tears welling up. "You're going to think I'm crazy, but I was just thinking about how lonely I felt."

My breathing began to slow. "I don't think that's crazy. I'm Kristen." I sat next to her.

"I'm Tricia."

Apostle Reid was right. That wasn't so hard after all. Tricia and I talked until her mother showed up. Surprisingly, we had a lot in common.

Early Friday morning, I was awakened from a nightmare to find gremlin-looking demons in my room. They were grotesque and stood about four feet tall. There were three of them, one by my door, one on the other side of the room by the bay window, and the other standing at the foot of my bed. Still groggy, I sat up to get a better look. I could feel fear coming over me.

"I rebuke you in the name of Jesus," I said softly, my eyes going from one demon to the next.

They began laughing hysterically and pointing at me. That's when I saw the same hooded spirit from before appear in the corner. He just stood there as if he were supervising. I focused back on the gremlin demons.

I began to get angry and I could feel the tears welling up in my eyes. I was tired of the torment. Why was I allowing this to go on? *It's your choice,* I heard in my head.

"That's right. It is my choice," I said quietly to myself. "I choose…I choose…." All of a sudden, it was like something in my brain clicked. "I choose," I laughed to myself. "It's just a choice." It was so simple. How did I not see that before? "I choose! I choose!"

The demons all froze at the same time. The one by my door still had his mouth wide open from laughing, but his facial features were changing into something else that I had never seen before on any of these creatures.

It was fear.

"No more," I said, staring into the eyes of the demon at the foot of my bed. I took a deep breath. "Fear, I cancel your assignment and I rebuke you back to the dry place in Jesus's name."

Immediately, the presence of fear was gone. I was no longer scared. Instead, I felt something different, something I had never felt before. Confidence.

"And as for the rest of you, I clear out this room in the name of Jesus. Go now!"

In an instant, the gremlin demons screamed in agony. Then out of nowhere, all three were consumed with bright flames of fire. I sat there, shocked at what I had just done. I glanced over at the cloaked demon who was also watching them burn. He shook his head in disgust and looked at me with fury in his eyes. He turned away and disappeared into the wall.

I was so excited by my victory, but I waited until Sunday after church to share the news with Apostle Reid and Bryn.

"Praise God!" Bryn shouted.

"That's awesome," Apostle Reid added. "Like I said, you are growing in leaps and bounds, keep it up. I'm especially pleased that you completed your assignment. That is what we rejoice in. Yes, it's exciting when you can cast out a demon, but the most important thing is saving souls, the ministry of reconciliation. It says in the Bible that when one soul is won, all of heaven rejoices. That's what we must follow after."

"I just talked to Tricia like you said to."

"Right, and that led her here where she was able to give her life to the Lord. That is something to rejoice over. You have grown tremendously in this short amount of time."

He was right, I have changed since giving my life to the Lord. And it wasn't superficial, like how Avery had changed, but a life-altering change. It felt so permanent. I couldn't remember how I ever functioned before. From the inside out, I was becoming a new creation, unrecognizable even to my own family.

That night I lay in bed thinking about all the Lord has brought me through in this short period of time. A feeling of peace washed over me. At that moment, it was like my life was flashing before my eyes. I was seeing all the times I felt alone, all the times I cried myself to sleep, all the times I felt like my life was hopeless, and all the times I pretended to be something I wasn't. The Lord revealed that He was there with me the whole time, never straying. I was astonished by the thought that there was hope. There was a purpose for me being here on this earth. I wasn't overlooked or forgotten. Tears of joy rolled down my face. The Lord was showing me He was keeping me safe because He loved me so much and had more planned for me. The feeling was so overwhelming that all I could do was cry as His presence soothed me to sleep.

* * *

Tuesday, after my AP Government final, I lounged out back by the pond under the flowering dogwood, watching the geese on the other side. Just then, the wind picked up and with it came a small bird feather that landed right on my leg. I held it up to my face for a closer look. It was soft to the touch, and its spine seemed so fragile. I wondered how something so tiny and insignificant could totally alter my world as much as it did. The fear was gone. That spirit could no longer project itself on me because I would no longer receive its feelings as my own. I held the feather out in front of me for one last look, then released it to the wind.

I focused on the geese waddling around, picking at the lush earth beneath them. I would be graduating high school in less than a week. I thought about my arrival in Georgia. Though it was only just over month ago, it felt like it had been an eternity. The Bruno Mars song I had kept on repeat my first week here came to my mind. In the song, he says that no religion could save him. About a month ago, I felt the same. I thought for sure there was no one who could help me, or even understand my situation. And I was partially right. There was no religion that could've saved me. I was looking for Jesus, but I was only finding religious beliefs and practices. So, when I finally found Him, it was the love of my Heavenly Father that saved my soul. It was my relationship with my Savior Jesus Christ that kept me daily.

His love is so real and tangible that it warms my innermost being. He saved me from the darkness that consumed my life and replaced it with a marvelous light that shone from inside out for all to see. He drew my brothers and sisters in Christ closer, so that I could, in turn, draw them closer to our Savior.

But they weren't the only ones who saw that brilliant light. Suddenly, a dark shadow was cast over me, but quickly disappeared. Like a small jet plane, it flew by just as fast and brought a volatile gust of wind with it. The hairs rose on my arms. I opened my eyes and sat up straight, causally turning my head to see who was standing behind me.

He stood a few feet away, towering at a height of at least seven feet. My tiny frame was miniscule in comparison. He was solid and thick, the color of soot. The muscles in his arms and legs were enormous. His wing span was massive, and I could see the detail of every feather as he brought them in closer to his body. His pupils were a solid bright red in contrast to the black of his skin. He scowled at me while slightly shifting his weight from one foot to the other, his hands balled up tightly. He might have been intimidating to others if they could see him, but I felt nothing but curiosity. Then, I thought about the hooded spirit in my room who was so upset by what I had done to those gremlin demons.

Why would this demon take time away from wreaking havoc somewhere else to come here and intimidate me? His eyes were inquisitive. I wasn't sure why he was scrutinizing me the way he was, but I wasn't going to let him intimidate me, no matter how much bigger he was. Fear no longer had its grip on me, but nervousness still fluttered in my stomach. *Well, Lord, I guess that means it's time to get back to work.* I stood up fluidly, facing the demon. He gazed at me, perplexed. What, did he expect me to run away screaming like a girl?

There was no way I was going to back down.

~~THE END~~
THE BEGINNING….

Epilogue

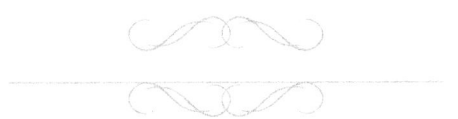

There were so many questions that were still unanswered, but there was one thing I was certain of. The darkness was gone. Instead, His light burned through the night, scorching what was once my midnight, replacing it with the light of dawn. So many questions I had wondered about my whole life had been answered in just a short month. I was no longer walking through life with uncertainty. Instead, I was on my way to walking with purpose. He preordained it before He even formed the world. He had me in mind all along. He knew this day would come. The day that I chose to lay down my heart, my opinions, my emotions, and my own comforts as a form of sacrifice. His all-consuming fire ravished me, purifying me. I knew now that I would have to die, so that I could truly live....

Acknowledgments

Without my Lord and Savior Jesus Christ, this book would have never been a reality. He took me from a life that seemed hopeless and gave me beauty for ashes. He completely transformed me and gave me purpose. I am eternally grateful. All the glory goes to Him.

Thank you to my loving husband, Ron, for your longsuffering and obedience to Christ. Others wrote me off or just didn't know how to help me. And even though you didn't have the answers yourself, you sought the One who did and He answered your prayers for me. You never stopped encouraging me even when I felt like I wanted to give up. You are my biggest cheerleader. And on top of all that you made beautiful designs for this project. You are my helpmate, my best friend and my love.

To my son Donte, thank you for all your love and acceptance of me. You welcomed me in to your life with open arms. You have no idea the impact that made on me as a new wife and mother.

Thanks to Marisa, my sister, for being a good friend and helping anyway you could. For listening to me vent, and for a shoulder to cry on. You always tell me the honest truth and seek wisdom from the Lord on how to console me. I do greatly appreciate that.

Thank you to my Mom, Ruth, who has always been here for me and has always believed in me. For all the sacrifices you made for me. I know that I was a brat at times in my younger years, but I get it now. You are an amazing mom.

Thanks to Lisa and her team for doing a wonderful job with editing and interior design. Lisa, you rock. Not only did you do an awesome job with the editing, but you took the time to teach me a little about writing. You also took the time to answer all my questions. You were a complete ease to work with and I'm so glad I chose you out of the crowd.

Thank you to all the publishers and literary agents who said no. It opened the door to creating my own publishing company, Alive in Christ Publishing, LLC. I have to admit, I never would have thought in a million years that I'd accomplish such a feat. The Lord has led me to create an avenue not just for me but for all those writers like me who the Lord has called to be authors. God, you get all the glory.

To all my family and friends, thank you for your love and support.

About the Author

Minister and novelist Tina C. Brown is a prophet empowered by God with the gift of discerning of spirits. She was born Tina Camille Walker in Kingston, Jamaica to parents Glenford and Ruth Walker. After moving to the U.S. as an adolescent, she enjoyed reading and began writing her first novel, but it was never completed.

In her spare time as a young teen, she wrote prolifically in journals. Brown describes her young adult years as a dark time—depression and hopelessness plagued her. But little did she know that while attending City College, a writing assignment to create a short story would soon be the beginning chapter of her debut novel.

From the time she gave her life to the Lord, she has gone through rigorous spiritual warfare under the leadership of Apostle Ron Reuel Brown. The Lord revealed His purpose and delivered her from the sin and demons that tormented her. Tina and Ron Reuel Brown are now married and are the founders of Alive in Christ Ministries Worship and Training Center in Atlanta, Georgia. The ministry's focus is reconciling the world and the church back to God. Their mission is to equip the saints of God for purpose, with a strong emphasis on worship, healing, and deliverance. Brown is also the owner of Alive in Christ Publishing, LLC.

DISCERNMENT

www.ingramcontent.com/pod-product-compliance
Lightning Source LLC
Chambersburg PA
CBHW070918260626
47162CB00007B/2712

* 9 7 8 0 6 9 2 0 9 5 9 8 0 *